PRAISE FOR LYNN MESSINA

Fashionistas

"*Fashionistas* is quietly hysterical, a stealth satire of magazine and celebrity culture."
—*New Jersey Star-Ledger*

"*Fashionistas* has genuine style, plus wit and wisdom. Messina is an acute observer.... The premise—indeed, much of the book's affectionate satire of the magazine industry—is frighteningly believable.... Displaying a light touch, Messina has written a book that captures the idiocy and humor of the fashion-magazine world. Perhaps she's even succeeded in raising the stakes of jealousy—by proving that imaginative flair is clearly more important than wearing the latest Jimmy Choos."
—*Time Out New York*

"Delightfully witty."
—*New York Daily News*

"Get the inside scoop on the scandalous world of fashion magazines..."
—*Elle*

"Well-written, funny and sharp."
—*Pittsburgh Post-Gazette*

Tallulahland

"Lynn Messina's characters are smart and sassy, affecting and engaging. I thoroughly enjoyed my trip to *Tallulahland*."
—Meg Cabot, author of *The Boy Next Door* and *The Princess Diaries*

"A sweetly comic story of love and healing."
—*Publishers Weekly*

LYNN MESSINA

Mim Warner's LOST HER COOL

RED DRESS INK
™

First edition March 2005

MIM WARNER'S LOST HER COOL

A Red Dress Ink novel

ISBN 0-373-89513-5

© 2005 by Lynn Messina.

Author photograph by Chris Catanese.

This book is a work of fiction. The names, characters, incidents and places
are the products of the author's imagination, and are not to be construed
as real. While the author was inspired in part by actual events, none of the
characters in the book is based on an actual person. Any resemblance to
persons living or dead is entirely coincidental and unintentional.

www.RedDressInk.com

Printed in U.S.A.

For Mom.

Acknowledgments

As always, thanks to: my father, my brothers,
the Linwoods, Chris Catanese, Susan Ramer, Farrin Jacobs.

Along with: Alyce Rogers, Deena Rubinson, Alistair Cormack,
Christine Bonnell, Mandi Bierly, Karen Winter.

Too: Roell Schmidt, whose ability to always say the right thing
leaves me speechless.

PROLOGUE

Mim holds up the pink baby tee with the word *slut* emblazoned on the front in twirly, frilly sky-blue letters and declares it the perfect gift for third-graders trying to establish a distinctive sense of style. Her upbeat tone is relaxed and familiar despite the television crew that's following her around. The director zooms in on her smiling face as she unselfconsciously hands the tee to the salesclerk of the small NoLita boutique. The image is grainy and stylized and every so often it jumps to a wide shot before lurching back to a close-up, but Mim is unaffected by the frenzied camerawork. Wearing her usual uniform—Sigerson Morrison flats, Chanel slacks and a crisp white shirt from Ungaro or Prada—and sporting her customary loose French twist, she seems like typical Mim, archetypal Mim, the Mim you hold up in front of the class as a prime example of standard-issue Mimness. But something is wrong: You don't give *slut*-emblazoned T-shirts to girls in elementary school.

While the saleswoman wraps the present in vibrant yellow paper, Mim explains that the slut trend is going to be huge in the coming year. The hip-hop beat that has played with quiet menace throughout the entire segment stops with a comical screech but Mim, unaware of what will happen in postproduction, chats blithely on with her host.

"Lunch boxes, notebooks, pencil cases, stickers, backpacks," she says as she puts the present, now topped with a pretty pink bow, in her Kate Spade tote. "This is going to be the year that slut merchandising finally breaks through."

The camera jumps to the next scene, which is equally disastrous—Mim in the Metropolitan Museum of Art gift shop picking out a reproduction twelfth-century samurai sword for ten-year-old Timmy. The sword, sharp enough to slice effortlessly through a sheath of silk as Mim proudly demonstrates with her own Hermés scarf, will no doubt make Timmy a superhero in the schoolyard.

"It's fun but educational," Mim says to a nodding, confused Harmony Cortez. "It's never too early for men to learn about honor. The samurai lived by a strict chivalric code called Bushido—that's b–u–s–h–i–d–o for those taking notes at home—which valued honor above life. It's a worthy goal for everyone."

Harmony Cortez is a well-known clothing designer. She has a weekly cable television show on which she does fun, off-beat things with her celebrity guests. This year for her holiday special she gathered several of New York's shopping elite—the editor in chief of *Lucky,* the creative director of Barney's—and gave them each a portion of her Christmas list. Mim got the nieces and nephews. When she'd been invited on to the show two weeks before, her shopping assignment had seemed like a solid idea. Mim has her own pair of young nieces who can always depend on getting something chic from Bergdorf's juniors' department. But now the adventure seemed like a disaster.

Mim Warner is known for two things: her unquestionable good taste and the eerie way she can predict the future. As one of the most successful coolhunters in the business—some would say *the* most successful—people rely on her for a clear picture of what's coming next.

Calling trends is Mim's thing, and she's never gotten one wrong: the great Hush Puppy revival of '96, the celebrated tattooing craze of the early zeros, the illustrious terry-cloth fad of '03. She sees what's coming next so clearly that it sometimes seems as if she lives sixteen months in the future and beams back her image to the present in holographic form. Run your hand over her arm and you're almost surprised that your fingers don't pass right through her.

For almost fifteen years, Mim Warner has been at the top of her game—ever since she broke through with the Potter hightop. She'd been hired by the ailing sneaker company to answer phones for the marketing director, but within a year she'd reinvented the brand. It wasn't intentional. Mim only took the job to make enough money to return to Asia, where she'd been bouncing around since college. Her life savings finally ran out in the middle of the Gobi Desert—somewhere near Gurvansaikhan National Park in Mongolia—forcing her to wire her parents for the airfare home. The plan was simple: Work hard, live cheaply, hop a plane to Bangkok as soon as she had enough cash to cover the flight and several months' worth of pad thai. But then she noticed that the kids at the pizza parlor where she picked up dinner every night were wearing bulky sneakers with thick rubber soles. Potter had a similar model—the Kong—which it was in the process of phasing out.

Mim, in a flash of intuition that's become her trademark, realized this was a terrible mistake. Wrestling shoes had been huge for more than a year, but their run was almost over. Teens, tired of the exaggerated sleekness, were looking for something a little unwieldy. That's what she saw coming—the backlash against the odd compact daintiness of the wrestling shoe.

Her plans to travel deferred indefinitely, Mim stayed another year at Potter. She struck gold a second time with its square-toed tennis sneaker but decided against heading up the development department. Instead, she hooked up with a friend who had start-up cash and an MBA and opened Pravda, a youth-focused research service that predicts what consumers will be buying in a few months.

Under Mim's watchful stewardship, Pravda has flourished. The steady and inexorable rise of youth culture—the way lust for the teenage dollar dictates most of our consumer choices—has created a thirst for the kind of information Mim provides. She makes it look effortless, but it's not. Knowing what to watch for and understanding what you're seeing—it's actually pretty tricky. Sometimes there's only a hairbreadth between one person's idiosyncratic taste and the next revolution in embryonic stage. This is the void that Mim stares into every day without flinching.

Or so we all thought.

ONE

I arrive at the office to what has become a familiar scene—all four junior employees of Pravda gathered around Josh's desk with the *New York Times* spread open before them.

I drop my tote bag on my chair, walk over to the fridge, take out a can of Coke and lean against the edge of my desk as I flip open the tab.

"What's the count today?" I ask before taking a sip.

Norah glances up. Her expression is somewhere between a frown and a smile—a frile, maybe, or a smown. "Two. There are only two."

"That's good," I say. "It's tapering off."

Josh turns to me with eyebrows drawn in violent, slashing lines. There's no doubt about his look—it's a scowl, pure and simple. "Not friggin' fast enough. We lost another client this morning—our fourth. I had the message on my voice mail. Modern Fife is breaking their contract and going back to Young and Younger," he says, an angry sneer curling his upper lip. Josh can't mention his former employer without some sort of extreme facial distortion. That he left the fellow trend-forecasting company of his own volition does nothing to soften his anger at the way they treated him.

Unlike Pravda, Young and Younger is a family firm. Josh had known this going in but since the oldest Younger was seven years his junior and still an undergrad, he didn't worry about the detrimental effects nepotism would have on his career. He didn't realize that as soon as Hildy Young Younger graduated with a 2.8 from Richard Stockton College of New Jersey, she would be given a corner office and the title of senior account manager. Josh, summa cum laude from Brown, tried to stick it out, but the first time Hildy asked him to fetch her a cup of coffee, he was on the phone with Mim discussing employment possibilities. Mim wasn't looking to expand her staff, but they worked out a formula—low base salary plus commission for new business—that suited them both.

"Still, two is better than three," I say reasonably. When Josh first started working here, I found him a little hard to take. Part of it was the condition of his employment—that he didn't start at the bottom as Mim's assistant like the rest of us. I was used to being the only fully independent coolhunter in the house; Liz still has to run things by Mim. But it was also his attitude. Josh has been trend-forecasting as long as I have but he hasn't lost his enthusiasm. Nothing had ever made him question the social usefulness of coolhunting, and he goes after things with an eagerness I used to feel. I think I was jealous.

Josh shakes his head at me now, impatient with my optimistic, glass–half–full rhetoric. As far as he's concerned, there is no bright side. Perhaps, in the very beginning, Pravda might have been able to squeak through the *Har-*

mony Cortez debacle without too much damage. The show typically gets low ratings—on average, less than a .25 share (around two hundred and fifty thousand viewers)—and rarely receives mainstream attention. Unfortunately, though, one of the quarter-million viewers who caught the Christmas special that night was an outraged mom from Forrest Hills who had the home telephone number of the *Times* Metro editor (her husband's cousin's first wife). In a vitriolic op-ed piece, Lydia Williamson held Mim personally responsible for the country's pedophilia problem.

The newswires picked up the story and repeated it over and over until even grandmothers in Edgeley, North Dakota, were raising their voices in shrill condemnation of Mim Warner. Disgusting pervert, depraved maniac, immoral corrupter—Mim has been called everything in the last week.

Helen Souter wrote a letter to the op-ed pages supporting the sword ("an opportunity to teach children about history"), and the shirt ("a self-consciously ironic statement on today's permissive culture"), but her defense of Mim only made matters worse. America wasn't ready yet for porno kitsch, and when readers saw her title, "Chief Operating Officer, Pravda Inc.," they sent in a fresh new flurry of letters condemning the judgment of Pravda's entire staff. Helen's big mistake was identifying herself as a member of the organization. Her opinion would have carried much more weight if she'd pretended to be a concerned citizen from Buffalo.

"Well, I think it's a good sign," Wendy says, brushing her auburn bangs out of her eyes. She's long past due for a haircut but refuses to get one until she receives a much-deserved raise. Her one-year review is only five weeks away, and she's confident she'll be nicely compensated for her fortitude. Wendy is Helen's first assistant to last a full year. It's symptomatic of the position—menial, demanding, iso-lated—that its occupants rarely stay. The revolving door ro-tates so quickly that I usually don't learn the name of the new employee until his or her four o'clock goodbye cake in the conference room. I only found out recently that Wendy is Canadian and performs stand-up comedy every Tuesday at the Comedy Cellar. "With Christmas two days away people finally have something better to worry about," she says. "I bet there won't even be a letter about Mim on tomorrow's op-ed page."

Josh sighs heavily. This is precisely the sort of upbeat thinking he's been trying to squash for days. His co-work-ers just don't get it—Pravda is now the byword for sex and violence. That's not something current and potential clients are likely to forget.

We all ignore Josh's theatrics. He's not the only one who's had a tough week.

The elevator dings and Mim enters the office. She's wear-ing wide brown sunglasses, a parti-colored scarf and a leather jacket she bought at a charity fashion auction last spring. Her cheeks are rosy from the chilly air, and her blond hair, usually tightly gathered in a sleek twist, is loose and windswept. The bracing weather has undermined her cus-tomarily pristine look, but it doesn't matter—even at her most disheveled, Mim's still quite sheveled.

Seeing us huddled over the newspaper, she raises an eye-brow for the count.

"Two," Norah says quickly. As Mim's admin, she's used to supplying all the answers.

"Only two?" she asks. There is disappointment in her voice, a tiny amount but detectable.

"Only two, but one is particularly vicious," Norah says

in a rush to offer consolation. "You were called a wicked degenerate by a man from North Salem. He says someone should take a samurai sword and Bushido you."

Mim nods and then turns away with a cynical half smile. When the *Harmony Cortez* piece first aired—on December 15, two days after the disastrous shopping segment was filmed—Mim seemed as surprised as the rest of us by her performance. For two days she walked around the office with a mystified look on her face while her poor-judgment gaffe was turned into a major brouhaha by the national media. She didn't talk about it to any of us, but we could all tell she was deeply disturbed and losing sleep. By day three, however, the disconcerted expression was gone, replaced by a cheerful outlook, and she announced soon after—on morning number four, when six letters and articles about her appeared in the *Times*—that all publicity was good publicity. Putting on a brave face is how Mim responds to all setbacks, but I was particularly impressed with how effortless she made it seem. Since then she's been getting some perverse enjoyment out of her notoriety. She knows it will fade soon enough. Josh's prediction, that Pravda will have to fold within two months, doesn't worry her one bit. She knows we're not going to lose four clients every week.

Norah straightens up, stretches her back and announces she has a ton of work to do. Mim, in the act of pouring coffee, nods and says she left some memos for her to type up.

Wendy, realizing playtime is over, makes dutiful noises. Liz also returns to her desk, but not before getting my attention and rolling her eyes at Josh's back. Although she didn't have the same adjustment issues with him as I did, Liz had her own list of grievances about Pravda's new employee and many lunch hours were devoted to the scrutiny of his most irritating traits: the way he turns molehills into mountains, the way he makes up nicknames for his clients, the way he talks loudly on the phone, the way he chortles at his own jokes, the way he *chortles.* In recent months, the Josh bashing had tapered off completely and Liz had returned to her favorite lunchtime activity—shopping—but with this new spate of mountain building, her wardrobe is once again suffering. *Women's Wear Daily* ran an article almost two weeks ago about the popularity of reindeer-skin Viking boots, but Liz is still wearing her mukluks.

Smiling at Liz, I swing around my desk, put my tote on the floor and sit down. I switch on my computer and wait for it to boot. Everyone has returned to the usual morning routine except Josh. His eyes are trained on Mim. Whatever she does—takes the milk out of the fridge, opens the sugar, stirs her coffee—he watches. He's been like this for days. Sometimes it seems as if he's afraid to let her out of his sight.

"He's got to calm down," Liz says softly to me a few minutes later as she reapplies lipstick in the bathroom mirror. Despite the out-of-date Uggs, she looks sleek and hip. Tall, boyish, thin—Liz has the ideal shape for today's fashions. I'm shorter and rounder. My frame is thicker, and although often draped in some seemingly unsuitable style—lace, fringe, ruffles—I always manage to pull it off with a sort of Mim-like elegance. "The way he stares all the time is starting to creep me out. He hardly ever blinks."

The image this statement immediately brings to mind— Liz watching Josh watching Mim—is so absurd it makes me smile. I hide it by bending down to readjust my new Sven ankle boots. Unlike Liz, I do my best clothes buying during fits of extreme temper; the more annoyed I am, the better I shop. "He's a little intense right now but I think he's better this week than last."

Liz turns her head to look at me. "Really? You think he's better?"

"Well, he's stopped talking to himself. That's a good sign."

Liz shrugs and puts away her lipstick. She clearly doesn't agree.

A half hour later Josh drops by my desk. I'm trying with little success to write a letter to the marketing director of Marconi-Vinzetti, the high-end sunglass manufacturer. A few weeks ago I noticed that kids in Williamsburg were buying Strikers—the thick-framed black classic that Tom Cruise doesn't take off in his latest flick—removing the arms and replacing them with cheap tortoiseshell ones found at five-and-dimes and thrift stores. The result was quintessentially teen: an uncompromising rebellion against the sleek perfection of the glossy Hollywood images foisted on them daily.

Now I'm trying to pitch the company on the idea of a mass-produced product that somehow maintains the imperfect homemade look of the street version. In recent years Strikers' stake in the fifteen-to-twenty-five demo has fallen off and this seems like an excellent way to revitalize a sagging line. Or at least that's how I want to position it to Marconi-Vinzetti. Getting the wording exactly right is turning out to be a challenge, and I don't appreciate Josh's interruption.

He sits on the edge of my desk, looks around to make sure no one is listening and leans in. These are more Josh theatrics.

"I'm worried," he says quietly.

"What?" I ask, my mind still focused on the troubling first paragraph.

"I'm deeply worried."

I scan the first line. It's still a little too informal. "Huh?"

"She's up to something."

"Who?" I ask, finally looking up. The sooner I finish this conversation with Josh the sooner I can get back to work.

"Mim," he says with more than a hint of exasperation.

"Mim is up to something?"

"Yes, I can see it in her eyes."

His tone is grave and sincere, and I smother the impulse to laugh. Mim's eyes are summer-sky blue, with thick lashes and a catlike slant on the outside corners. They're pretty and deep but I've never seen anything in their depths.

"You can see it in Mim's eyes that she's up to something?" I say, when I have the amusement under control.

Josh nods, relieved that I'm finally getting his drift. "Oh, yeah, she's definitely working on something."

"Of course she's working on something," I say coolly, hoping to rein him in. "She has a business to run."

He shakes his head emphatically. "No, it's bigger than that. *The Harmony Cortez Show* was just the beginning. She's plotting something much bigger and more terrible."

I lean back in my chair and consider him carefully. In the seven months I've known him, Josh has never shown a propensity for paranoia. He's brash and ambitious and sometimes impatient. His coolhunting credentials are good—the Maybe Makeup account, the Up Yours T-shirt Company account, the Wavy sandals account—and his instincts are solid. He doesn't have Mim's innate sense or talent, but he knows this and compensates with hard work and creative thinking. During his short tenure at Pravda, he's already brought in five new clients, two of which left Isabel Young and Marty Younger to follow him. Modern Fife was one of these. "What's she plotting?"

"Our downfall."

I've only asked the question to be polite, and this answer of his, extreme and absurd, proves that you should never humor anyone. "Mim is plotting our downfall?" I repeat slowly. The idea is ridiculous. Mim likes to maintain a professional distance between herself and the staff, but she's open and honest. I can't imagine her plotting anything, let alone someone's downfall.

He nods seriously, without irony or self-consciousness.

"Like yours and mine?"

Josh nods again, more enthusiastically this time. "Yours, mine, Helen's, Norah's, Wendy's, Liz's. She's plotting our downfall."

"Of everyone?"

"Of Pravda," he explains calmly. "The entire organization. I can tell. It's in her eyes."

After eight days of the Mim scandal and its attendant humiliations, it's obvious that Josh is starting to fall apart. The Modern Fife contract, which seven months ago he carried away triumphantly from Young and Younger and which has now gone crawling back with its tail between its legs, was the last straw. "Josh, right now you're under a lot of pressure—"

He holds up a hand. "Don't bother. I know what you're going to say and you're wrong. Mim's got something brewing. Ever since *Harmony Cortez,* she hasn't been herself."

"She seems fine to me," I say almost defensively. Mim was a little off her game right after the big event—really, who wouldn't be?—but she rallied quickly enough and was now back to normal.

"She isn't. She's up to something."

"Then maybe you should talk to Helen about it," I point out reasonably.

He turns to me with a sharp look. "Helen?"

"Well, she does have a vested interest in our downfall."

Josh thinks about this for a moment. I understand his reluctance. Helen is Pravda's part-time chief operating officer and Mim's full-time business partner. She drops by two or three times a week and makes her assistant tremble with nerves. Because she's only here half the time, Helen tries to maximize her hours, which usually means making Wendy do three things at once. Her haphazard working style doesn't leave much time for pleasantries or getting-to-know-your-co-workers chitchat. Even though Helen writes the paychecks, it's doubtful she knows Josh's name.

"Hmm," he says after a long pause, "I don't think it's come to that just yet."

Of course not. Few things come to the point where you need to have a one-on-one with Helen. "Then what are you going to do?"

"Wait," he says softly, sliding off my desk and shuffling back to his own, "and watch."

TWO

When Mim arrives at the office on the morning of
snuffgate, she finds us all in the conference room watching the video.

"Oh, excellent," she says, beaming widely at us as we take
in for the fourteenth time the unlikely image of Mim on
the *Today* show promoting the use of pulverized tobacco
for the nose. "You caught it. I tried calling Norah this
morning to ask her to tape it but I missed her."

"I got it," says Wendy in unusually good humor as she
spreads cream cheese on a sesame bagel. It's not often she
scoops the entire staff, and she made us all wait until everyone was present before showing the video. Norah didn't
come shuffling in until ten-fifteen. "I heard them tease
your name as I came out of the shower and ran to find a
tape."

"I didn't know you were scheduled," Josh says casually.
He's trying to seem offhand and indifferent but he's not.
Every time he watches the footage of Mim assuring Matt

Lauer that snuff is going to be the biggest trend of the new year, his left eye twitches.

Mim smiles. "I thought it best not to tell anyone in case it didn't happen. Surprises are so much nicer than disappointments."

"Did your publicist arrange it?" he asks.

"Publicist?" Mim furrows her eyebrows in intense concentration as if she's not quite sure what the word means. "No, I don't use one of those. I arranged it myself with someone I had lunch with this week. It was actually very easy."

Josh has more questions about the *Today* show booking process but he doesn't get to ask them. Just as he opens his mouth to pursue the matter further, Norah compliments Mim on how natural her makeup looks.

"They did an excellent job. Your complexion's perfect. You don't see any wrinkles or spots. I wish I had a makeup artist come to my apartment every morning to hide my imperfections," she says with typical, unsubstantiated self-deprecation. Norah Jenkins is twenty-three and unmarred save for a beauty mark to the left of her mouth, which is as disfiguring as Cindy Crawford's. Her skin is milky white and her eyes are dark brown, and they both go great with her black, short hair. Her look is mainstream goth, with a little street Betty Boop thrown in for good measure.

Mim stares at the screen for a few seconds without responding. She seems almost transfixed by her image. Josh has to ask her twice if there's anything else big like this in the pipeline that we should know about.

"What?" she asks, pulling her eyes away as her TV doppelgänger thanks Matt for having her on the show. "Uh, no, nothing that you should know about. Now if you'll excuse me. This late start has put me behind. Norah, I'll need you in twenty minutes to make some telephone calls."

As soon as she leaves the room, Josh picks up the remote and rewinds the tape to the beginning. Watching the interview makes his left eye twitch but not watching it makes his whole body convulse. He has two favorite parts, as evidenced by eye-movement speed: when Mim explains how useful the miners in Northwestern Pennsylvania find snuff ("They can't light matches with all those dangerous gasses in the tunnels.") and when she talks about the almost limitless possibilities for designer snuff accessories ("My favorite, next to the cloisonné snuff box, is this eighteenth-century gold antique box with pavé diamonds.").

The snuff announcement crowns a week of erratic and bizarre predictions from Mim. Ever since New Year's, she's been tossing out trends like they're numbers in a lottery drawing. Orange is out. The bustle is back. Knickers are next. The careful forethought, detailed research and reasoned thinking that has made her the leader in trend-forecasting is absent. Abandoning entirely the methodology she drummed into me—thesis, antithesis, synthesis—Mim is making stuff up at whim. Or at least that's how it seems to the staff.

"This has to be stopped," Josh mutters as Mim smiles delightedly into the camera. Although she hasn't done much television work, she's a natural. Her posture is relaxed and comfortable; you could never tell by looking at her that she's talking absolute nonsense. "It can't go on."

Josh has had a particularly difficult week, thanks to Hildy Younger, who keeps calling about the transfer of Modern Fife from him to her. Her questions are basic and fundamental, and it's impossible to tell if they're the product of gross incompetence or malicious taunting. He's tired and stressed and has gone to worst-case-scenario-land in his head. First sex and violence, and now this—drugs. The op-ed pieces practically write themselves.

He can feel Lotus Jeans, the other account he brought over, slipping through his fingers.

"What do you suggest?" Liz asks, straightening in her chair. She's not as given to doomsday prophesies as Josh, but she's noticed a new resistance to what she does since the *Harmony Cortez* scandal. She's not the only one. My meeting with Strikers is set for mid next week but it wasn't easy to arrange. People are wary of us. Pravda has a reputation now and it's not for excellence.

Josh shakes his head. He's very good at foretelling Armageddon but he's not as adept at avoiding it. But that's understandable. I don't have any ideas for heading Mim off at the pass either.

On-screen, the interview draws to a close for the fifteenth time. The shot jumps to Rockefeller Center and Al Roker, but before he can say hello to a redheaded woman wearing an American flag sweatshirt and carrying an oak tag sign that reads "Bringing Home the Macon, Georgia," the image cuts off.

We listen to the snowy static for a few seconds before Liz gets up and turns off the sound. The remote is in front of Josh. I'm expecting him to rewind and watch again but he doesn't. He turns to Norah, who's examining her nails. "Who did Mim have lunch with this week?"

At first she doesn't respond—her chipped black polish is that fascinating—then she bites her bottom lip and shrugs. "Couldn't tell you off the top of my head. I'd have to check the book. Why?"

"Mim said she arranged the appearance herself over lunch. I'm wondering who it was with."

This curiosity is easy enough to appease, and Norah gets

up to retrieve her calendar. On the way back she picks up a Coke.

"Wednesday," she says after a moment. "She went to Lever House with the lifestyle producer of the *Today* show."

Josh opens his mouth several times to respond but for the moment he's speechless and appalled. Finally he finds his voice. "Oh, my God. And you *let* her go?"

Norah takes a sip of soda and lowers the can slowly to the table. She knows as well as the rest of us that Josh has been on edge lately, and she doesn't take offense at his tone, even though the implication that she has any control over Mim is ludicrous. I should know. When I was twenty-three I was Mim's assistant, too, and the only time I exerted influence over her life was when I forgot to pass along telephone messages from her husband. "Excuse me?" she says.

"On the morning in question, she announced that capes were the new must-have accessory. Capes—those silky polyester things that superheroes tie around their necks—as a fashion staple. Clearly this was a cry for help. And yet you *let* her blithely go have lunch—lunch!—with a producer for the most popular morning show in the country." The contempt in his voice is thick but I'm not sure who it's for: Norah or Mim. "Man, that's irresponsible. You're her assistant. You're supposed to look after her. You wouldn't let her get behind the wheel when she's drunk, would you?"

Norah doesn't know what to say to these charges, and the look on her face as she tries to figure it out is comical. She hasn't been Mim's assistant for very long—only three months—and she's still trying to sort out the requirements of the position. This is Norah's first office job. Previously she worked at a designer boutique on Gansevoort. Something about her impressed Mim—her instincts, her sense of style, the smooth way she maneuvered Mim into buying a kelly-green taffeta dress—and she was hired on the spot.

This is how Mim finds all her employees—plucking them from other callings. I'd been studying journalism at NYU when we met. Toward the end of my senior year, I arranged to interview her about trend-forecasting for a series of articles I was writing on interesting and unusual jobs. I spent a week tailing her and asking questions and feeling increasing awe at the way her mind worked. When the article was written—seven hundred and fifty words on how some things just can't be predicted, although it was certainly fun trying—she called and offered me a job. At first I said no. I was still waiting to hear from the *Times* and *Newsweek* and imagining myself as a glamorous international reporter. But neither job came through, and the glamour of charting trends—of actually making the dots on the bell curve— started to appeal.

Norah continues to think of a reasonable response. Josh sees her struggling and relents. "Look, there's no use crying over spilled milk," he says. His voice is clipped—he's still angry—but he's trying to be kind. He knows this isn't Norah's fault. If Lotus Jeans also defects to Hildy, he has no one to blame but Mim. "Let's look ahead to the future. Who's she meeting with next week?"

Norah flips the page of the calendar and briefly glances down. "Monday she's tied up all day in meetings with the people from Stellar. Tuesday she has a three o'clock with Loretta Garcia. Loretta's a segment producer, but only for NY1."

Norah's tone is dismissive—no reason to worry about a small local cable channel—but Josh tenses. He's learned his lesson: In today's global media complex, there's no such thing as small and local. He nods abruptly and tells her to continue.

"She'll be out Wednesday morning—hair color and trim at Fekkai. Client meetings in the afternoon. Uh-oh." She looks up. "Drinks date with Harold Kelly."

Josh doesn't know the name and repeats it.

"Yeah, he's a culture writer for the *Times*," Norah explains.

At the mention of the newspaper of record, Josh shudders and closes his eyes. He can't hear that name without having flashbacks. "Cancel it."

"What?" Norah says, her jaw dropping. But she's not the only one who's shocked. We're all amazed by his autocratic tone.

"Cancel it," he orders again. "Tell him that she has a dental appointment or a burst appendix or whatever. I don't care what you say. Just cancel that appointment. And the one with Garcia."

"But be careful not to use the same excuse for both," advises Liz smoothly. "You need to mix these things up a little. My favorite is a death in the family. No one ever has the bad taste to question it."

Wendy, her hair in a long ponytail, shakes her head. "No, lying about something like that is only tempting fate. I find that an unexpected trip to somewhere off the beaten path like Halifax or Antwerp works well."

They're having a little fun at Josh's expense—twin broad grins attest to this fact—but in his current state he's not hip to undercurrents. He nods enthusiastically and tells Norah to do whatever she thinks is best. "I trust you to sort it out. Now, moving forward. What does Thursday look like?"

Norah consults the book as a voice near the doorway ahhems to get our attention. We all turn around.

Helen is leaning against the wall, looking as dictatorial and annoyed as always. It's impossible to tell how much she heard, although it almost doesn't matter. Sabotaging our boss's meeting schedule is a huge no-no, of course, but the greater sin as far as she's concerned is the way we're sitting around the conference table being unproductive layabouts who don't earn their paychecks.

Wendy opens her mouth to utter some excuse to explain her idle behavior—as the only one at the table who reports directly to Helen, she has the most apologizing to do—but Josh doesn't let her. He's too close to a solution to the problem with Mim to act cautiously. And maybe he's the only one who can get away with it. The amount of his paycheck actually depends on the amount of work he does.

He's barely gotten the word *snuff* out of his mouth when Helen holds up her hand. "No, no, I understand. I saw the segment myself. It was interesting, to say the least."

Helen is short, barely five feet tall, and she favors traditional business suits that hang unflatteringly on her frame. Although not a particularly svelte woman, the clothes she favors—jackets with shoulder pads, slacks with pleats— make her seem wider than she is. Helen likes the girth. It adds physical weight to her moral authority.

The room is silent as we wait for her to say something cutting or censorious. Wendy is stridently avoiding eye contact with everyone. That Helen's here at all today—on a Friday of all days!—is somehow her fault.

Helen takes a seat at the table and turns to Josh. "You were saying…"

He coughs nervously. "I…uh…*we* thought, well, with the, uh, unreliable declarations Mim has been making lately, it might be best to cut down her, uh, contact with producers and writers."

She nods abruptly and tells him to go on. Helen lacks

the affable friendliness of Mim—she never bothers to make benign chatter or put people at ease—but her ruthless efficiency inspires confidence. She knows how to keep the trains running on time.

"I…uh…*we* were just batting around some ideas for rescheduling her appointments until she's feeling more like her old self," he explains, growing more assured as Helen nods encouragingly. When she doesn't like an idea, she usually cuts you off midsentence.

"We thought it would be best if we varied the excuses," Norah adds helpfully. She's in Josh's corner, playing it straight.

"You know, though, if we're really going to make it stick, we'll have to reroute her telephone calls," Liz says. Her tone is no-nonsense and practical but there's a little mischievous curve to her lips. She likes egging Josh on. He's an easy target because he takes everything so seriously. "No point in canceling appointments when they can easily be followed up on."

"And her mail," says Wendy, with a quick dart in Helen's direction. Her boss's relaxed composure—the way she hasn't singled out her assistant and embarrassed her yet—emboldens her. That she's not completely in awe of her demanding employer is one of the secrets to her longevity. "Wouldn't we also have to reroute her mail?"

"Yes," agrees Norah, "she gets a ton of invites every day. And don't forget her e-mail. Mim's in-box is constantly dinging."

"Oh, I have it." Liz waves her hand excitedly. "We move her to another office on another floor. We cut her off completely so that she has no contact with the outside world."

It's obvious from her sarcastic tone that Liz is drawing attention to the absurdity of the idea, but Josh is nodding enthusiastically. He's not getting it. He's thinking this could work. For the first time in a week, he's wondering if perhaps everything might actually turn out all right.

His fist tightens around Lotus Jeans.

"And we'll watch her," he says with a sort of uncontrolled eagerness. His left eye is twitching again but in a good way. "We'll draw up a twenty-four-hour schedule in which everyone gets a shift and we'll keep an eye on her at all times."

I listen to the brainstorming session without interrupting, but my feet are firmly planted in Liz's camp. This is absurd. Mim's behavior has been strange and unpredictable and somewhat damaging, but after thirteen years of steadfast dependability, she deserves the benefit of the doubt. Whatever's bothering her, she'll figure it out. She doesn't need us tinkering behind the scenes, saving her from herself.

Helen ah-hems for a second time, reminding us of her presence, and everyone falls silent. "Are you done?" she asks mildly.

Josh doesn't blush—his sense of shame doesn't work that way—but he has the grace to look embarrassed. He glances around the table and then nods slowly. Yeah, he's done.

I sit up in my chair and brace myself for the inevitable outburst from Helen. This sort of behavior from underlings—the word-by-word building of a Mim pen, even partly in jest—isn't something she takes calmly. And it's not just the blatant disrespect it shows toward a superior that's the problem. The slight is personal. Helen and Mim are lifelong friends. They grew up in neighboring houses and shared a white stretch limo to the prom and copied off each other during their Intro to Bio midterm. They keep the relationship professional in the office, but they go back more than thirty years.

Helen makes eye contact with everyone at the table, including me, even though I haven't said a word. "If you're done, I'd like to propose another solution." She waits until we all agree. Josh is the last one to nod but he does it eventually. "I could talk to her."

The suggestion, practical and uncomplicated, is so shocking, we stare at her as if she's just suggested a lobotomy.

Liking the effect, Helen smiles. "Good. I'm glad you're in agreement. I'll take this matter up with Mim and promise to have it all sorted out by the end of next week. How does that sound?"

Although the question is aimed at the entire staff, we all look at Josh to see his reaction. He's surprised at first and almost annoyed by Helen's interference. But then his expression changes. He leans back in his chair and smiles. "Good. It sounds really good and doable," he says as if the vastness of the proposed enterprise—canceling meetings, intercepting mail, rerouting e-mail, cutting off telephone service, renting new office space, duping boss—is just now hitting him. "Thank you."

Helen shrugs it off. "I'm here to help," she says, as if this graciousness were not an extraordinary event. I'm amazed it happened at all—that Helen, sensing trouble among the rank and file, could actually rise to the occasion of leadership. Her actions aren't completely selfless, of course. As co-owner, she has an equal stake in Pravda. Still, I didn't think she had it in her.

Helen accepts our thanks with unaccustomed good humor. When the gratitude tapers off a few minutes later—there are only so many ways you can verbally express appreciation—she reminds us that we all have work to do and leaves the room. Wendy runs after her with a worried frown on her face.

THREE

Ian drops by the Pravda office on the afternoon of the *Today* show debacle just as I'm about to run out for lunch, sits down on the overstuffed Ultrasuede couch in the waiting room and tells me he wants a two-bedroom apartment with a terrace—and that I have to make it happen.

"Excuse me?" I say, leaning against the wall several paces away. I don't want to get too close to him. We broke up almost a year ago, but there is still a lingering attraction. It's a small spark that ignites whenever we're lonely and drunk. Although this usually happens in dimly lit bars at midnight, it doesn't hurt to be careful. The sunlight pouring through the windows is no guarantee of clear-headed behavior.

"I want a two-bedroom apartment with a terrace somewhere south of Fourteenth Street but north of Houston." He leans forward as he talks and rests his arms on his knees. There is an odd jumpiness about him, an intense energy barely contained, and his eyes flicker erratically as he watches me watching him. This is Ian at his most engaged.

A thirty-something New Yorker, he's mastered the art of ironic detachment. Although it's no longer cool, he's a post-modernist. He believes everything in the world is dead, even the notion of death itself. It's one of the reasons we didn't work out. "And the terrace thing is optional. I'm perfectly willing to accept a two-bedroom apartment with a fire escape."

Pravda's waiting room is in a high-traffic area—on the way to the elevator and right outside Mim's office—and Ian falls silent as my boss breezes by with a shopping bag from MoMA's downtown design store and a tossed green salad. Mim doesn't say anything but she notices our arrangement—Ian on the couch, me against the wall—and wonders at it. She isn't the only one to raise an eyebrow. Two minutes before, Josh ran by on his way to a meeting and paused to examine us. We look silly with half an office between us but I don't get closer. The circumstances are all wrong—the sunlight is shining and I'm completely sober—but all of a sudden he's terrifyingly appealing. With his elbows on his knees and his eyes jumping, he's the Ian I rarely get to see—the eager Ian, the interested Ian, the Ian who isn't afraid to want something more than clean boxers and a medium-rare cheeseburger.

"A fire escape?" I ask, when Mim disappears into her office and closes the door halfway. "You want a two-bedroom apartment with a fire escape?"

"Yeah, but not one that overlooks a shaftway or a dingy courtyard where the building's garbage piles up," he explains quickly. "But that's only if we can't find a proper terrace."

Ian lives in a two-hundred-and-thirty-six-square-foot tetrahedron on Mott Street. He has a loft bed and a kitchen that he shares with an artist named Olivia, who spends most nights in her painting studio in Little Italy. The room has two windows, but they both look out onto wells so narrow and deep that sunlight has never touched their panes. Fresh air is scarce and the only view he has is into the neighbor's brown living room. It's no surprise he wants something new.

"Have you looked at anything yet?" I'm trying to figure out why he's here. Advice? Guidance? Either notion is ridiculous. I'm not anyone's idea of a real estate guru. I found my apartment in the *New York Times* and wrote a very large check to a charlatan named Nita who had lived there before me. "I can give you the name of the broker who helped one of my friends find his place. The fee was a little less than standard. I think it was only twelve percent of the annual rent."

Ian shakes his head. "I don't want to rent. I want to own."

Renting or buying—the principle is the same and neither involves me. "I'm sure his agent has for-sale listings as well."

"But I need you to make it happen."

There it is again—this odd conviction that I have anything to do with it. "Ian, I don't know what you're talking about it. How? *How* can I make your apartment—"

"My two-bedroom apartment with a terrace."

I roll my eyes. It isn't like him to be pedantic, and I humor him because it's so out of character. "All right, how will I make your two-bedroom apartment with a terrace happen?"

"Jawbones," he says.

My shoulders stiffen and I stop leaning against the wall. *"Jawbones?"*

He nods emphatically.

Jawbones is the name of Ian's soon-to-be-published novel. It's about an unscrupulous petty thief who gets sucked into

New York's violent underworld and discovers that he has a few scruples after all. It's dark and brutal and seething with an anger that pulsates under the calm surface of Ian's detached writing style. The book is chock-full of sleazy pimps, slimy slumlords, dirty cops and murdering drug dealers, and amid this encyclopedic catalog of street filth who populate the novel, the true villain is a socially irrelevant, morally bankrupt coolhunter. This is another reason we broke up.

"What about *Jawbones,* Ian?"

The elevator dings, the "up" light flashes and Wendy steps onto the floor. Ian waits until she's out of sight. "Well, I thought you could take it and do that thing you do," he says. He's now at the edge of the couch. There is nothing laid-back or relaxed about his stance. Even his earlobes look tense with expectation.

Although I still don't know what he wants, I'm pretty sure I'm not going to give it to him. He might be eager, interested Ian, with his enthusiastic green eyes and his hopeful smile and his open demeanor, but he's also the creator of Delilah Quick—seducer of men, betrayer of promises, destroyer of kingdoms.

"What thing do I do?" I ask. Before I say no, I'd like to know what exactly I'm turning down. It's unlikely that I'll have a chance to find out afterward. Ian doesn't know how to fight. He never defends his territory or stands his ground, but he's exceedingly accomplished at walking away. There are few things in the world I know as well as the back of his head.

"Popularize something, make it hot, give it a cultural identity, turn it into that thing everyone's talking about," he says. And he doesn't blush. He seems completely immune to the irony of the situation. He doesn't realize that you don't do this—dismiss someone's profession as trivial and exploitative for two years and then avail yourself of her skills. Ian doesn't even believe I have skills. He thinks I stand on a street corner like a crossing guard watching traffic go by. That he would come here like this, tugging his forelock, is an indication of how much *Jawbones* means to him. I should be angry or gleeful but I'm neither. Ian caring about something more than his meticulously constructed self-image—it's not a state of affairs I ever thought to see.

"Ian, I don't think—"

"Please," he says, his eyes wide with hope. "You do it all the time—poof, and something is popular."

This isn't exactly how it works. Most days I spend hours in stores talking to kids, showing them products, watching their reactions, observing what they wear, writing down what they say and trying really hard to get a sense of what they like. Then I take that information and attempt to gauge what will be popular in a few months. Every single conclusion I draw is based on fact. I don't pull rabbits out of hats or make gold from dross. I just forecast trends. I see a tiny green sprig growing in a field and predict that one day a tree will stand there. If I happen to get the type of tree right, so much the better. Ian doesn't understand this. He thinks coolhunting is a really neat trick done by a magician with very quick hands.

"You know it's not that simple."

Ian nods agreeably—more proof of his commitment to *Jawbones*. I've defended the complexity of coolhunting a hundred times before and he's never once conceded the possibility that it might actually be true. "Right. Of course. But you know what to do. I mean, it's what you do."

"Why?" I ask, crossing my arms across my chest.

He blinks at me several times before responding. "Why what?"

"Why is this so important?"

"I told you, I want to buy a two-bedroom apartment with a terrace. I've been living in a closet on Mott Street for almost four years. I'm tired of not seeing the sky until I step outside. I need sunlight."

It's a good response and it makes perfect sense but I'm not buying it. "Why?" I ask again.

Ian hates being pressed and his lips tighten as he struggles with an answer. "You know," he mutters finally.

The truth is, I do know. I'm perfectly aware of what has provided the impetus for him to come here asking for help from an unlikely source, but I refuse to let him gloss over it. That *Jawbones* is the only thing he cares enough to fight for hurts me in a way I didn't know I could be hurt anymore and makes me determined to do this the hard way. Ian was supposed to fight for me. The way I ended things— calm little speech about the relationship not working any longer, quiet shutting of the door as I walked out of his apartment—was an opening salvo in an air-clearing argument that never came. It was a retaliatory strike for Delilah Quick's immorality. It was a grandstanding play. It was not supposed to be the end.

"Do I?" I ask, petty enough to draw it out. I spent five minutes in his hallway waiting for him to come after me. Five minutes. Even now, the thought of it makes my cheeks warm with embarrassment.

Ian sees my expression—the raised eyebrow, the blank look—and realizes I'm not going to relent. He doesn't understand why but is annoyed just the same. He sighs irritably and gives in. "I need an edge."

"An edge?"

"An edge," he repeats with quiet emphasis. The nervous energy is still there but it's contained now that the topic has switched from his cover story to the truth. "You know, something that will make *Jawbones* stand out from the other Butcher Kane knockoffs weighing down the bookshelves."

Of course. Butcher Kane—drug addict, murdering scum, literary sensation. The hero of *The Ballad of Butcher Kane* went from nobody to pop icon in less than sixty seconds. The book marked the triumphant return of the antihero and the birth of a new literary genre, magical nihilism. In very little time, magical nihilism—pronounced with a long "e" to rhyme with realism and to preserve the wit and ingenuity of the *Vanity Fair* writer who coined the term—has become a huge publishing force. Every house now has a bevy of thirty-something males writing about how hard it is to live by a moral code in today's corrupt world.

"Yours isn't a knockoff," I say with some asperity. I no longer have to cater to his feelings, but I'm still annoyed by the suggestion. *Jawbones* is an excellent book, with crisp, quiet passages that cut you in half, and I told him so— thirty-six hours after finishing it and seventy-two before finishing us. I couldn't not tell him. You don't date a novelist for a year and fail to get a tiny glimpse into what it all means: the whalelike importance that can't be articulated because it's somehow beyond the scope of ordinary language. That I could do this at all—separate my hurt over Delilah Quick from my admiration for his writing—surprised me. I didn't know I had it in me. Neither did Ian. The shock was on his face for only a moment but that was enough.

"It'll be called one."

"But it's not one," I say, insistent. *Jawbones* is magical nihilism—it has too many of the elements to be called anything else—but it doesn't dress up its hero in Butcher Kane's army fatigues and send him out with a Colt .45 in his waistband. Bones McGraw is different. He longs for the comforts of middle class and the calm of middle age and he refuses to measure himself, or any man, by how well he faces death. *Jawbones* is still Hemingway—and it can't not be, since the magical nihilism protagonist is just the code hero updated and angered—but it's more "A Clean Well-lighted Place" than "The Short Happy Life of Frances Macomber."

"It doesn't matter," he says. His tone is petulant and he refuses to smile but I know he appreciates my quick defense of his work. He has always liked having me in his corner, even though he's never been able to say so. "It will be perceived as a knockoff and you know as well as I do that perception is everything. The very best I have to look forward to is *Publisher's Weekly* calling it a competent entry in the Butcher Kane look-alike contest. Competent," he says again, practically spitting out the word. "I'd rather be universally panned than damned with such faint praise."

Ian treats everything with either a shrug or an all-purpose "whatever," so I'm not sure how to take this statement. It doesn't seem possible that he's telling the truth. Nobody would rather be slammed by reviewers than called competent. Competent at least is a starting point. It implies that with the right equipment—perhaps a compass and a high-powered telescope—you might be able to find your way to ingenious or skillful.

If Ian were anyone else—my brothers or my roommate or even Josh—I'd tell him to stop being such a drama queen. But Ian's drama-queenliness is something to be encouraged. Perhaps if he were capable of the big argument scene, with its climactic yelling and name calling, he and I would still be together. "What you're describing is publicity," I say. "I don't do that. I don't know how to."

He leans forward. He's now sitting on the very edge of the couch. "But you do it all the time. Poo—"

"Don't say poof again," I growl through clenched teeth. "It's not poof."

"It is poof."

"Ian, it's a matter of agency," I explain, struggling to hold on to my temper. This just proves my point—he never listens to me. If he did, he'd know it's not poof. "It's a matter of control, and I don't have any. Making things happen isn't my job." But Ian continues to stare at me with a steady, hopeful expression. I take a deep breath and wonder how many times I can say the same thing with different words. "I don't do, Ian. I watch. I identify what is already happening and shine a light on it. That's not poof. That's turning on a light switch."

He's quiet for a moment. "So turn me on," he says softly, earnestly.

I sigh and close my eyes. The desire to turn him on is real and sharp but I won't do that again. "Doesn't your publisher have a person who's supposed to do this for you?"

Ian smiles wryly. "Yeah, they've got a person but he represents every book on the imprint, which is almost like saying he represents none of the books on the imprint. His complete contribution consisted of sending out copies for review. They don't even follow up with editors. He's got an assistant who's well-meaning and nice, but she doesn't know a thing about publishing."

"*I* don't know a thing about publishing," I remind him.

"But you're clever and you learn fast and you're never, ever wrong," he says quickly. "You're like Nostrodamus."

Like Nostrodamus? For God's sake. "Ian—"

"You're good, Meghan. You're really, really good at what you do."

The words are nice and sincerely spoken but that just isn't enough. This puddle is too deep for him to lay his cape over it now. "Oh, is that why I got cast as evil incarnate?" I ask angrily. I don't want to talk about Delilah Quick—I'm *so* over Delilah Quick—but I can't help myself. The situation is too much. The unexpected compliments, the appealing eagerness, these sudden, surprising reminders of how unimportant I am—they all combine in a perfect cocktail of impatience and disgust. "Because I'm so darn good?"

Ian flinches at my venomous tone but he maintains eye contact. He doesn't turn his head when the elevator dings and he doesn't look down as Liz breezes past. He simply waits silently with his eyes trained on mine until we're alone again. "She's not you," he states with quiet emphasis.

"Yes, she is."

"No, she's not. She's a character," he says slowly, pedantically, as if I'm a small child who doesn't understand basic arithmetic. "She's a piece of fiction. She doesn't actually exist."

Ian and I have never discussed Delilah Quick before. Even though she's been living in the back of my mind for almost a year and the quiet hum of her refrigerator has often lulled me to sleep, this is the first time I've let her name pass my lips. In one moment of stunning anger, eleven months of practiced self-control vanishes like a bunny rabbit in a magician's black hat. Poof. But that's the problem with dignified silence: It's a short-term solution.

A telephone rings in the next room, making me keenly aware of my surroundings. We shouldn't be doing this now—airing the Delilah Quick laundry in the reception area of Pravda's offices. My boss shouldn't be little more than six feet away behind a half-closed door. And yet I'm happy to take what I can get. Ian is stingy with words. He hoards them in a small burlap sack that he carries over his shoulder and rarely unties. "Are you sure she doesn't exist? Because, you know, she looks like me and she sounds like me and she acts like me and I'm pretty sure that I exist." I take skin from around my wrist and pinch. Ouch. "Yep, that hurt. So I guess I am flesh and bones. Imagine that—a flesh-and-bones person being angry that she was portrayed as evil incarnate in her boyfriend's book."

To no one's surprise—neither his nor mine—Ian stands up to leave. It's not as easy to make a grand exit with an elevator as it is with a front door that snaps satisfyingly behind you, but Ian is clever. He'll figure something out.

With his back toward me, he presses the button. He's walking out again. I know it doesn't matter anymore, but it still bugs the hell out of me. Even though it's better this way—after almost a year, there's nothing he can say about Delilah Quick that would make her shady existence palatable to me—I still detest it.

The elevator dings and the "down" light flicks on. The doors open. A few seconds later they close. Ian hasn't moved. He stands by the button with his back toward me. "You've never lied to me," he says.

I don't know which is more unexpected—his continued presence or his statement—and I stare at his back, wondering what both mean. "What?"

"You said she acts like you. You've never lied to me." His tone is quiet but insistent. "You've never slept with my brother. You've never stolen a hundred thousand dollars from a mob boss and framed me to take the fall. You've never conspired with a dirty police officer to send me to Leavenworth. You've never stabbed me in the gut with a sharp kitchen knife and tossed my body into the East River." He turns around, leans his body against the wall and looks me in the eye. "So it's pretty obvious to me that you're not Delilah Quick."

Ian is trying to make me feel ridiculous. By highlighting Delilah's most appalling deeds, he's distilling her down to a series of sins and washing the dirt of context from beneath her fingernails. His Delilah is a cartoon villain. She's a plastic action figure you buy in a children's toy store. But I'm not fooled by this subtle maneuver. The shadow she casts is absurd. My feelings are not.

While he waits for me to say something, Ian rests his shoulders against the wall. He is perfectly still—no twitching eyebrows, no jumping legs, no fingers compulsively playing with the zipper of his hooded sweatshirt. The agitation from earlier is completely gone and he's familiar again. This is the Ian I know—stubborn Ian, detached Ian, the Ian who doesn't give a shit about anything. But even as he looks at me with shopworn disinterest, I know something is different: He's still here. Despite his proximity to an escape hatch, he is still in the room, his natural inclination to walk away trumped by a fear of being lumped in with magical nihilism imitators.

Poor Ian—denied the dignity of a majestic exit by one Butcher Kane.

"It's not that simple," I say quietly, looking down at my hands, at the floor, at the frayed edges of the couch. I want to explain in detail how Delilah Quick made me feel, but I don't trust him to understand. Upon brief perusal, her rap sheet reads like a series of petty misdemeanors: vanity crimes, ego offenses. But her trespasses extend further than the outline of my bruised pride. The humiliation I felt when reading the book cut through the muscle around my heart. There they were—all the things that I'd ever said about coolhunting: the giddy comments about how great it feels to be right about a trend, the thoughtful observations about enjoying the challenges of my job, the gushing monologues about how fabulous Mim is to work for. He took it all, everything, and put it through his meat grinder so in the end it came out like a burned-out hash of cynical thoughts and actions.

It's mortifying to realize that someone is taking notes on your life and that they're not even transcribing it faithfully. And the worst thing about it all—worse than the overcooked mince patties and the avert-your-eyes embarrassment—is this unsquashable inkling that he might be right.

I take a deep breath. Since I can't say all of it, I won't say any of it. "It's not that simple."

It's a weak statement, the sort I used to hiss angrily at my parents when I was punished for breaking curfew or coming home drunk from a party in high school, but it's the way I feel.

"Perhaps," he concedes. "But it's not that complicated either."

I nod. It doesn't mean that I agree. It just means that I'm too drained to argue.

Ian stares at me silently for a moment. He looks as though he wants to say something more—explain, perhaps, why it really isn't that complicated after all—but he only glances at his watch and mutters excuses. "I should get going. I've got to be at the bar in an hour and you probably want to get back to work. Or go to lunch."

"Yeah," I agree vaguely. Work or lunch—either one would do right now.

He presses the elevator button. "All right, so I'm gonna take off now," he says somewhat unnecessarily. There's no need for him to narrate—it's pretty obvious what's happening—but he's feeling awkward. Now that Delilah Quick is out in the open, he can't stand being here.

Ian presses the button a second and a third time with little success. Despite his best efforts, he can't make the car come any faster. I watch him scrambling to escape and feel a fresh burst of anger at the fact that he doesn't get it. He based Delilah Quick on me. He gave the symbol for the decline of Western civilization my face.

The elevator finally arrives and Ian darts into the empty car. With escape only seconds away, he can now bear to look at me. His smile is somewhat self-conscious as he presses the button—at least he has the sense to feel shame.

"I'll think about it," I say.

The doors are closing and he stops them with an arm and looks at me with a confused expression. How quickly he forgets.

"Publicity ideas for *Jawbones*," I say. "I'll give it some thought."

He smiles widely, no longer quite so ill at ease. "Thank you," he says, then disappears behind sliding doors.

I lean against the wall and exhale a deep breath. I shouldn't have done that—tell him I'd help. My reach in the world doesn't extend a fraction of an inch beyond my fingertips, but Ian doesn't understand this. He thinks I pull strings and people dance.

Just as I'm about to return to my desk, Mim's door opens and she steps out of her office. She has a newspaper in one hand and a gleaming black coffee mug in the other. She's striding purposefully toward the kitchen area with a deeply pensive look on her face. To the casual viewer, Mim is oblivious to the world around her. But she's not. She knows I'm here. She's thoroughly aware that I'm standing in the reception area with my back against the wall. From the corner of her eye, Mim is watching me. Her sly behavior is odd, but I don't question it. These days, everything she does is odd.

FOUR

Vicky is having a cocktail party on her terrace. She's put the bar against the north wall, lined the perimeter with chin-high ferns and arranged candles at regular intervals along the ledge. She's placed her tiny Bose speakers in opposite corners and Frank Sinatra is wafting up the courtyard and over the building.

For the third time in ten minutes, Bonnie stops in front of our kitchen window and watches the scene across the courtyard with amazed curiosity. She's supposed to be getting ready for dinner—her hair isn't done and her makeup isn't on and she still hasn't decided which dress she's going to wear—but she's too busy marveling to worry about things like that. "I mean, dead mice," she says.

I'm sitting on the couch in a half-prone position watching the news. The dead mice aren't a breaking story. Bonnie has been talking about them for almost fifteen minutes. "I know."

"That is, actual mice that are dead," she explains needlessly. "Yikes. One of the cocktail-goers, a well-dressed man in what looks to be—can it be? yes, ladies and gentleman, I believe it is—an Armani suit is about to step on one. I can't watch." But this isn't exactly true. She can't watch without her Canon EOS Rebel and its superlong zoom lens that she'd bought for a safari in Kenya, and she runs into her bedroom to fetch it. Although she was in Africa for almost a month, she took only two rolls of film. Wildlife doesn't interest her nearly as much as city life, and we have more pictures of Vicky's apartment than we do of the Masai Mara.

My voyeuristic tendencies aren't as well developed as my roommate's, but I have a natural interest in the bizarre and I get up to look. Vicky's terrace is nothing more than the black tar roof of the Italian restaurant she lives above. It's a five-foot ledge that collects rainwater in stagnant puddles and rotten banana peels from the apartments above. One neighbor even throws her used glue traps with struggling mice onto it. The ledge looks out onto a narrow cement courtyard that's really the dumping ground for the four apartment buildings surrounding it.

"I don't see the Armani guy," I say, my elbows resting on the wide, white ledge. The crowd on the terrace is thick and it's hard to distinguish anything except the glue traps with the dead mice that line the perimeter. "Do you suppose she just doesn't realize they're there?"

Bonnie returns with her camera and slides in next to me. "I saw her sweeping the roof yesterday. I think the real issue is that she underestimates the extent of her upstairs neighbor's rodent problem." She looks through the viewfinder and frowns. "I don't see him. Drat. I knew I should've kept the camera on the windowsill."

I take one long last look at the spectacle and then glance

at the clock hanging on the kitchen wall. It's a quarter after seven. "Don't you have to be at the restaurant in fifteen minutes?"

"No," she says, unconcerned, as she snaps shots of the party. As far as photography subjects go, the scene is a good one. The contrast between the lush elegance of the guests and their rundown surroundings is particularly eye-catching. Bonnie has never considered showing the gallery owners on West Broadway her photos, but she should. The pictures she has taken over the past eighteen months would make an interesting one-woman exhibition, particularly to the one woman who unknowingly stars in them. "Dinner isn't until seven-thirty."

"And what time do you think it is now?"

She focuses, clicks and shrugs. "Six forty-five."

"Close," I say, taking the Brita water filter out of the fridge and filling a glass. "You're only off by a half hour."

Bonnie doesn't flinch. She doesn't jump up and rush into the bathroom to blow-dry her hair. She simply turns the lens one half degree to the right and takes another shot. This is why she's always late.

"It's because I don't want to go," she says a minute later. She's left the camera on the windowsill next to the open window. The sky is clear now but showers are expected later. "If this weren't some boring dinner with potential funders, I'd be dressed and out the door."

There's genuine conviction in her voice but it's misplaced. The occasion and the company aren't what's making her late. It is Bonnie herself and an internal clock that hasn't been wound in years.

"I'd much rather stay here with you," she says, calling from her bedroom, where several different outfits are scattered on the bed, "and talk about Ian."

I pick up the camera and move it to higher ground. The kitchen is small and crowded but there's always room for one more thing on the cluttered tile counter. "There's nothing to talk about," I say. My voice is calm and unemphatic, and there's no reason for Bonnie to assume that I'm protesting too much. But she does anyway.

She comes out of her room in a black knee-length cocktail dress. Her not-quite-dry brown hair is falling over her shoulders. There is an old-fashioned elegance about Bonnie—like Elizabeth Taylor in her late teens just seconds before she married Nicky Hilton—that appeals to society ladies and corporate sponsors. This is why she's so good at getting money for the struggling theater company she works for. Although she's only twenty-nine, she's the best development director Exit Stage Left has ever had.

"Please. You can't fool me," she says, taking my hand and leading me to the couch. "His visit today upset you. It's so obvious." She has only seven minutes to get to the restaurant, but she wants to sit down and have a heart-to-heart anyway. "Tell me about it."

The possibility that Ian and I will reconcile is a little bird that's constantly fluttering a few feet above Bonnie's head. No matter how many times I tell her it's over, she refuses to believe me. The reason for this is simple: Bonnie likes Ian. She likes him more than any other guy I've ever dated. She thinks it's because he's intelligent and funny; I think it's because Ian is the only one she's gotten to know. My previous dating experience consisted almost entirely of three- to four-month cycles of infatuation and boredom. These minirelationships, as Bonnie likes to call them—microrelationships when she's feeling snide—never gave her a chance to exchange more than a few words with the object of my affection.

"I'm not upset," I say, pushing her toward the front door. She grabs her purse as we move through the kitchen.

"Just don't stay home and brood," she says on the threshold of the apartment. "Call Marcy or Dawn and go out."

"I can't, even if I wanted to. My father's coming in for dinner."

At this news, her face brightens. "Oh, in that case, I'm not worried. You'll be fine."

Bonnie likes my father, too. In fact, all of my friends like him. But they've never stood next to him in the crowded bars on Bleecker Street while he trolls for women. It is an experience that is far from fine.

"Yeah, fine," I mutter, imagining the long evening ahead.

"Okay, going now," she announces, checking one more time to make sure she has everything she needs—money, ID, lipstick, keys.

"Have fun," I say over the unrepentant creaking of our front door.

Bonnie rolls her eyes and tightens her grasp on her little black handbag. "Yeah, fun."

My father requests Thai food and I take him to my local favorite, but before we cross the threshold, I review the rules with him.

"Don't ask out the waitress," I say as the light changes on Seventh Avenue. "Her name is Lisa and she's twenty-four years old."

Dad considers this for a moment, then nods. He's a letter-of-the-law man, which means that his agreement doesn't preclude flirting. This is something he can live with.

"Don't ask for fortune cookies."

My second demand hits closer to home—playing the country bumpkin is one of his favorite pastimes—and he considers his answer carefully. Dad doesn't understand the notion of cultural insensitivity. To him "Chinese, Japanese…what's the difference?" is the perfect punch line. "All right," he says finally, crossing the street.

"Don't ask for twenty percent off."

This rule gives him pause and he stops on the corner of Grove and Bleecker to argue with me. "Come on, Meghan, that's taking it too far," he insists with a laugh.

I don't agree. Bullying a restaurant that used to give customers twenty percent off coupons during its freshman year into giving you a discount all the time—that's taking it too far. "No asking for twenty percent off," I say again, folding my arms across my chest. This point is not debatable. Bangkok Green is my restaurant. It's my stomping ground and he doesn't get to play his little games here.

Dad consents. He seems deflated and sad, but he promises not to ask for twenty percent off.

"Or any percent off," I add. Dad looks at me with his eyebrows drawn closely together. He wants me to think he's confused, but he isn't. I know that look. It means I've ruined his fun. "You can't ask for anything off, not twenty or thirty or even five percent. Nothing off. We pay full price or we don't go in."

"I told you that was fine," he says, peevish and petulant and a little impatient. We resume walking to the restaurant, and even though I'm staring straight ahead, I know my father is looking at me with a baffled expression on his face. He's trying to figure out who I am. After all these years, he's still not quite sure how he wound up with me, a daughter who can't enjoy a good joke. This is always the problem—I'm a stick in the mud. It's never that he isn't funny.

The restaurant is crowded by the time we arrive, and the hostess seats us by one of the large windows that line Grove Street. Bangkok Green is dark and cheerful. Empty bamboo birdcages hang from the ceiling and water trickles down a marble falls in the far left corner. There is none of the aluminum kitsch that you often find in Thai restaurants.

Dad examines the choices, settles on an old favorite and puts down the menu just as our waitress stops by to fill our water glasses. She's tall and pretty with a long, thin face and a severe ponytail. I've never seen her before.

She greets us enthusiastically—it's still early in her shift—and asks if we're ready to order.

"Yes," I say, "I'll have the papaya salad and green curry with chicken."

She nods amiably, writes it down and looks at Dad. He orders quickly—wonton soup, basil chicken, Singha—and then asks the woman her name. The answer isn't Lisa—it's Jenny or Ginny—which makes him smile widely. Suddenly, there are opportunities afoot.

"What's your real job, Jenny?" my father asks. This is one of his favorite questions and it never fails to solicit an animated response. So far Dad has been lucky. He has yet to come across a career waitress in the Village.

Jenny works in a small clothing boutique in NoLita where she's a designer. It's only a part-time gig now but she hopes that will change as soon as the summer rolls around. Dad loves answers like this one and spends the next five minutes asking follow-up questions. Jenny is pink with delight and ignores several pointed looks from patrons who would like their water glasses refilled.

"My daughter works in the fashion industry," he says.

Jenny turns eager eyes my way. "Really?"

"Sorta," I say, resisting the urge to deny it outright. Dad's understanding of what I do is as imperfect as Ian's. A veteran reporter and the editor of a community weekly, he can't quite get his head around trend-forecasting. Dad knows hard facts and evasive answers and scandals that erupt in small, bedroom towns. The type of reporting I do, less concrete and more open to interpretation, doesn't strike him as useful. Telling companies where to put their logos—it's not the kind of impact he wanted his daughter to have on the world.

"She's just being modest," my father assures her. "Meghan decides what's popular and what's not. Magazines get her opinion all the time."

"It's not that simple," I tell her. "As I'm sure you already know, there is a lot more involved than the opinion of one person."

"Yeah, I know that. There are several people whose opinion matters and we try to get our stuff into their hands but most of the time it's just im—" She breaks off as her gaze settles on the woman at the table next to us who is holding up her empty glass and waving it vigorously. "Oh, excuse me."

Dad watches her walk away, then leans forward. "It constantly amazes me how you just have to talk to people. They never fail to have something interesting to say. Your mom knew it. She talked to everyone."

I nod. Mom was very outgoing. She was always striking up conversations with strangers—in the pizza parlor, in the supermarket line, at the beauty salon—and in the seven years since her death, my father has cultivated this habit. Where he was once withdrawn and distracted, he's now gregarious and engaged. There's something feverish about his sociability, a hyperaggressiveness in his manner, that makes me uncomfortable. Neither my brothers nor I quite understand it. Sometimes I wonder if he's trying to fill the hole of silence Mom left with as many words as possible.

"Ian's book is coming out soon," I say in the lull that follows Jenny's departure. "Three weeks."

"Wow, less than a month already?" he asks, surprised yet again by how quickly time flies. "It seems like he just sold it yesterday."

"Yeah, I know," I say, although in many ways the year has been long and slow. "He's completely freaking out over publicity. He doesn't think his publishing company is doing an adequate job."

"So you're talking to him?" Dad asks casually. His interest is paternal and he cares for my well-being, but there's more than that at work: My father is a fan of Ian's. Smart, decent, easy to talk to—this is someone he'd want to hang out with even if his daughter weren't dating him.

"Not really," I say, giving the sort of nonanswer that used to drive my mom insane. Dad accepts this. He doesn't dig or pry or try to shake things loose from their moorings. He listens and talks and nods wisely when he's feeling wise but he never offers advice or questions your choices. At first I took this for indifference. When Mom died and we were left staring at each other across red-and-white-checked tablecloths, I thought he didn't care. But that wasn't it. Dad believes that each person knows what's best for herself. This is his cogito: I am, therefore I think.

Jenny swings by with our drinks. She lays two glasses and a bottle of beer on the table and quickly dashes off to take the order of a family along the back wall. Every table in the restaurant is now occupied and she has no time to talk about her real career.

"It's just that he dropped by the office today," I add, looking out the window at a young woman who's handing out fliers for the piano bar next door. She's wearing a green duffel coat—a little warm for the oddly mild winter weather—and making eye contact with every person who walks past. "He wants me to help get the word out about *Jawbones.*"

"Will you?"

I shift my gaze to inside the restaurant. Dad is pouring the last of the Singha into my glass. "I told him I'd think about it, but I don't see what I can do. I have no experience with publicity. Also, it seems to me that if his book is coming out in three weeks, it's already too late to create interest."

"Who knows? You're creative. You might have a few ideas."

"I suppose I might," I say without conviction. My creativity is limited to discovering where teenage hipsters hang out. I can do it in any city in the world but it's still a rather limited talent. It's not breaking a story about statewide corruption or even citywide malfeasance. "Things are a bit of a mess at the office right now. My boss is behaving very oddly. Did you happen to catch the *Today* show this morning?" He nods. "The insane woman hawking snuff? That's my boss."

My father laughs. "I'm sorry to say I missed that. It must have been during the second hour. Did she demonstrate how to use it?"

"Yes, and with a very graceful flick of the wrist, too," I say, taking a sip of beer. "We got several irate telephone calls from public-welfare groups complaining that we were glamorizing a carcinogen."

Dad nods. He gets it. "So things are crazy in the office."

"Right. I want to stay focused. But I think I'd like to help Ian." Although this is the last thing I want to admit, it's true.

The new Ian, the one who digs in his heels and fights, fills me with a quivering optimism that's as disconcerting as it is novel. But I know that this Ian isn't real. He's not flesh and bone and pulsating heart valves. He's just a four-color image projected on a wall.

"Whatever you do, I'm sure he'll appreciate it," Dad says.

I nod. Despite Ian's many conversational shortcomings, he's always been able to say thank you. "Yes."

We both fall silent. I fold my napkin neatly in my lap while looking around the room. Dad takes a sip of beer and smiles pleasantly. There was a lot of this at the beginning—silence and wandering eyes and blank smiles. We'd go out to dinner, do our best to avoid eye contact and wonder what to say next. Talking helped. It was the only thing that over-came the awkwardness and the awfulness and the pene-trating sadness of life without Mom. At first we didn't make sense—we were just chickens squawking in a hen-house—but then something happened. The words formed sentences and the sentences formed conversations and the conversations formed a relationship. It was an accident, like amino acids colliding in the primordial soup.

After Jenny returns with our appetizers, the conversation shifts to Dad and he tells me about a woman he went out with the night before. Her name is Sylvia and she's a travel agent from Peoria.

This is one of Dad's ongoing problems with New York—it's too much of an international city. Most of the women he meets are just passing through. He could hang out on Long Island—there are singles bars everywhere—but he loves the energy of New York. Dad's a night owl and nothing makes him happier than a jammed Bleecker Street at two in the morning. He's mentioned getting an apartment several times in the past seven years but the talk has grown more frequent in recent months. In November, right before Thanksgiving, he ended a long-term relationship. It wasn't that he was no longer interested in Sarah, it was simply that he was equally interested in other women.

I was sorry to see Sarah go. I didn't know her very well—even after three years, we still treated each other with the cautious politeness of fellow travelers sitting next to each other on a very long flight—but she was familiar and kind.

The first woman Dad dated after Mom's death—a VP of advertising named Lydia—was brittle. After twenty-five years of clawing her way to the top, she was suspicious of everyone. Whenever she entered a room, her eyes, beady and blue, always raked the corners as if looking for secret cameras. She was difficult to talk to, thanks to a preference for one-word answers punctuated by long silent pauses, and I gave up after the first few months. I complained about her often to my brothers, but they were too far removed from the situation, both physically and emotionally, to care. They only had to deal with her during infrequent visits from the West Coast and couldn't understand what all the bother was about. I like my brothers a lot and get along with them really well, but they're still distant figures. Mark and Brian are only guest stars on *The Meghan Resnick Show.*

"How often does she get to Manhattan?" I ask.

Dad shrugs. "She says twice a year. I can go there for a weekend, but I don't know if it's worth it. We'll see. I might have meetings in Chicago in October."

"Are you seeing her again before she leaves?"

"I don't know. She's here with her cousin and there's some complicated story about theater tickets and a paralyzed dog. It all sounds fishy to me," he says, laughing slightly, as if he's not sure whether it's funny or not.

Dad's plans with women are often upset by complicated

stories, and I'm never sure if he's being blown off with overthought excuses or if he isn't paying attention when his dates call to cancel. Of the two, I'd much rather lay the blame at the feet of poor listening skills. However, the possibility of rejection is always there. It's a run-of-the-mill dating risk, a banality that all single people have to deal with, but it somehow seems dire when applied to my sixty-two-year-old father. There's something almost unbearable about that sort of vulnerability in a parent.

Dad starts talking about another woman he recently met—a fifty-something lawyer who lives in the city. He rambles on for some time about her apartment and her job and her svelte legs. I'm his confessor. Even though he has two sons, I'm the one he tells his stories to. The barrier that separates parent and child is gone. It was washed away in a flood, leaving this terrible free flow of information. I don't want to be in this position. I'd much rather go to my room and slam the door, but Dad needs me. This energy has to go somewhere or it'll tear through his body like a whirling dervish.

After dinner we walk over to Bleecker Street and listen to jazz in a crowded bar. The room is dark and smoky and everywhere I stand I'm in someone's way—the bartender, the waitress, the guy from New Jersey who's loading in a drum kit. I hate coming here. The club has a fifteen-dollar cover, music that's too loud and a bridge-and-tunnel crowd that's too cheap to pay for coat check. My scene is more low-key than this. I tend to hang out in basement bars with stale popcorn and bartenders who tell the same stories over and over again.

Dad strikes up a conversation with the woman next to him. She has a youthful appearance—tight blue jeans, flowing red hair—but her makeup is caked on and thick. She's trying to hide crow's-feet and laugh lines and the last ten years of her life.

I play with the straw in my ginger ale and pretend to be fascinated by melting ice. After a few songs, the band takes a break and I look at my watch. It's only ten o'clock.

"Your father's a very nice man," someone says. The words are spoken in my ear but I'm still not sure they are directed at me. I look up. It's the redhead. She's looking at me with a kind smile and an air of expectation.

The room is buzzing with small talk and laughter, but it's curiously quiet without the piano and the saxophone and the steady bass line. "Yes," I say.

"You shouldn't be embarrassed by anything he does," she assures me, smile firmly in place and a few stray hairs in disarray. She brushes them behind her ear. "He's a very nice man."

This is not the first time I've been told this—Dad uses me as a prop in his woman hunting: "Hi," he says as an opening line, "I'm going to embarrass my daughter now by talking to you"—but I still don't know how to respond. I return her smile with a pleasant one of my own and hope she goes away. She doesn't. She lingers to ask me what I do and where I live. Rather than try to explain trend-forecasting or encourage further conversation, I say I'm an accountant for an insurance company. I talk for a few seconds about actuary tables and her eyes glaze over. She wanders off and I glance again at the time. It's now ten-twenty. This is the home stretch. In ten minutes I'll find my father, tell him I have to be at work early in the morning and say goodbye.

It's not a perfect evening but it's better than trying to talk billionaire society ladies into giving you cash.

FIVE

I'm shutting down my computer when Mim assures Helen for the third time that she's fine. "Really. You're lovely to be so concerned," she says sweetly, "but there's nothing the matter."

Helen growls frustratedly. I can't see her—they're in Mim's office on the other side of the three-quarter wall that separates reception from the rest of the office—but I can easily envision what she looks like: teeth bared, color high. Helen spends much of her life irritated with bank managers and health insurance representatives. "Perhaps you feel that way now, but you haven't seemed quite yourself lately," she says coolly, managing to hold on to her temper despite the extraneous sounds that suggest otherwise.

"Not quite myself? How dramatic you are," Mim says with a laugh. It's a dismissive sound, flippant and glib, and I wait for Helen to snarl again, but she restrains herself.

"Come on, Mim. This is me. Helen. You know you can tell me anything."

"But there's nothing to tell. Everything is going very well. Actually, it's going so well I have a million things to do tonight before leaving."

The hint is clear but Helen doesn't take it. "Keeping it bottled up inside isn't healthy. You need to let it out. Tell me. Just tell me and it will all be better. You'll see. I just want to help." There's a new element in her tone, a wheedling note that's on the verge of begging.

All week long she's been trying to get Mim to open up. On Monday she scheduled simultaneous manicures and dragged a very confused Mim to the beauty parlor. On Tuesday she insisted on treating her to post-lunch cocktails. Neither tactic worked—not girl talk over nail polish, not confessions over drinks—and all Helen had to show for her efforts were acrylic tips and a hangover.

This is the third component of the female-bonding trifecta: the earnest heart-to-heart, and although the conversation is compelling and part of me wants to stick around until the end, I know I can't. Eavesdropping is wrong, but the karmic punishment is nothing compared with what Helen will dole out if she finds out I've witnessed this final humiliation.

I only dropped by the office after my four-o'clock appointment with Strikers to pick up my stuff. My meeting ran long—the creative director loved my idea for the new line, which he's already calling Mutants, and detained me for two hours with his marketing plan, including his product placement brainstorm ("I have a call in to the producer of the *X-Men* movies. We'll have a pair of our babies on every mutant freak who walks across the screen.")—and I assumed the office would be empty by the time I got back. I certainly didn't expect to overhear a personal conversation. The acoustics in the Pravda offices are simply too good for privacy.

My computer finally shuts down, and as I switch it off, Helen tries a different approach. She reminds Mim of all the things they've been through together and appeals to her sense of history, but Mim remains resolute in her insistence that nothing is wrong. Whether this is the truth or just the party line, I can't tell. That's how it is with Mim: She projects calm sanity at all times. That you can never tell what she's thinking is one of the things I admire most about her.

"Why do you *always* have to be like this?" Helen asks, her temper so frayed she's actually whining. "You never tell me anything. Remember fifth grade? When Danny Zimmer broke up with you a week before the Valentine's Day dance? I *knew* something was wrong—you were so sulky— but every time I asked you said, 'I'm fine, Helen.' And then you turned around and told Tina Gorka."

I put my tote bag over my right shoulder and walk to the staircase in the back of the office. The insight into the Mim-Helen dynamic is fascinating but vaguely discomforting. The polished veneer of happy accord they show us two or three times a week—the united front of warring parents (*"Pas devant les enfants."*)—is a nice fiction. I like it. I don't need to know about the seething underbelly and leave before any more secrets are unwittingly revealed.

By the time the accordion-rock mêlée breaks on Thursday morning, we're all too used to this sort of thing to care. Wendy has the *Times* with Mim's two-thousand-word treatise on the new music that's going to change the world, but nobody bothers to read it. We all saw Pat Kiernan mocking the article this morning on NY1 ("Accordion rock— isn't that just polka?").

"The guitar is played out," Wendy says, rehashing the item in her own words. "It's been all downhill since Hendrix but the A&R people at the labels won't admit it. It's the dirty little secret music industry insiders refuse to talk about. Enter the accordion. It's fresh, it's unique and its sound is practically unexplored. Mim predicts it'll be bigger than grunge." She finishes her summation and looks up. "An interesting premise. I might use it in one of my stand-up routines."

Norah walks by Wendy's desk on her way to the coffee-pot. "So the point is to replace guitars with accordions?" she asks, filling her cup. "Teenage boys in flannel and Converse All-Stars are going to pound the accordion keys in their parents' garage?" She adds milk, stirs and tosses away the spoon. "I gotta be honest. I don't see it. 'Accordion Rock Saves World' is like a headline you find on the front page of the *Onion*."

Liz and I laugh but we don't say anything. Mim's bizarre predictions have become commonplace and to comment on them seems like a waste of breath. Even Josh is uncommonly mellow about the whole thing. With a control-relinquishing, Mim-will-be-Mim shrug that was like the first step in an AA recovery program, he said it would blow over quickly enough.

He's probably right. Compared with Mim's other two major faux pas, there's something refreshingly harmless about this latest: It's only rock and roll. An editorial by Jann Wenner isn't nearly as damning as one by C. Everett Koop.

Helen arrives at eleven o'clock. She steps off the elevator in a noisy huff, with the newspaper tucked under her arm, and pounds on Mim's door. The sound is loud, repetitive and unproductive.

"She's not in there," says Norah, handing me an expense report and closing the file cabinet.

Helen rounds on her angrily. "What?"

Norah takes her seat at the desk and I pretend to be reading the form. I should go discreetly back to my desk but hiding in plain sight seems the better way to avoid attention.

"She's not in there," Norah says again.

"Then where the hell is she?"

Norah shrugs. "I don't know. She hasn't come—"

"Yeah, I bet you don't know." Helen's voice is rough and accusatory as she grabs Mim's calendar from a stunned Norah's desk. Then she stomps off to her office and slams the door.

"Wow," says Norah.

I sit down on the suede couch against the three-quarter wall. "Yeah."

"I guess that conversation with Mim didn't go too well."

"No," I say, revealing nothing, "I guess it didn't."

"I mean, otherwise the *Times* thing wouldn't have happened, right? Helen was supposed to put a stop to this."

Helen stays in her office for the entire day. For a while we speculate about what's going on behind the closed door—a novelty in itself because when she's here Helen likes to make her presence felt—but after a while we get bored and return to work. Despite the recent falloff of clients, we all have things to do.

At five forty-five, just when Josh is putting his backpack onto his shoulder to head out, Helen emerges from her hole and calls a staff meeting in the conference room.

Everyone wants to protest but nobody is brave enough. Even when Helen isn't thrashing around the office like a

raging bull, she's a hard person to question. We content ourselves with disgruntled looks as we take our seats.

"The situation with Mim is out of control," she says
grimly, opening a leather-bound folder. "Here's what we're
going to do. Norah, you're to cancel all her appointments
for the rest of the month. Use whatever excuse you want—
business trip to Halifax, dental appointment, death in the
family, burst appendix. I don't care. Tell Mim that the other
person canceled. Again, be sure to vary your reasons. I've
spoken to the telephone company and they're going to forward all her calls to Wendy. If anyone asks, tell them she's
on vacation and I'm handling things in her absence."

Norah nods as Helen barks out instructions but there's
a confused expression on her face. "But I thought you were
going to talk to her."

Helen looks at her with intense dislike. I didn't know that
a lip could curl like that. Norah slides down in her chair.
"This is what we're going to do." She pauses and waits for
dissent. None is forthcoming. "Josh, here's a key to a post
office box on Varick. All Mim's letters will be forwarded
there. Go through her mail every morning and separate out
the pieces that seem harmless. She can have catalogs and
brochures and basic junk mail. Everything else goes to me."

Josh stares at the small key while Helen issues instructions. He doesn't pick it up or put it in his pocket for safe-
keeping.

"Wendy, here's the number for the management company that oversees the building. They said there'll be a
space available downstairs on the fifteenth of next month.
I think it's the travel agency next to the yoga ashram. It's
not a whole floor like ours, but a small office. Follow up
with them and make sure they don't go back on their word.
We'll set Mim up there as soon as it's available." Helen folds

her hands on top of her leather folder. "Any questions so far?"

The general reaction around the table is a sort of shell-shocked amazement. There are a million holes in Helen's plan—isolate Mim so she could get up to more mischief while nobody is looking?—but we are all too stupefied to list them. Even Josh, who started us down this path, doesn't seem to know how to react.

I take a deep breath and raise my hand. I don't like putting myself in front of charging bulls, but I can't stay quiet. This treatment isn't fair. Mim's behavior of late has been embarrassing, bizarre and erratic but it doesn't justify this—banishment to an obscure outpost at the edge of the Pravda empire. She's not a disgraced British soldier in the mid-nineteenth century.

"I don't think this is right," I say quietly. "I think we should be more up front with Mim and—"

"You came to me for help," Helen says, her color rising as she rewrites history. "I'm helping."

I look around the table for moral support but everyone is averting their eyes, even Liz, who a week ago thought this plan was ridiculous. "But Mim has never been anything but kind to me and I don't like the idea of going behind her—"

"We've been losing money," she states impatiently. "In the last three weeks we've lost six clients—and that's over the holidays when nothing's supposed to get done. Just this afternoon Lotus Jeans called. They're going back to Young and Younger."

Across from me, Josh freezes. He didn't know about this latest defection.

"Right now Mim isn't good business," she continues, unaware of the blow she's just dealt. Her voice softens as she looks me in the eye. "You invest in something for thirty years and you think it's going somewhere but then—"

"Thirteen years," I say.

Helen tilts her head, confused. "Huh?"

"Pravda's been around for thirteen years. You said thirty."

"It doesn't matter how long," she snaps impatiently. "The point is you invest in something and you have the right to expect certain things. Mim's reneging on those promises and until she gets her head back into the game, she's in total lockdown." The harshness of the sentiment hits her as soon as it does us and she coughs. "What I meant to say is, who here wants to be unemployed?"

Nobody raises their hand.

"Who here wants our company to fold?"

Again, nothing.

"Who here wants to find another job?"

I think about what I'd do next. Perhaps return to journalism. The skills I've nurtured coolhunting—the watchfulness, the eye for detail—would serve me well at a newspaper, and the switch would certainly make my dad happy. Still, my arm stays firmly at my side.

"Who here wants to do something to save Pravda?"

Slowly, one by one, the arms go up. It starts with Josh, continues through Wendy and Norah, and ends with Liz.

"Traitor," I say softly under my breath. I don't expect much from the others—they're strangers and new employees—but Liz has worked here for three years. Mim hired her right after her law-school breakdown, when she was confused and incoherent and thankful to be away from Cornell's supercompetitive environment. Even though she frequently got messages all wrong—her psychiatrist parents identified this confusion as post-traumatic stress disorder— Mim remained patient and encouraging.

Liz stiffens her shoulders in response, but she makes no other acknowledgment of my comment.

"Good," Helen says, reaching for some pages in her folder. I haven't raised my hand but she doesn't notice. She's too caught up in her Mussolini moment to care. "Here's the schedule for watching Mim. I've broken the month down to four-hour blocks. First shift starts immediately after this meeting. You'll see it's color coded by name."

My co-workers each take a schedule and examine it carefully. Nobody protests or complains. Wendy is on the first shift but she has plans for tonight and trades with Norah, who doesn't go on duty until six tomorrow morning. But then Norah remembers that they don't actually know where Mim is—a violation of the twenty-four-hour watch's central tenet—and she and Wendy trade back.

Although it's well after six now, Helen makes us stay. She reviews the new procedures and spot-quizzes us on our familiarity. I'm a halfhearted participant but I'm here. I haven't gotten up from the table and stalked out of the office in outrage. I stay for two reasons. One: I don't actually believe that Mim containment will work. There's too much technology in democratic, first-world countries to cut someone off completely. Perhaps if we were in China, a scheme like this would go off without a hitch. Plus, the twenty-four-hour-watch schedule is destined for failure. The compartmentalized order of it appeals to my turncoat colleagues now—the 168-box grid seems like a feasible way to save the company—but it won't at three in the morning when one of them is standing outside her apartment in the freezing rain.

Two: I'm worried about Mim. Something has happened. Some monumental event has turned the savant of coolhunting into a fortune teller with a crystal ball. Thir-

teen years ago Mim reinvented trend-forecasting. Before she
hit the scene with her bimonthly Mim Report docu-
menting the trends in ten key U.S. markets, coolhunting was
a decentralized enterprise. Now it's national and every firm
in the country, even one-man operations in small cities like
Des Moines, has some sort of newsletter. And it was talent
that brought Mim to the top of her profession, not luck,
as some envious people have been small-minded enough
to suggest. It wasn't that she was at the right place at the
right time—New York City in the early nineties, when the
long-forgotten Potter was looking to reclaim its stake in the
sneaker business—it was that she took the time and place
and made them right.

Now she was falling apart, and her business partner was
dismantling her dignity in a fit of pique.

There has to be a reason for this. People don't flip out.
Reliable, stable, intelligent women like Mim don't just wake
up one morning and overthrow a career's worth of hard
work for the heck of it. Events have explanations. Effects
have causes.

I want to help but I don't know how. My position at
Pravda is far from privileged. Mim is my boss. I run client
problems by her and discuss trend reports and listen to her
advice. Sometimes the topic slides to more personal things—
holiday plans, weekend trips, favorite movies—but that
doesn't alter the nature of our relationship. We are always
what we are: employer and employee, teacher and student.
There are moments when we are almost more. The day I
came back to work after my mom died—the day Helen and
everyone else in the office avoided looking at me—Mim
pulled me aside. She put her hand on my shoulder, stared
me straight in the eye and struggled with what to say. "I was
your age when my own mom..." Pause. "If you want to

talk…" Longer pause. "If there's anything I can…" She couldn't quite get the words out, but it didn't matter. I knew what she meant. Her hand was warm, her gaze was steady and I knew exactly what she meant.

When I first started at Pravda I was confused by Mim's behavior—the way she offers friendship with one hand and pulls it away with the other—and it took me a while to understand what was happening. Mim masks a closed nature with an open demeanor. She's friendly and warm but separate. A tall chain-link fence edges her property line. It's well hidden behind ivy and azaleas, but it's always there at the tip of your pruning sheers. I respect that. Mim's the boss. She has the right to keep a professional distance. Her relationship with her partner—what she chooses to tell her, what she chooses not to tell her—is none of my business. I won't be an instrument in Helen's reprisal.

SIX

Every year at gala benefit time, Bonnie presses me into service. She doesn't present her case or pitch her cause or even give me the option of refusing. She simply tells me where to go and when to be there and how to behave: Venetian Room, seven o'clock, charming.

"It's not the place in Rockefeller Center," she says, hovering in my doorway as I look through my closet for a cocktail dress I still like. My wardrobe is extensive and varied and filled with lovely clothes but it's boring. I'm tired of every single thing I own, even the items that still have price tags. This is an unfortunate side effect of coolhunting—everything enters and leaves my life at an accelerated pace. I'm like Mercury circling the sun.

"Broadway and Seventeenth. Got it," I say.

"You might get confused because the place in Rockefeller Center is called Venetian Rose," she adds. "The place in Rockefeller Center is a cheesy tourist trap and I wouldn't invite the Astors to a gala in a cheesy tourist trap."

"If I promise not to go anywhere near Midtown today, will you go away?" I ask, trying with little success to find an appropriate outfit and feeling increasingly bad tempered about it. My clothes are organized in chronological order of purchase—new in front, older in back—and looking through them now I'm struck by the historical record they present. All you need to know about the past twelve months of fashion can be read in these cloth fossils: the blue period, the fringe period, the bandeau period. Seeing it like this, as an arrangement of layers in sedimentary rock, makes me impatient with my life. I always thought it was fun, being au courant. But maybe it's not. There's something mildly ridiculous about it all—the way every two weeks some overlooked color is always the new black, even black.

Annoyed, I reach into the dark closet and grab the first thing my fingers touch: a black tuxedo shirt. It's ruffled and tailored and festive in a strolling mariachi way. I go in for a second round and withdraw a black skirt, which I compare with the shirt. The two shades aren't a perfect match but I don't care.

Bonnie holds her position in the doorway. "But you promised to help," she says, her voice a high-pitched whine. This always happens on gala day. She gets nervous and preoccupied and squeaky.

"I am helping. Look, I'm packing my outfit in one of those zippered plastic things you carry suits in." I hold it up for emphasis. "Now I can go straight to the party from work."

Bonnie acknowledges my contribution with an abrupt nod, but it isn't enough. "You have to help me come up with something to say to the chef."

I hunt through the pile of shoes on the closet floor and consider the challenge of schmoozing a chef. It hardly seems like a challenge at all. "First you thank her for all her hard work, then you say something about how you couldn't have pulled off the event without her."

"But what about the picture?"

"What picture?" I ask. I've found only half a pair of stiletto-heeled Jimmy Choo sandals but I remain hopeful that I'll stumble across the other sooner or later.

"The one in *Time Out*." She pauses. "The one where she's standing in the kitchen of the Venetian Room completely naked?"

I look at her. "Huh?"

"God, Meg, I just told you about this," she says, exasperation raising the pitch of her voice to an impossibly high level. The mice in the walls are probably scurrying for cover in the building next door. "Sabrina Carpenter, the Venetian Room's executive chef, is completely naked in this week's *Time Out*. She's standing in front of a cutting board with her pert little breasts."

Bonnie had told me about it, just as soon as she'd gotten over her shock. It's not something you expect to see while flipping through your local weekly listings mag—the pert little breasts of your favorite chef.

"What should I do?" she says now, while I tear about my closet looking for the recalcitrant Jimmy Choo. Thanks to this evening's party, I'm going to be late for work. And I can't be late for work. I have the first Mim shift—from 10:00 a.m. to 2:00 p.m. "Should I tell her she looks great? Should I compliment her on her body? She has a great body. God, that sounds so creepy. And we're supposed to have a professional working relationship, which means my saying she has a great body can be construed as sexual harassment. So maybe I should just pretend I didn't see it at all. But that will be weird, too, because I *did* see it and she'll know I saw it because I'll be too embarrassed to look her in the eye and then I'll really seem like a creepy pervert. God," Bonnie says with a sigh, throwing herself on my bed, "I can't believe she did this to me."

The contents of my closet are now strewn across my bedroom floor and still I can't find the shoe. Either it's lost or it's hiding under my bed. I get down on my hands and knees. "Tell her you admire her bravery."

"Hmm?" she asks absently. Bonnie is so wrapped up in the awful turn Sabrina Carpenter has done her that she's forgotten I'm here.

"Tell her you admire her bravery. She was the only female chef, right? The four others who posed for the naked chef article were men who put absolutely nothing on the line. Oh, look, topless men. Isn't that risqué?" My bed is on heavy-plastic risers so that I can have more storage space but I never clean it out. I only push more and more junk underneath until everything is crushed and misshapen. This has worked with mixed results: My luggage has seen better days but the air conditioner is pretty much unscathed.

Bonnie is quiet as she mulls over my suggestion. "I like it," she finally says. "I think it could work. You're a genius, Meghan."

My shoulders are half under the bed but I shrug them anyway. "Thanks."

"So I'll see you later then?"

"Yes."

"At the Venetian Room."

"Right."

"At seven o'clock."

"You got it."

"And you'll be charming."

"My most charmingest."

"Perfect, I'll see you there," she says, walking away. I can hear her footsteps as she crosses the living room and goes into the kitchen. A few seconds later she's back. "That's Venetian Room on Broadway and Seventeenth, not Venetian Rose in Rockefeller Center."

I sigh but don't say a word. I just push a clear plastic storage box to the side and look for the damn shoe. It has to be here somewhere.

Despite my best intentions—outfit on by 6:26, makeup on by 6:31, hair brushed and twisted by 6:38—I arrive at the party more than a half hour late. The traffic and a telephone call and a last-minute meeting with Helen to discuss the success of Mim containment are all responsible. But Bonnie doesn't care about my excuses. She hands me a clipboard at the door.

"This is the list of high-profile donors and board members," she says, looking over my shoulder at the entrance. There isn't a large crowd of people waiting to get in— maybe ten at the most—but they're a throng to her. Bonnie hates the check-in process. No matter how quickly the line moves, some millionaire mucky-muck is always left waiting in the foyer. "Go find the photographer and make sure she's getting pictures of all the important people."

"All right. I've got it covered," I say as I take off my coat. I'm about to check it, but Bonnie isn't having any of it. Time is too precious to waste seconds getting a claim ticket.

"Here, give me that," she says, her tone exasperated and impatient as she grabs my wool coat and tosses it under a table. Then she turns and smiles ingratiatingly at a Broadway actress who's just stepped into the restaurant.

I track down the photographer and explain my purpose. She's testy and annoyed and insulted by the implication that she doesn't know how to do her job. I assure her it's nothing personal—last year I trailed after Patrick McMullan—and point her in the direction of some board members.

The cocktail hour passes in a flurry of flashes and forced smiles. When it's over, I lean against the far wall and listen to the quartet play the final notes of Vivaldi's "Spring."

"I couldn't tell from across the room if you like red or white," a voice says in my left ear, "so I brought over one of each."

I turn my head. A man in a well-tailored dark suit is holding out two glasses of wine. He's tall and streaked with blond and smiling hopefully. I reach for the red.

"Hmm, that's what I thought," he says as he hands me the glass.

I wrap my fingers around the stem and look at him. He has a West Coast look about him—a revealing sun-splashed goldenness—which is intriguing. Stage Left fund-raisers are always a familiar collection of East Coast money and establishment. "What gave me away?" I ask.

"A certain polished sophistication," he explains. "White wine is easier to like. I knew you'd have more depth."

He's handing me a line, and although I know it, I don't walk away. I watch the waiters clear the floral centerpieces from the tables.

"I was just about to adjourn to the dining room. Care to join me?" he asks, offering his arm. It's a disconcerting gesture, the sort made in the drawing rooms of country estates that are listed with the national registry, and I think for a moment of refusing. I don't have anything against lovely manners in general, but his actions are overkill. Still,

I accept his escort. The novelty of the moment overrides the faint absurdity.

"Did you see any of last season's Stage Left plays?" I ask as we climb the stairs. This is my usual opening line. It's safe and reliable and always sparks a discussion.

"Actually, no," he says, with an abashed smile that seems at once calculating and sincere. "But I have a very good excuse. I'm not from around here. I live in California. The last play I saw was a big, splashy musical—and I mean that literally. There was a swimming pool on the stage."

I laugh. The musical adaptation of Esther Williams's life is one of those Broadway success stories. It was panned by the critics, who took issue with the Cirque du Soleil derivativeness and the predictable triumph-over-adversity plot line, but audiences love it. They pay $110 to sit in the front row with a plastic tarp over their legs and don't complain when they leave the theater soaking wet.

"Where in California?" I ask as we reach the second floor. Guests are milling around the room, reading place cards and finding their seats. The tables are decorated beautifully, with small, tasteful arrangements of hydrangea and candles.

"Los Angeles," he says, once again pulling out his apologetic, charming smile. "I'm third-generation Hollywood, if you can believe it."

I look at him again, trying to find something familiar about his streaked hair and friendly dimples. I draw a blank. "Are you an actor?"

"God, no. Producer. My name is Harrison Gordon," he says. Then he pauses for a split second to let name-recognition happen. But it doesn't and he continues as if the tiny silence gap were a figment of my imagination. "You probably know my father—Lucas Gordon."

I nod. Everyone knows Lucas Gordon. His name is connected to almost every movie ever made. "So producing's a good gig?" I ask.

Harrison puts his hand on the small of my back and leads me gently through the crowd. "Yeah. It's hard work but it's rewarding," he says. "Dealing with monstrous-size egos is the hardest part."

"Feel free to name names," I say, scanning the floor. I'm supposed to sit at the staff table by the kitchen but Harrison has other ideas.

"One of our party had to leave early," he explains as he holds out a chair for me at his table. "Perhaps you'd like to join us?"

The truth is I'd rather not, but I smile cordially and say I'd be delighted. I'm here as a favor to Bonnie and don't want to be rude to potential donors.

Harrison introduces me to the other people at the table as the waiter fills my champagne glass. Thanks to his interference, I'm now sitting with pharmaceutical executives and their wives. The company is glittering: I see sapphire earrings and ruby necklaces and diamond signet rings everywhere I look. These people are superwealthy. They live in penthouse apartments on Central Park West and sprawling mansions in Great Neck.

I ask them if they caught any of last season's productions.

Everyone at the table except Harrison has seen at least one play and thoughtful critiques of the four different productions carry us through the first course.

"They do such innovative work," says the woman to my left. Her name is Lila or Lily and she speaks with a faint British accent. All her vowels are long. "The physicality of the roles." She shakes her head in wonder. "I simply don't know how they do it."

Stage Left is known for two things: their physically grueling roles—almost every ensemble member is a former trapeze artist or ballerina or college football star—and their rigorous adaptations. The former was an unexpected development that evolved over time but the latter was intentional. The school they went to taught them only one way to write a play: Find a text, break it down to its elements and reassemble. This is all they know: tailoring narratives to the stage. The challenges of adaptation—representing internal thought, compensating for a visual medium—are not insignificant but in the end it's just putting flesh on someone else's bones.

In a recent production of *Middlemarch,* Dorothea spent half the play doing back flips—a literal interpretation of her willingness to bend over backward for Casaubon. Stage Left loves Victorian novels. They always have plot to spare.

Bonnie knows this from personal experience. A few months ago, fed up with corseted waistlines and eviscerated Hardy tales, she started writing a play. "Coming up with what happens next has always been the hard part, hasn't it?" she observed. "It's staring at a blank sheet of paper that's the terrifying part."

At the moment it's still a convoluted mix of themes—appearance versus reality, the undeniable allure of fantasy, disappointment and its attendant hardships—but she's slowly paring down the hodgepodge into something interesting and compelling. Based on Bonnie's compulsive spying on our neighbor Vicky, the story delves into what happens when watching someone else's existence takes over your own.

Although a rough draft is almost done, she's never mentioned it to anyone at Stage Left. Making the transition from administrative to creative in the theater world is almost impossible, and she's not ready to deal with the resistance she's sure to encounter.

"It's all those circus performers they hire," Lila or Lily's husband explains now. "They have the proper training."

Harrison leans over and whispers in my ear. "This is unbearably boring," he says. "I'm sorry."

"It's fine," I say honestly. I like helping Bonnie.

My answer fails to convince him, and he gives me a dubious look before noticing my wineglass is empty. He offers to refill it.

"No, my turn," I say, grabbing the glass before he can. My reflexes are faster or less impaired than his. "What would you like?"

Harrison requests a scotch and soda. The bar is across the room and as I walk over to it the twelve-piece band starts playing "My Way." Several couples take the floor while I wait for the bartender to pour my drinks.

"Here you go," he says.

I thank him, pick up the glasses and turn around. I'm not paying attention—the music is too lovely—and I bump into the person standing behind me. "Whoops," I say as scotch and soda dribbles down the side of the tumbler and over my fingers. My first impulse is to wipe the glass on the side of my skirt, but I resist the urge. I might not appreciate a surfeit of manners in West Coast producers but I do have some sense of proper etiquette. I curl my hand in a ball and look up as I apologize. "I'm sorry. I wasn't paying attention."

"That's all right," he says, giving me a napkin.

His voice is familiar and it takes me only a second to recognize Mim's husband, Peter. He realizes he knows me at almost the same moment and smiles warmly. "Meghan, what a surprise. I didn't know you supported the arts." He smiles delightedly and pecks me on the cheek as he hands me another napkin.

Although I know very little about Mim's nonwork existence, I'm quite familiar with her spouse. We were in almost daily contact during my three years as her assistant. Peter was always calling to make a plan or rearrange one. Sometimes he'd drop by the office unannounced to take Mim out to lunch. He'd buzz the intercom and not say a word in response until she impatiently opened her door to see what was wrong. The rapid-fire change in expression when she saw him lounging unexpectedly by the reception desk—from irritated huff to giddy delight in one hundredth of a second—was the most insight I got into her private life.

"I'm not really a supporter of the arts," I explain, stepping away from the bar. A small thirsty crowd has gathered behind me, and despite the polite, understanding smiles on their faces, they're hovering impatiently. "My roommate works for Exit Stage Left and needed some help. Is Mim here? I'd like to say hello."

He shakes his head. "No, I'm not with Mim."

An awkward silence follows this statement. I'm waiting for him to elaborate, to say what kept Mim away, but he doesn't. He just looks at my wet hands around the dripping tumbler and offers me another napkin. I take it and ask how work is to smooth over the moment. Peter Kreisky is a successful photographer. He's preternaturally skilled at catching the frenetic energy of great metropolises just seconds before they start decaying. Several of his most famous works are hanging in museums all over the world.

"Work is good," he says. "The last few weeks have been very busy. I've been out of town mostly."

I want to ask if he's noticed anything funny with Mim—

is she behaving just as oddly at home—but I don't have that kind of courage. Mim is my boss. Peter is my boss's husband. "That's good." Another weird silence. I hold up my drinks. "Well, I suppose I should go back to my table."

"Yeah, me, too," he says. Then he turns around and walks away without ordering a drink. Whatever he came here to get has completely slipped his mind. This strange behavior arouses my interest, and I watch him return to his table. I watch him sit down next to a redheaded woman, who looks petulantly at his empty hands. I watch him whisper something in her ear that makes her laugh. I watch him kiss her cheek.

I'm so surprised by this development, I forget my manners. It's rude to stare, even worse to glare openly and shoot death rays from your eyes, but I don't care. I stand there, rooted to the spot, thinking of Mim. After a moment, Peter realizes he's the object of my attention and he looks at me. His eyes meet mine without flinching and he raises his chin rebelliously. Now he's defiant—from thirty feet away.

I'm not with Mim. No, I can see that he's not.

After a prolonged staring contest—Peter averts his gaze first—I return to my table of pharmaceutical execs, preoccupied and less inclined to make small talk. I'm smiling and agreeing with every word said but I'm really worrying about Mim. Does she know? God, what a silly question. Of course she knows. Your husband doesn't show up at a high-profile, media-saturated event with a redheaded floozy if all is cheery at home. It's hard to tell from watching Peter and his date—and, yes, I'm watching Peter and his date with uninterrupted steadfastness from my unexpected position at table number 7—how long they've been together. They seem like a thing. They're comfortable with each other and unselfconscious—hallmarks of a longstanding attachment. This relationship isn't new. Poor Mim.

Harrison's aunt Judith asks me about my day job, and I tell her I work in marketing. She asks how so and who for, and I rattle off a scripted answer about a consulting firm. If my ex-boyfriend and my father cannot understand coolhunting, I doubt a society wife from Great Neck will.

Aunt Judith coughs and asks another question. There is a mild strain of annoyance in her voice and I have the awful feeling that she's repeating herself, that I missed the question the first time around. I straighten up in my chair, pull my eyes away from Peter and explain that I find the challenges of marketing very satisfying indeed. Harrison's aunt is far from appeased by my belated, enthusiastic reply. She's not accustomed to split attention spans and wandering interests. I ask her several questions about herself and pretend to be fascinated by the answers to make up for my inattentiveness, but it doesn't really work. Although she's polite and friendly and happy to tell me about their recent winter travels, she's no longer warm. I had one chance to ingratiate myself and I blew it. I won't regain her good graces no matter how many times I ooh and ahh over her description of Christmas festivities in Athens.

I finish my third—or fourth—glass of wine while Judith tells me in riveting detail about their charming villa on Lipsi, a devastatingly quaint island in the Aegean Sea. Her vacation was long, almost four whole weeks, and just as I'm convinced it will never end, her husband interrupts to ask her a question about their gardener. She's too distracted by this new topic of conversation to return to the old and I welcome the opportunity to go back to my previous occupation: watching Peter and his date. In the intervening minutes, they've progressed from mild flirting to aggressive canoodling. The sight is so horrifying I almost look away.

"Do you want to dance?" Harrison asks softly.

I'm staring across the dance floor at Peter's table, but Harrison thinks I'm pining. I don't have the energy to explain, so I say yes. The band is playing another Sinatra tune, "Strangers in the Night," and he wraps his arms around me. Harrison is a good dancer—his grip is light and his steps sure and he doesn't hum the tune in my ear—but something is missing. Maybe it's the humming. Ian always sings along. He can't hold a note or find the right key, but he has a nice singing voice—strong and smooth and soothing.

The song ends and the band announces it'll be taking a short break during dinner. The waiters then suddenly materialize around the edges of the room to serve filet mignon and perfectly cooked salmon steaks.

Harrison holds out my chair for me, yet another unnecessary courtesy that irritates me. I don't mind being wined and dined and I don't object to receiving flowers and chocolates, but this hyperpoliteness is grating on my nerves. Ian never pulled out chairs for me. He never offered his arm to escort me into dinner like I needed help finding the way, but he always held my hand while we walked to the movie theater in Union Square.

Dinner is good, and while we eat, Harrison tells me about the production he's working on. It features several well-known WB stars who are trying to shake free of the small screen. The dangerous stunts sound exciting but the plot is hard to follow. Rather than try, I drink wine and nod politely. Before I know it, dessert is being cleared away.

Yay—another fund-raiser over. Despite the free food and flowing wine, these things are never as much fun as they're supposed to be. They're always more work than play, even when you're a halfhearted recruit in your roommate's army. Only last year was good, when Ian came.

Several people at our table get up to leave. The men dig through their tuxedo pockets looking for the coat-check slip while their wives touch up their lipstick. Their perfectly painted lips signal the end of my tour of duty, and I turn to Harrison to thank him for a lovely evening.

"You're taking off?" he asks, his aristocratic eyebrows rising again. "I thought we could go somewhere quiet and get a drink."

After this evening's excesses, the last thing I need is more alcohol. I'm not completely drunk—all my faculties are present and accounted for—but I'm not entirely sober either. I'm something else: pleasantly tipsy and pleasingly dizzy and terribly distracted by how easily Peter has replaced Mim. I've had enough of the high-society circus for one night. The diamonds and these plastered-on smiles that don't bend at the corners are making my head ache. All I want right now is a club soda in a dark bar. "That sounds lovely, but I have plans." I look at my watch. It's after ten—right in the middle of Ian's shift.

"Are you sure? I know a great place around the corner," he says cajolingly, coaxingly, and for a second I get a glance at producer Harrison, the money guy who convinces WB starlets to take a hundred grand less for a role.

"Very sure." I open my bag and start digging around for my claim ticket. I usually put them in the change compartment of my wallet but it's not there. "I'm meeting a friend downtown. I told him I'd be there around ten-thirty."

Harrison isn't prepared to give up and he takes my hand, despite the fact that it's buried in a sparkly black purse. "I can't convince you to break your date?" His voice is softer now, perhaps even seductive, but I'm immune and impatient and annoyed that I can't find my coat-check ticket. Where the hell did I put it?

"No, I make it a policy never to cancel plans at the last minute," I say, standing up. "I'm sorry. But do have a lovely stay in New York."

But Harrison isn't paying attention to my well wishes. He's too busy trying to make sense of my abrupt leave-taking. This isn't the way it's supposed to happen. He wasn't plying me with wine all evening so that I'd fall into someone else's arms.

I shrug and walk away.

After I explain my problem to Bonnie in more words than necessary, she reminds me that I never checked my coat. "I threw it on the floor, under a table, remember? I think it's still there. I saw it about two hours ago."

I nod tepidly. I have a vague memory of black wool flying. "Thanks," I say before wrapping her in a hug. "It was a great party. Congratulations."

Bonnie sighs and then laughs. "It was, wasn't it? Let's hope everyone else agrees." Sometimes she's convinced an event is a great success only to find out the next day that the creative director of the company thought the miniature camembert walnut puffs were soggy. "So I'll see you at home?"

"Well, I thought I might stop—"

She doesn't let me finish. She doesn't have to. "Meghan, you're awful," she says, amused.

I blush. No matter how many glasses of wine I've had to drink, I'm always embarrassed by this—by how much I want to see Ian when my defenses are down. "It's just that I've had a really rough evening. Mim's husband was here but not with Mim, who's been acting strangely and—" I stop myself from rattling on and on. Bonnie has more im-

portant stuff to do than listen to me stress about things I
can't change. "And I'm going to find my coat and get out
of here. I'll tell you all about it tomorrow or the next day."
I wave goodbye but a new drama—a board member, missing keys and a terrified busboy—has already grabbed her
attention.

By the time I get to the Cardinal Rule, it's almost eleven
o'clock and the place is half-empty. Wednesday nights don't
draw a big crowd—not like the packed houses of Thursday
and the weekend—and Ian spends most of his time playing
songs from the jukebox and eating popcorn. When I enter,
he's pouring bottom-shelf whiskey into a glass with ice and
reaching for a lime wedge. I sit down at the far end of the
bar and wait until he sees me. He never looks at me or even
glances my way but a minute later he's putting a glass of club
soda down in front of me. I always think I'm a mystery, but
I'm not. My aura is letters arranged in short, precise sentences.

"Hey," he says.

It's been four weeks since I last saw him—four whole
weeks since he came to the office and pleaded for something
that mattered—and I'm not sure how to behave. I hate that
I've let him down. He came to me with expectation and a
glorious excitement in his eyes and I sent him away with
vague promises of I'll see what I can do. I've done nothing.

"Hey," I say, not sure where to start. I can't just jump into
it. I can't run him over with the Peter and Mim car. "How
are you?"

He shrugs. "What's up?"

I make another effort. "How's the crowd tonight?" I ask.
Ian knows I'm struggling for things to say. I've spent too
many Wednesday nights on this bar stool not to know the
status of the crowd.

He shrugs again. "All right."

The front door opens and a large man wearing a down jacket enters. Sweat is dripping from his temples and he orders a Guinness before he even gets to the bar. Ian grabs the tap, which is within easy reach, fills a glass, puts it on the bar and makes change without taking his eyes off me.

It was this stare of his—steady and still—that first attracted me, and it set the stage for all the things I'd eventually learn about him. Whenever he told me stories about his Boston Brahmin upbringing, I'd default to this look. Like the time he was found in the inner sanctum of the statehouse signing bills into law—I can see it clearly: five-year-old Ian looking up at the governor of Massachusetts with that inscrutable, unwavering intensity.

His childhood, though privileged and pleasant, wasn't an advertisement for the advantages of wealth. Ian comes from a long line of businessmen. His ancestors were old-fashioned captains of industry—clever, exploitative, lucky—and even before he was weaned off his mother's milk, the course of his life was laid out. Straying from the plan wasn't an option. Cumberlands have destinies. And Ian accepted this. With that familiar stare on his face, he stood silently as his father announced there would be no more writing classes for him at Harvard.

"So what's going on?" he asks, resting his elbows on the bar for a moment.

There's a congeniality about Ian that gives no hint to the battles he's fought. He has enough sense to realize that the obstacles he's had to overcome—Ivy League business degree, trust fund, overly involved parents—are precisely the sort of impediments most people wish for. Leaving Boston with only a backpack and the cash in his wallet didn't put him at a disadvantage. It just leveled the playing field.

"How's your sister do—"

"Meg," he says, impatient with my burnt offerings to the social graces. We are beyond that. Ian and I have known each other too long to waste words. They say familiarity breeds contempt, but it doesn't. It just breeds familiarity.

I take a sip of club soda and tell him about Mim's erratic behavior and Peter's infidelity and the redheaded floozy who looked to be about twelve years old. I ramble on for a while about Helen's colossal temper tantrum that has resulted in Mim containment. I rant angrily for twenty minutes about my awful co-workers' willingness to go along with the unscrupulous plan. I complain for ages about Harrison and his boring, judgmental aunt. I babble and blather and stray from the topic so often that the topic itself becomes a vague notion. Ian listens and serves drinks. Sometimes he makes intelligent, useful observations, but mostly he lets me get it all out. Ian is good at letting you vent, and in the bright red glow of the bar's Budweiser sign, he seems almost perfect. A surreal vermilion halo is hovering over his sandy head and for a little while I forget about Delilah Quick.

The rest of the night rushes by in a flurry of words. Suddenly it's three o'clock—the bar is empty, the front door is locked—and I'm following Ian back to his place.

SEVEN

I'm on the phone with Roger Cooley the next morning when Norah summons me to Mim's office. He's the director of research and development at Potter, and because this is the first time we've actually spoken to each other after three weeks of phone tag, I wave her off. Norah leans against my desk, prepared to wait. I hold my hand over the receiver while Roger runs through next season's models. "Five minutes. Ten tops. We're almost done."

Norah looks at me dubiously and walks away. I return my attention to the conversation, which has carried on nicely without me. Being able to listen without interrupting is one of the keys to trend-forecasting success, and sometimes you don't even have to have your ear in the game to do it well.

"We're very excited to work with you," he says, when he's done with the summer-catalog highlights.

"Thanks. I'm excited, too," I say. And it's true. Potter has always been Mim's exclusive domain, and I was ridiculously flattered that she entrusted it to me.

"I felt terrible asking for a new account manager," he adds with a sigh, "but after the Killington it was either that or go with a new firm. The department manager, John Purcy, wouldn't hear of it. And with good reason, of course. He used to work with Mim in the old days. But Potter prides itself on its street cred and we couldn't risk another disaster."

"Of course not," I say agreeably, although I have absolutely no idea what he's talking about. The Killington? "In your business street cred is everything."

"Exactly. It's one thing to have the *New Yorker* make fun of you. I mean, even if our customers saw the cartoon, they wouldn't get King Kong snowboarding down the Empire State Building. Actually, I didn't get it. But it's something else entirely when *Teen People* devotes an entire spread to lampooning your newest model. We can't ride that out, not when they're putting Killingtons on hobbits."

While he talks, I pull up Google and search for Potters and Killington. Several thousand hits come up. I click on the top one, which is the Potter official site, and wait for the page to load. "On hobbits? How terrible. What'd you do?" I ask. Keeping the chatter going seems like a good way to get information. It always works in crime novels.

The page finishes loading and I get my first glimpse of the Killington—silver, thick, high, fat.

"We pulled the model. There weren't many left on the shelves anyway. Most of the stores had already sent them back. They weren't moving," he explains, his voice weary. I look again at the picture and understand his fatigue. Even in cyberspace, the Killington looks draining. Sneakers are supposed to be light and fleet of foot, not laced-up anvils. "We should have known better. I mean, a street version of a snowboarding shoe sounds unworkable. Our designers were leaning toward something different, an aquatic shoe or even a wrestling shoe, but Mim was adamant that sneakers were going to get fatter before they got thinner, and she'd never steered us wrong in the past. I felt terrible about asking her to remove herself from the account but my hands were tied. We need someone who is still in touch with the youth market. It's like I said, Potter has street cred. We can't afford another misstep."

"No, of course not," I say soothingly because he's the client, not because I agree. Mim made one bad call in fifteen years. One bad call. I made more than that my first month on the job. "I'm sure Mim understood." This is also a lie. Your flagship client telling you you're too old—there's nothing to understand.

"She handled it beautifully. It was right in the middle of the dreadful to-do over *The Harmony Cortez Show.* I'd been putting off making the call for almost a month, but then the story broke and the head of the department insisted that I tell Mim right away. She was completely sympathetic. I'm very sorry this had to happen. Mim really is a pleasure to work with. But we've remained loyal to Pravda. That's what matters."

He says this in a smug tone—as if he should be thanked for his generosity—and even though we've never met, I can easily imagine his self-congratulatory smile.

"Yes, that's what matters," I say.

"But that's all water under the bridge now," he says, switching the topic to more upbeat things like what's on the drawing board for next winter. Roger has lots of ideas—neon colors, swervy stripes, rubber eyelets—that I want to pay attention to, but I can't. I'm too troubled by the previous topic to do anything other than say "uh-huh" every so often. Finally he wraps up the conversation. "So I'll see you next Wednesday? Three o'clock?"

I have no recollection of setting up an appointment, but I agree to it anyway and promise to see him in a few days. Then I put down the receiver. The Killington is staring at me, and I close the window because I can't bear to look at it. Mim's other misfires are distant—snuff boxes with gold-embossed lettering are remote objets, like priceless figurines under museum glass—and unreal. But the Killington is thick and bright and only inches away from my face. It's so close I can feel its hot breath on my cheek, reminding me— no, making me really aware for the first time—that Mim is not infallible.

This proof of her humanity should be comforting in an oh-well-nobody-is-perfect way but it's not. One blunder makes way for a million others. One mistake refutes unde- niably the immovable permanence of her gift. I believed in Mimness. I subscribed to it wholeheartedly. That it could be something unstable—more the needle on a compass than the *N* indicating north—never occurred to me.

"Hey, Meghan," Norah says. I look up to see her stand- ing over me with an uncharacteristic scowl of impatience. "You said ten minutes and now it's been over a half hour."

For a moment I have no idea what she's talking about— the destabilization of the Mim-verse has driven everything else from my mind—but I remember quickly enough. "Yeah, I'll be right in."

She nods and walks away. A few feet from my desk, she stops and turns around. "Are you okay?"

"Huh?" I ask, reaching for my calendar to mark down the Potter meeting.

"Are you okay? You were staring at your computer like you were trying to bore a hole through it with your mind.

I had to call your name five times before getting your attention."

"Yeah, I'm fine." Norah doesn't need to know that I'm disturbed by what Roger just told me.

She hesitates, then shrugs. "All right. Mim's waiting for you."

I grab a pen and scribble "Roger Cooley" and "3:00 p.m." on Wednesday before it slips my mind. It's bad enough I don't remember making the appointment. Part of the forgetfulness is exhaustion—I got very little sleep last night—but only a small part. Most of it is Mim.

She's on the phone when I enter her office and she waves me in. "Have a seat," she says. "I'll just be a minute."

I nod and sit down across from her. Irrationally, I'm expecting fallible Mim to somehow look different from her infallible twin, but there's no appreciable change. The toppling pedestal didn't wrinkle her clothes or muss up her hair.

Rather than stare rudely, I search through the pamphlets on her desk for a suitable diversion. Underneath a small booklet instructing one on the care and use of one's new Uniden Bearcat police scanner—more Mim oddness—is a West Elm catalog. I'm flipping through the pages with the appearance of rapt interest, but it's all for show. I'm more interested in who she's talking to. Norah isn't supposed to put through any calls.

"No, no, I like the way that sounds. Can you read it back to me again?" Extended pause. "But make it clear that's King's College London. I don't want to be accused of falsifying my CV."

Mim containment has been in effect for three weeks and so far it's a qualified success. There have been some failures—a 92nd Street Y panel where she defended *slut*

T-shirts as free speech, which aired on C–SPAN 2; a quote in *USA TODAY* about hibernating being the new co-cooning—but on the whole Helen's plan has worked. To some extent we have Mim to thank for its smooth implementation. Although she's noticed that things are unusually quiet around the office, she hasn't shown any particular interest in the cause. This passive complicity—the way she accepts Norah's explanation that all mail in the building is being temporarily diverted to the Varick Street station for safety reasons—implies that Mim's mind is elsewhere.

Containment is working even without one hundred percent compliance with the Mim-watching schedule. Only Helen, who gave herself the cushiest shift—from 2:00 to 6:00 p.m., Monday through Friday—follows it. Josh did his first two dead-of-night stints with enthusiasm, but gave up on day three after Mim's doorman, taking him for a homeless person, kicked him out for sleeping in the lobby at four in the morning. Norah hasn't done a shift yet but lives in perpetual expectation of fulfilling her obligation—just as soon as she has the time. Wendy shows up for the handoff from Helen, waits five minutes, then goes home.

Across from me, Mim hangs up the phone, apologizes for the wait and jumps right to the point. She hands me a file and tells me that I'll be in charge of the Stellar Soft Goods account from now on.

"Vivian's a tough customer," she says, referring to the head of the clothing company. Usually Pravda works with department managers and division supervisors. It's rare that the president of a company gets directly involved with the everyday aspects of product development. "Working with her will be a challenge but I think you're ready for it."

In the past few weeks, Mim has given me three other accounts to manage. She always puts the handover in terms of my development as a professional coolhunter—she thought I was "ready" for the Potter challenge, too—and I took these statements as the compliments they were clearly meant to be. But now I'm not so sure. In light of the Cooley revelation, it seems as though Mim is divesting herself of responsibility. Rather than get back up on the horse, she's deeding the ranch over to me.

"Vivian has a new project she can't wait to get started on: baby tees with decals. I told her you'd call today to set something up for early next week. I hope that's all right."

Mim looks at me with polite concern and I consider telling her the truth: that no, it's not all right, not at all. I'm too tired for this. My responsibilities at Pravda have tripled in the past month. Not only do I have more projects than hours in a day, I have to give up valuable minutes to Helen, who requires twice-weekly Mim reports. Yesterday I received the first prototypes of Strikers' Mutants in the mail, and the thought of hitting the street to get opinions wipes me out completely. The enthusiasm I used to feel for this job is buried under snuff and Delilah Quick and Helen's 168-box-grid Mim-watching schedule.

I want everything to go back to the way it was—Mim perfect, Helen indifferent, me undisillusioned. More than anything else, I want to have the simple clear-sightedness I had on my first day of work back. Better information for better products—that's the bill of goods I was sold. And I believed it. For a very long time I bought it hook, line and sinker. But it's not true. In today's market, companies aren't selling anything as simple and basic as well-made products. Potter isn't selling sneakers. It's selling an image. It's selling yourself back to you, only with clearer skin, a hipper haircut and funnier friends. But this ideal doesn't exist. It doesn't have limbs or homework or an outline you can trace with a crayon. It's absolutely nothing at all. Hip itself is a man-made construct like the Hoover Dam and capitalism, and I'm not sure anymore if it even exists. Coolhunters, treasure hunters, ghost hunters—we're all chasing chimeras.

Sometimes I still think it's a fairly harmless way to make a living—at least it's not testing eyeliner on cute little bunnies or increasing the breast size of insecure sixteen-year-olds—but I can't always fool myself. After eight years on the street, I know the effects are slightly more insidious. The vaguely comic image that coolhunting has always called to mind—Mim and I with rifles on the Serengeti Plain tracking big-game cool—has been supplanted by something more menacing: teens being stalked for their authentic experiences. And there's no doubt about it: They *are* being stalked. Cool is continually on the move—by the time the Mutants hit the street, the hip kids from Williamsburg will be on to something else—and it's a constant struggle to hold it in your crosshairs. This is what keeps Pravda in business.

I'm too tired for this, I think again. My crisis of faith coinciding with Mim's crisis of confidence—it's too much to deal with on a quarter night's sleep.

Mim notices my lack of response and smiles encouragingly. "Is everything all right, Meghan?"

I look at her. She's hardly changed since the day she hired me: hair in place, shirt pristine, expression concerned. I don't know how she does it. Last night her husband kissed a redheaded bombshell at a public event, and I really don't know how she does it.

I close my eyes for a moment, feeling frustrated by the situation. I want to offer sympathy or outrage or solace, but I can't. The humiliations she's suffered are painful enough in the quiet dark of a lonely room. She doesn't need me shining a concerned flashlight in her eyes. If she'd wanted to talk about it, she would have told Helen weeks ago.

Mim tilts her head. "Is there something I can help you with?"

I sigh and put down the catalog, wishing the fatigue I felt was just sleep deprivation. "Do you ever think it's wrong?" I ask.

"Excuse me?"

"Coolhunting," I say. "Do you ever think it's wrong the way we insinuate ourselves into the lives of kids in order to sell their likes and dislikes to corporations?"

Mim answers without pausing to consider her words. "Better information for better products. You know very well that's what I believe. And," she says, smiling in a self-deprecating way I rarely see, "please don't say insinuate. It sounds sinister."

This answer, taken verbatim from the Pravda stump speech, is disappointing, and I examine her silently for a moment, wondering if I should leave it there. But I can't. Mim is smart. She has to have given her career more thought than that. "Right, but it's not better products we're making, it's better brands."

Mim disagrees with a quick shake of her head. "That's a false distinction, Meghan. Products are brands," she explains wisely, her kind, reassuring smile urging me to trust her on this.

But I'm not reassured. Mim is an excellent role model: an intelligent, attractive woman at the peak of her profession at thirty-nine. She represents the future. Her talent, her success, her poise—it's where I want to be in ten years. Or so I had always thought.

"Do you have other concerns?" she asks. "I'm happy to talk about them." Her tone is patient and gentle, as if she'll cheerfully devote the entire day to easing my mind. And she probably would. Mim never rushes you out of her office. Our first interview lasted almost three hours. She asked as many questions about me as I did about her.

"No, that's all," I say quietly. It's not the whole truth, but it doesn't matter. Despite whatever personal reservations she may have, Mim won't engage in a discussion about the ethics of coolhunting. The calm, reassuring smile—that's the garden gate.

I close the door, feeling an odd sort of sympathy with Helen. Perhaps this is how she felt when nail polish, liquor and heartfelt sincerity failed to elicit the truth.

Helen calls us into the conference room for a meeting at one o'clock. I try to get out of it by claiming Mim detail, but Helen shakes her head. She wants the entire staff present, even Norah, who usually stays at her desk in order to maintain the appearance of normality. "Don't worry, she has lunch plans at one-thirty with an old friend from college," Helen says as she puts her laptop on the table. Then she pulls down the screen—a surefire indicator that we're going to be entertained by a PowerPoint presentation. Helen's two years at business school seem to have been devoted exclusively to the mastering of software—I've never seen her amortize an expenditure—and she incorporates these programs into her life whenever she can, whether appropriate or not. "All right. Today we're going to talk about the tricky business of trend-forecasting."

The first slide is a collection of black silhouette stick figures with menacing-looking questions marks over their heads. It's impossible to determine from their height how old the people are, but Helen's notation at the bottom, "America's teens," clears it up nicely.

"As you all know, I can no longer rely on Mim," she says, adjusting the image on the screen even though it's already perfect.

In the past month, Helen has made it remarkably clear that Mim containment is all about soothing her own hurt feelings. It's difficult to believe that anyone can be so petty, but it's not unheard of. California governors have been recalled for less.

"Don't you mean *Pravda* can no longer rely on Mim?" I ask. Although I'd rather pass this and every other meeting in quiet contemplation, I can't let a statement as blatant as this one slip by.

Helen looks at me with dislike but holds on to her temper. She's trying to present a new image of strong, resourceful leader and doesn't want to fall back on old habits. "It's the same thing," she explains calmly. "I am Pravda."

The statement is calm and forceful but comical—she might as well have said "I am Caesar" for all the armies it actually commands. But I let it pass with just a smirky smile.

Helen waits a beat, then continues. "As I was saying, I can't rely on Mim, so I need a new system. Trend-forecasting has always been an inexact endeavor, more like reading tea leaves than a scientific process. It relies heavily on intangibles like instinct and gut feeling and tingling spider sense. I find this unacceptable." Flip. Next slide: stick figures with thought bubbles over their heads. "The only way to find out what teens are thinking is to ask them." Flip: stick figures at computer screens. "I have designed a program called MAD B 4.0." Flip: the words Mega Annotated DataBase, version 4.0, in black Helvetica bold. "A superdatabase of teenagers will allow us to chart their likes and dislikes without ever leaving the office. It will allow Pravda to conduct a constant two-way dialogue with teen taste-makers." Flip: stick figures with ties (marketing execs?) standing over stick figures at computers. "Through the program, clients will take their products directly to their ideal target market." Helen stops here to take questions. She wants to make sure we're all still with her.

Wendy waves her pen; she's been taking notes. "What happened to the first three versions?"

Helen is caught off guard. She was expecting praise. "What?"

"This is MAD B 4.0. What happen to MAD Bs one through three? Weren't they super enough?"

A few smothered giggles but nobody laughs outright. Still, Helen's look is quelling. "Nothing happened to them. They had unfixable imperfections in their code."

Wendy thinks about this for a moment and then nods. "All right."

"Any other comments?" Helen is still waiting for the admiration to pour in, maybe even a small ovation.

I raise my hand. "Isn't this Josh's idea?"

Again Helen is nonplussed. "What?"

"E-mailing polls and surveys to thousands of paid teenage consultants across the country—isn't that Josh's idea?" He smiles at me, trying to look innocent, and I wink in return. I heard all about the superdatabase when Josh first started. It was another reason I didn't like him. Masses of teens hooked up to Pravda through their computers—it's a little too Borg Collective.

Helen recovers from her shock and answers the question. "Josh might have mentioned it. I can't remember. Anything else?"

"When will we implement it?" Liz asks. "Is the program ready to go now?"

"No, we need to work out the kinks in the software first and build the database of ten thousand teens. It should be ready in six months."

"Six months?" Liz says softly. She's doing the math in her head: How long after the implementation of MAD B 4.0 will Helen fire her.

"Six months and then we'll be up and running," Helen chirps. "You'll be amazed by how smoothly everything will go with the new system. Coolhunting is about to enter a golden age."

This, too, she stole from Josh. "Golden age" is part of his rhetoric, as well as "the unreliability of field work" and "the rise of precision info gathering." Josh is convinced that his database is the wave of the future. Maybe it is. Recent articles in the *Times* and elsewhere have pinpointed a new phenomenon: the instantly passé trend. Thanks to constantly accelerating life cycles, trends are now lapping themselves on the culture track—they are in and out at the exact same time. Fads are hailed as hot and lamented as not in a single breath. Within that split second before the exhale lies the end of cool.

The only solution is for trend-forecasters to pick up the pace—to get info more quickly and with greater accuracy. No doubt teenagers will be happy to comply. Give them a little money and tell them their ideas are important, and they'll happily answer product survey after product survey. Mim's one-on-one approach isn't much better. We don't hook kids up like dairy cows to a tank but we still milk them for all their worth.

I'm enough of my father's daughter to realize there's a story here—about the marketing of youth culture, about the exploitation of today's teens. There's so much material regarding the way corporations brand and brainwash that there might even be a book. Sometimes I even think I will write it myself, but I don't have the time.

Norah asks how the megadatabase will be created and Helen smiles. "Excellent question." Flip: stick figures in caps (baseball players?) holding clipboards and standing in front of a squat black building. "I will come up with a list of questions for potential teen consultants to answer. The staff will go to malls across the country and distribute the questionnaires, then enter the ones who qualify into the computer."

"Data entry," Norah says, her smile disappearing. "Cool."

The comment is facetious but Helen doesn't care. She'll take the acclaim any way she can get it. "We'll talk more about that as the time draws nearer. This is just a preliminary meeting to give you an overview."

"An overview of what?" asks Mim. She's standing in the doorway with a steaming cup of coffee in her right hand.

Helen freezes at the sound of her voice, then scrambles to block the screen with her body. She doesn't answer until she's reasonably confident Mim can't see the image clearly. "Life insurance. I'm just giving them an overview of our new life insurance policy. I thought you were having lunch with Marsha?"

Mim shrugs and leans against the door frame. "I was. She canceled. The flu, which seems to be going around. We're lucky nobody in the office has come down with it yet."

"Yes, we're very lucky," Helen says, inching backward until the hanging screen is in her grasp. Without turning around, she gives it a strong tug and it curls up with a satisfying snap. Pleased with the smooth disposal of the incriminating evidence, she steps aside. The conference room walls, however, are white and the lack of screen makes no difference.

Mim examines the image of the clipboard-bearing stick figures with interest. "New life insurance?" she says.

Helen realizes her mistake a second later and darts back into position. "New life insurance. I was just explaining to the staff that they'd have to answer some questions before they find out their premium. You know, things like do you smoke and does cancer run in your family."

"Hmm. This sounds like something I should know about, too," Mim says, putting her coffee on the table and reaching for a seat.

"No," Helen says sharply.

Her tone is so abrupt Mim stops sliding out a chair to look at her. "No?"

Helen coughs and tries to fix her blunder. "No reason to waste your time. You've already been filled in on all of this."

Mim draws her eyebrows together. "I have?"

"Of course. I sent you a memo last week. I wouldn't make such a drastic change without consulting you first."

"I don't remember a memo," Mim says softly as she tries to recall the events of the previous week.

"Well, I gave it to your assistant. Norah," she barks, "didn't you give my memo to Mim?"

Norah jumps at the sound of her name and looks at Helen. She, like everyone else at the table, was busy pretending to be invisible. Nobody wants to witness the exchange between co-owners. Their perfidy is bearable as long as it's done from a comfortable distance. Watching Mim struggle a few feet away to recall something that doesn't exist is a little too real for them.

Norah is quiet for a while as she considers the question. It's impossible to tell what's responsible for her prolonged silence—surprise at being called on or reluctance to lie. "Your memo?" she says finally.

Helen nods emphatically. "Yes, my memo."

"Oh, yeah, your memo," she says. Norah turns to look at Mim, but her eyes are focused somewhere over her left shoulder. "I left it on your desk."

It's obvious from Mim's confused expression that she can't recall anything at all about the new life insurance policy, let alone the memo that detailed it, but she doesn't press the matter. "All right, good. Helen, I'm glad you've got everything under control." She picks up her coffee and steps away. "I've got some stuff to do, so if you'll excuse me."

Mim leaves with a baffled look I've only seen once before—in the wake of the *Harmony Cortez* fiasco. Helen's smile is wide and pleased as she pulls down the screen again; she continues with her presentation as if the interruption never happened. The room is silent now but not out of deference to Helen or the genius of her super mega-database. Her staff is avoiding eye contact with each other and looking studiously down—at their hands, at the table, at the carpet—in either acute embarrassment or shame.

Nobody says a word when the presentation wraps up. Helen looks around the table, disappointed yet again by the lack of response. The mood in the room has changed but she doesn't notice. "Well, if nobody has anything else to add, then please return to work. I know you all have much to do. And remember—" flip: stick figures with bandanas tied over their eyes (hostages?) "—this project is very hush-hush. Let's keep it between us for now."

The staff shuffles out of the conference room. I return to my desk and ostensibly work on the proposal for Stellar Soft Goods. After an hour of trying to write the opening sentence, I give up. I turn off my computer, throw my Filofax into my tote, grab my jacket and go home.

But the change of scenery doesn't help. I'm still appalled that I let them do that—play with Mim's mind when I know she's already doubting herself.

EIGHT

Bonnie insists on cleaning the apartment on Saturday morning. By the time I get up, she already has the contents of every kitchen drawer scattered across the living room floor. I walk gingerly to the stove and put on water for a cup of tea. Intent on removing a layer of dust-laden grease from a Ketel One bottle that's stored on a shelf over the range, she hardly notices me. She says hello in an absent way and reminds me to wash and put away my spoon when I'm done with the sugar. It's okay that every kitchen appliance we own is on the floor, but not all right that one spoon stays in the sink for a second longer than it has to. I hate cleaning days.

Fortunately Bonnie doesn't do this often. We're both relatively clean people—not neat, of course, but clean—and we maintain visitor-ready conditions at all times. We wash the bathroom sink once a week and vacuum the jute rug in the living room every Sunday. It's the other stuff that gets ignored—the dust bunnies under the couch, the tiles along the back wall of the bathtub, the scuffs and scratches on the black-and-white vinyl kitchen floor. Except when Bonnie finishes a huge project at work. Then 186 MacDougal is spick-and-span central. Bonnie puts on her yellow rubber gloves, finds the Comet and attacks dirt with the dogged enthusiasm of a three-star general bucking for a promotion. It's not a pretty sight.

The water for tea starts boiling vigorously and I take it off the heat. I reach for a coffee cup without looking and come up empty. Mugs, glasses and random pieces of stemware are being temporarily housed on the couch while Bonnie lays new contact paper—red gingham, only fifty-six cents a roll at National Wholesale Liquidators—and I have to go into the living room to fetch one.

Before drinking my tea, I wash the spoon, dry it on a pink towel that's seen better days and throw it on the living room floor with the others. Then I lean against the sink and watch Bonnie work. Satisfied with the sparkling shininess of the vodka bottle, she's moved on to whiskey, a considerably smaller bottle.

"You can help, you know," she says, her attention rigorously focused on removing the thick coating of grease. Her tone is conversational and informal, despite the stiff-backed peevishness of her words. Bonnie knows I carry my own weight. I'm not a heavy Pig Pen albatross around her neck.

I take another sip of tea and contemplate the kitchen mess. I'd planned to take it easy today, but suddenly heading uptown and talking to kids about the Mutants seems like the better option. That coolhunting is the lesser of two evils is ironic and sad. I used to relish being in the field. Now it's just a good way to get out of cleaning. "Can't right now. I'm working today. Maybe when I get back."

Bonnie nods and turns the bottle ninety degrees—one-fourth done. "I'll probably still be here," she says, sighing as she looks at the disarray around her. Our kitchen is small—try making a three-course meal for eight and you'll quickly realize there aren't enough surfaces for soup bowls and wineglasses and dessert plates—but it suddenly seems huge.

After I finish my tea and wash the mug, I jump into the shower. The bathroom has been likewise overturned and it takes me a while to find shampoo, conditioner and body wash. It's a good thing I'm not in a rush.

A half hour later, I'm throwing sunglasses into a backpack and grabbing my camera. It doesn't have a fab zoom lens like Bonnie's but that's okay. I don't need the stealth element. The people I'm photographing are perfectly aware that I'm taking their picture.

I hop on the 6 train and go to the Bronx. The first place I hit is Carmine's, a sneaker store with a hip-hop vibe that does extremely brisk business on the weekends. I spend a couple hours there showing the Mutants to boys and girls and getting feedback. Although most of the kids I talk to seem to like them, the girls are a little less enthusiastic.

"It looks like they're broken," says a twelve-year-old named Jasmine, with pretty green eyes and a shy smile, as she tries on a blue pair. "If I wear them, it'll look like I can't afford new ones."

My next stop is an arcade. It's loud and crowded and has the faintly sweaty smell of a boys' junior high locker room. I walk around for several minutes, getting a feel for the place before talking to three fifteen-year-olds who are waiting for a videogame called Monkey Karate Death Car to become available. They're pimple-ridden and smart and their sensibility is ironic. With their fisherman's caps and their dull-colored, short-sleeved collared shirts from thrift stores, they're not quite the ideal target market for the Mutants.

I'm looking for teens who are a little less savvy, but I take a mental picture of them anyway. Their nonstyle is increasingly common among urban kids. The nameless hat, the purposely logo-free shirt—it's a way of hiding from large brands that want to put your life in a box and stick it on a shelf in Target. But they won't fly under the radar forever. Eventually corporations will take the too-cool-for-cool slouch and straighten its posture.

I sit at the snack bar, buy a Coke and look over the room. This arcade, unlike the one Delilah Quick frequents in *Jawbones,* is well lit and bright. A thirty-year-old woman, even a hottie with a superyouthful appearance, couldn't pass for fifteen here. But that's what Delilah does—passes for fifteen, befriends high schoolers and uses them as her own personal focus group. She earns their trust and summarily betrays them. When things get particularly dicey, she has her new chums make drops in her stead. They think they're buying Hello Kitty purses at drastically marked-down prices, but they're really picking up kilos of heroin. One girl, the naive and wistful Drusilla Walker, gets shot in the head. At the end of the book, she's still in a coma.

Delilah's duplicity is twofold. Even before she put teenagers in mortal peril, she'd sold them out to giant corporations greedy for their allowances, and Ian lingers on this fact for several pages. The extremeness of the betrayal is necessary—it moves the plot forward—but it's also pointed, and the implication, simple and dramatic, is that it's only a matter of degrees. Delilah Quick is a literal manifestation of a more abstract truth: that commodifying teenagers is wrong. Their experiences—their likes and dislikes and the painful prom night disappointments—are more than a catchy slogan for selling sneakers.

I know this. You can't crouch behind an acacia tree on

the coolhunting veldt and not be aware of the exploitation. But every job has its downside. Every career, calling and occupation has its black-sheep edge that nobody wants to run her finger over.

I finish my soda and approach two boys who are watching their friends play a brutal game of air hockey. They say they have a minute but their attention is divided until I take out the sunglasses and hand them each a pair.

"Hey," says one of the boys, looking them over. He's wearing dirty blue jeans and an olive ski cap even though it's sixty-two degrees outside. "I like these."

His friend is silent as he tries them on. He walks around for a minute and checks out the look in a dark window nearby.

"These are mad," he says quietly.

The boy, Carlos, isn't much for words but his inflection is dead on, and I spend several minutes asking him questions about what he's into now. While he talks, I feel a tingle of the old excitement. Some people know cool. They have a cool gene that the rest of us lack, and because of their uncommon genetic makeup their opinion matters tremendously. Viral marketing, mimetic theory, the stickiness factor—they're all attempts to explain how trends catch on. The few influence the many and it's these alpha consumers—the superspreaders, in epidemic terms—who you want to reach.

Carlos is one of them. He looks like the other kids here but he's not. There's something about him—the way he words his answers, the way he looks me in the eye, the way he examines the sunglasses—that makes him stand out. I can't pinpoint the quality; it's simply a series of familiar intangibles that I've made a career out of reading. But this is how it works—Peggy Guggenheim seeing a Jackson Pol-lack painting and just *knowing*.

I show Carlos a few other pairs of sunglasses and he con-siders them all carefully, as if this is very serious business indeed. His friend, Jonah, rolls his eyes. "Man, you are too *into* it," he says, rocking on his heels.

The air hockey game finishes with a loud crack as the final goal is scored. A boy in a baseball cap raises his arm triumphantly and Jonah walks to the table to play the win-ner.

"These are the maddest," Carlos says, holding up a pair of classic Mutants—tortoiseshell arms, black frames. "I could use these right now." He reaches into a pocket and pulls out a pair of Nomads. They're wide and thick, with brushed-steel frames and dark purple lenses. "I can't wear these no more. Everyone in the world has 'em."

This is true. Just last week, Madonna was on the cover of *Rolling Stone* sporting a pair. Youth culture signals don't get any clearer than this. All that's left is for your mom to show up at your sister's soccer match wearing them.

His friend, the recently defeated Ricky, examines a pair with interest, and I jot down notes while the two talk. Within a few minutes, Jonah is knocked out by the champ, and Carlos picks up the paddle. I watch the game for a lit-tle while and then return to my job. Even though I've lost my enthusiasm for trend-forecasting, I'm still good at it. Fil-tering out the noise and knowing who to listen to—it's not something everyone can do. It's a talent. It's my talent.

My stomach growls, reminding me that I haven't eaten yet, and I head outside to grab a bite because the hot dogs at the arcade are gray and unappetizing. I wind up at a Mex-ican hole-in-the-wall with outdoor seating. The tacos are spicy and delicious and dripping with so much grease that

I can see through the paper plate by the time I'm done. I sip ice-cold water and watch people walk by. It's another unusually mild winter day—mid-sixties and sunny—and almost everyone is outside enjoying the weather.

Deciding it's time to get out of here, I pick up my mess, drop it in the trash can and head to the subway to go home. It's only when I get off at West Fourth Street that I realize it's too early. Bonnie's still cleaning. Her arms are elbow-deep in soap suds and she'll no doubt want me to help. She won't get angry if I don't—she knows she started this project as a way to clean out other demons not so literal—but she'll make me feel guilty. She'll look at me reclining on the couch among the mugs and plates with an expression of longing. It's always like that, and then suddenly I find myself with a mop in hand asking if I should use Lysol or lemon-scented Clorox.

I make a right onto Bleecker and walk west toward the river. If I'm going to do more work today, it might as well be the income-earning kind.

The office is dark and warm when I arrive. It's rare for one of us to come in on a Saturday, even Helen. Almost all Pravda-related business can be done on a PC and e-mailed to work. I turn on my computer and get a glass of water. Just as I'm sitting down at my desk I hear the elevator ding. Now, that's odd.

Seconds later the doors open and Mim's voice, reasonable and calm, drifts through the room. "Yes, Peter, I know you still have to collect the rest of your things." Pause. "Of course I realize your key doesn't work anymore but I can't help you with that." Another pause, longer this time. "A court order sounds lovely. Have your lawyer get in touch with mine and we'll see what happens." Short pause. "How you do go on, darling. Your camera equipment is in perfect working order. I used it just yesterday. Some little metal doohickey fell off when I dropped it but I glued it back on and you almost can't tell the difference." Very short pause. "Peter, are you there?"

When Mim first entered the office, I meant to announce my presence and warn her that the walls have ears before she said something indiscreet, but I didn't get a chance. The first words out of her mouth gave away everything and all I could do was listen with intense fascination (again).

I sit still for a second, listening for Mim movements. I'm prepared to hide under my desk if she wanders over here for a cup of coffee, but she doesn't. She turns on the radio and sticks to her side of the wall. I'm getting ready to duck out the back staircase when the strangeness of her radio selection strikes me. She's not listening to a classical station or a talk station or a news station. She is instead listening to the police station. Hurried voices are reporting crimes in progress and calling for backup and talking to the dispatcher. The cacophony of static and distress is so far removed from the opera or whale sounds that she usually listens to that I find myself walking away from the staircase door and toward Mim. I still don't want to be seen but I'm too curious to walk away without taking a quick peek.

Standing on Wendy's desk on my tippy toes and looking over the three-quarter wall isn't the best way to spy on Mim but it's the only one that presents itself. I have to pile two phonebooks and a dictionary to get my eyes over the wall. The jerry-built pedestal isn't the most sturdy solution—it shifts every time I breathe—but it provides a front-row seat to Mim theater.

The first thing I notice is a tall frappuccino on the reception desk. Excellent. This takes care of my number one concern—Mim coming to this side of the office for coffee and seeing me hanging on the wall like a rock climber without equipment.

The view into Mim's office is limited by doorways and walls, but she's sitting on her couch, which is in plain sight against the far wall—more good news. I watch her for a while. The radio is on the coffee table and she's listening to it intently. Her pose is classic fascinated theater-goer watching a brilliant Broadway production—at the edge of her seat, elbows on knees—but she's not watching anything. She's staring at her Uniden Bearcat police scanner, and I'm disappointed by the mundanity of the scene. I didn't risk life and career-ending embarrassment to watch Mim do nothing.

Just when my toes are about to give out underneath me, Mim moves. She grabs a thin book from the coffee table and flips through it quickly. There's a jumpiness to her movements—an animated excitement—that I've never seen before. Mim is always calm. Despite the bottomless cups of coffee she drinks and the sugary snacks she munches on constantly, she's immune to the jitters. The only time her hand shakes is when she's meeting someone new.

I watch her for several minutes, fascinated by the randomness of these seemingly disparate elements—the scanner, the book, Mim herself on the couch with elbows on knees. The scene is like a brainteaser from the Mensa Society: What do these three things have in common? The answer is nothing. The answer is I don't know. The answer is they're all here on a Saturday afternoon in February. But so am I. I'm here on my tippy-toes with painfully stiffening fingers wrapped around a Sheetrock wall. The real question is: What do I have to do with them?

I'm trying to figure this out when my left foot starts to cramp, making me keenly aware of the long-term untenability of my current position. No matter my intentions, I can't stay here. It's physically impossible for me to hang on this wall watching Mim for the rest of the day. Sighing deeply, I sit down on the stack of phonebooks and stretch my left arch, which is now pulled into a tight knot. I lean my head against the wall as the pain subsides and sigh again. My feet ache—it's not just the arches, it's my toes, as well, which have been crushed mercilessly under my curios-ity—and my fingers hurt. This is stupid. Spying on Mim is stupid.

I slide off the pile of telephone books, annoyed with my-self. Mim has never been anything but kind to me. From the very first time we met—when I showed up two hours late for our interview because the E train got stuck under Times Square—she's been unfailingly thoughtful and pa-tient. Even when I was following her around Washington Heights asking exasperating questions about the mysteri-ous erraticness of trends—why fashion novels? why now?— she kept her cool. Mim took me seriously and treated me professionally and saw something, a spark of talent, that she wanted to nurture. She didn't know I'd be good at this but she took a chance anyway. I've always been grateful for that.

Climbing off the desk, I think again of the morning I returned to Pravda after my mother died—those sentences so full of meaning they couldn't be completed. Mim doesn't deserve this shoddy treatment, this secondhand Helen behavior.

The police scanner drones and whirs in the background as I carefully put the telephone books and dictionary back on the reference shelf. I'm suddenly eager to get home. The moral simplicity of cleaning the kitchen floor now appeals to me in a new way, and I walk toward the door to leave. This is what I should have done fifteen minutes ago.

At the ground floor, I step into the lobby and lean against the wall to dig out my wallet. My apartment is close by— only a fifteen-minute walk from here—but I'm drained enough to consider taking a taxi. I count singles: eight. More than enough to get me home.

I'm putting my money back and readjusting the tote bag on my shoulder when the elevator bell dings. I glance up, expecting to see a yoga enthusiast or a blue-clad janitor, and my heart stops again. There is Mim. She's walking toward me in wraparound sunglasses and a long, tan Burberry coat. I press my shoulders against the wall, trying desperately to disappear like a black moth against a soot-covered tree, but it doesn't work. The gray marble is too dull for my red jacket, and I wait tensely for her to stop in front of me. I should act natural—pretend I just entered the building and say hello like a normal person—but I don't. Instead, I hug the wall like there's a hundred-foot drop inches away from my toes.

As I'm trying to relax my shoulders and form a coherent greeting, Mim walks by. She brushes past me without stopping to ask what I'm doing here or glancing in my direction or even looking up. One second she's walking toward me at a dizzyingly quick pace and another she's walking away. In a matter of seconds, her hand is flush against the glass door, pushing it open.

I watch her go, stunned and relieved and a little bit insulted that I'm so easy to overlook. But I know it's not just my pale skin that has made me almost invisible. Her trench coat, with its raised high collar blocking all peripheral vision, also contributed to my— Wait a second. Why is Mim wearing a trench coat?

I run to the door to get a second look, not quite sure I believe my eyes. Mim doesn't wear trench coats. She's a

Prada fiend and Escada regular and Armani hopeful, but there's not a speck of Burberry in her closet. She hates its fussiness, its midlevel-bureaucrat-having-an-affair-with-his-secretary aesthetic. But there she is—Mim in an ankle-length Burberry trench coat and thick sunglasses waving down a cab. How bizarre.

After a short while, a cab stops in front of her. She climbs into the back seat, leans forward and gives the driver her direction. Then she retrieves a black makeup bag from her purse. She is reapplying lipstick as the car pulls away.

I'm so stunned by this wild development that for a moment I can't move. I can only press my nose against the glass door and watch her cab drive away. A second later, the elevator dings again and two yoga instructors in Adidas sweats and Puma sneakers step out. They walk by me, discussing where to have lunch in the area, and as they open the door fresh air sweeps into the lobby.

I know what I have to do. The answer is obvious and inevitable. I dash to the curb and wave down another taxi.

Spying on Mim is wrong. It's stupid and dishonest and immoral in a ruthless Helen way. But not knowing what's going on—that's unbearable.

I have only enough money to get me to the corner of Ninth and Forty-fifth, but that's okay. Several feet away, Mim's car stops in front of a sandy brown apartment building with a white fire escape. I check the meter one more time and hand the driver all my cash. His tip is a measly sixty-five cents, and I slam the door quickly before he finishes counting the singles.

Forty-fifth Street is narrow and crowded, and the cab has to inch slowly around two police cars that are parked in the middle of the road. Their lights are flashing but the sirens are off and the cars, which offer excellent cover, are empty. I hover behind them, half-crouching, as Mim approaches the apartment building, number 435. Her stride is purposeful and confident, and she doesn't seem the least bit self-conscious in her tan Burberry coat and her Sigerson Morrison flats. Mim doesn't spend a lot of time in Hell's Kitchen. Despite the bars and restaurants and stores that have opened up, Mim remains unimpressed with its gentrification.

The building is a six-story tenement, the fire escape such a vibrant white it seems as if someone had just added a fresh coat the day before. On the ground floor there's a small laundromat offering wash-and-fold for the very reasonable price of fifty-five cents a pound. Two of its employees, a young Asian woman and an older man with gray streaks in his hair, are standing in the doorway. They're watching the police. Everyone on Forty-fifth Street between Ninth and Tenth is watching the police as they unfurl yellow tape that says "crime scene." Everyone except me. I'm watching Mim.

Although the crowd isn't large, it's very interested in the scene. Nobody knows exactly what has happened, but several people are quite happy to speculate and I catch snippets of theories as I duck discreetly behind the police cars: gang war, jealous husbands, irresponsible parents. All they know for sure is that someone is dead. They don't even know who.

Mim doesn't appear to be bothered by these concerns. Her expression is familiar and placid, and it seems entirely possible that she doesn't realize what's going on around her, despite the flashing lights and the crime-scene tape and the hovering crowd. But then she swivels her head, looks left and right and slips calmly and smoothly under the yellow tape. Within seconds she's in the building, striding up the hallway. Although there is nothing particularly discreet about her—the Burberry was a nice tip of the hat to private detectives everywhere, but it serves no practical purpose—she slides past a distracted police officer without incident. She does this with so much ease that for a moment I believe she really is a ray of light projected back in time. Then she disappears up the stairs.

Mim is gone for two minutes and I lean impatiently against a police car, glancing at my watch every few seconds and fully expecting to see her being forcefully ejected from the building. When she reappears, it's with the same cool, composed expression as before. I have no idea where she's been or what she's done, but her lack of distress makes it seem harmless, as though the dead body and her presence are just a small coincidence. They aren't. You don't listen to police scanners and wind up at crime scenes as a matter of chance, but Mim almost convinces me that you do.

Another police car pulls up, sirens blaring, and I walk to the opposite curb to give it and Mim some room. The street is more crowded now with onlookers and as soon as a uniformed officer gets out of the car, he starts trying to get us to disperse. Mim isn't paying attention to him but she leaves anyway. She goes to the corner of Ninth and waves down a cab.

I want to follow her again. Tailing Mim this far hasn't yielded any answers and I want to see what happens next, but I can't. First I have to run into a convenience store and get more cash. By the time I do, Mim is long gone. She's probably halfway to another odd location preparing to do more bizarre things.

NINE

Bonnie adjusts the focus on her camera and tries to hand it to me. I'm not receptive. I'm in the act of putting on an earring and not the least bit interested in playing with her sophisticated surveillance equipment.

"It isn't sophisticated at all," she says, not as attuned to sarcasm as she usually is. This is what photography does to her—involves her so thoroughly that she forgets herself. "Here, you can do it. It's simple."

I slip on a second silver hoop. "I know I can do it. I just don't need to." I look at her in her stained T-shirt and cargo pants. Yesterday's cleaning frenzy extended well into this afternoon. "Are you ready to go? I'm leaving in ten minutes whether you're ready or not."

Bonnie makes another adjustment—changes the aperture—and leans over to show me. She's unmoved by my threat. "You can't stalk Mim without a zoom lens."

"I'm not stalking Mim," I say angrily. I've been telling

Bonnie this for almost twenty-four hours but she won't listen.

"I suppose you could buy binoculars but then you'd have no documentation. At a time like this you need paperwork. Trust me, this baby catches everything in the blink of an eye." She adjusts the camera's focus and looks across the courtyard to the neighbor's apartment. Vicky hasn't been home all weekend, much to Bonnie's dismay. "What if she's found some boyfriend with a huge apartment on the Upper West Side with a real balcony?" she'd asked me this morning while I ate cereal. There was a familiar note of sadness in her voice. Bonnie worries about this all the time. Some nights it even keeps her awake.

I pointed out that our neighbor only dates poets and musicians—they can barely afford apartments, let alone beautiful balconies—and asked if she needed help putting the plates back in the cabinet. The distraction worked and she stopped brooding for a moment about her possible lost subject.

I look at her now as she stares across the courtyard wearing that familiar unhappy expression. Not only is it unnecessary, it's time consuming. "I'm leaving in five minutes," I say.

Bonnie straightens her shoulders and while I'm not looking puts the camera in my hands. I have to grasp it tightly or it will fall. "Here, get used to it. The weight is pretty light for a camera of this size. It's perfect for stalking Mim."

"I'm not stalking Mim," I say through clenched teeth as the bathroom door shuts.

"Of course not," she calls back in a blithe, condescending tone as if she knows more than me. But she doesn't. All she knows is what I told her—that I followed Mim to 435 Forty-fifth and that I won't do it again. And I really won't. Voyeurism isn't a compulsion. It's a choice.

I want to shout back at her but I just mutter under my breath about some people not listening to reason and sit on the couch to wait. I put the camera on the coffee table without examining the settings. I don't need to know the settings. After a few minutes of not playing with the camera I get bored and turn on the television. I flip for a while, then settle on the local news channel as Bonnie slowly gets ready. I glance at my watch. We were supposed to meet my father at the restaurant more than ten minutes ago.

Bonnie pops out of the bathroom with wet hair—wet hair! who said there was time to shower?—and promises to be ready in just a few. I flip channels and wait impatiently and wonder what Mim is doing now.

The restaurant where my dad likes to sing is only a few blocks away and when we finally arrive he's sitting at the bar having a drink and flirting with the bartender Judy. She's blond and tall and recently engaged. We ooh and ahh over her ring after she takes our drinks order. Bonnie is better at it than me—she makes comments about the stone's clarity and provenance—and my eyes drift to the corner where the piano player is engrossed in a tune. This is Nico, Dad's accompanist. We haven't been introduced but I already know a lot about him—Italian, twenty-two, hopes to see something of North America before he goes home. He plans to take a Greyhound to Seattle in a month or so, but Dad is trying to convince him to stay in New York. He's never had an accompanist before—certainly not one who practices with him and follows his lead—and he's reluctant to lose him now.

Dad's singing is another post-Mom thing, like the manic talking and the compulsive flirting. It started in Puerto Rico three years ago, in a little piano bar outside San Juan where he finally got up the courage to perform a song—

"Winter Wonderland," despite the eighty-degree temperature outside. He left the safety of piano bars and cabarets four months ago when he discovered this place, a small Italian restaurant on Cornelia Street that had just opened. Now he shows up once or twice a week and sings to his heart's content. The staff doesn't mind. They love customers like him—the sort who throw fives and tens into the tip jar and raise the merriment quotient. That he has to pay for the privilege of singing for his supper doesn't bother him; he gets too much joy out of serenading bachelorette parties to even notice the quid pro quo aspect of the arrangement.

The front door opens as Nico starts playing "As Time Goes By," and I turn to my dad, expecting to see him jump up from his bar stool, catch a microphone that has been tossed to him by some unseen hand and stand in the middle of a bright spotlight. But that's not the way it happens. Dad barely notices the change in music and continues to chat with the bartender. Now he's asking her what her real job is.

I take a sip of whiskey and look around the room while Judy explains that she's getting her degree in library sciences. My father has never met a library scientist before and is full of questions about procedure and process. Ten minutes pass quickly as she pours Absolut and mixes martinis and talks about her classes at Columbia. The restaurant is small and dimly lit, with fluttering candles and an unused fireplace in a cozy brick corner. It's still early for New York—only eight-thirty—but the restaurant is almost packed and I watch a group of six women squeeze around a table for four. There are too many elbows and purses for the tight space but nobody seems to mind. They wave down a waitress and order drinks right away.

"Archiving is my favorite class, even though it meets on Sunday mornings," Judy is saying as she scoops ice into a shaker.

Bonnie is wide-eyed at the thought of a class that meets before noon on the weekend. The weekend! This is another reason why she'll never go back to school for playwriting or photography.

I smile and finish off the last of my drink. I haven't eaten much today—Bonnie threw out half the fridge's contents while defrosting it—and I can feel the effects of the whiskey almost instantly. My joints are fluid and languid, and I have to hold on to the side of the bar stool to keep from sliding off. It's a lovely feeling—comfortable and warm—and for the first time in hours, I forget about Mim and her Bearcat scanner and the easy way she glides past police officers.

Nico starts another song—a familiar Rodgers and Hammerstein tune—and Dad begins humming. The sound is quiet at first, only something under his breath, but after a few measures he's singing at the top of his lungs. He stands up and makes his way to the piano at the front of the room. He's in no rush to join Nico and stops at every table to sing a line or two. Dad isn't Elvis in Hawaii or the Beatles on *Ed Sullivan,* but he knows something about pleasing a crowd and they respond to his enthusiasm.

I order a second drink and watch Dad. I'm a little embarrassed—how could I not be embarrassed by this?—but the experience isn't as painful as I thought. Perhaps it's the whiskey. Perhaps it's his voice. Perhaps it's the delighted smile on his face. Singing fills a hole. It plugs a leak. Mom's death was like the magic Kennedy bullet, leaving five different exit wounds in its wake, and my father has been patching them up ever since, using whatever materials are handy. In this case, a twenty-two-year-old piano player and an audience.

The song ends, the diners applaud and Dad announces that he'll be happy to take requests. There's a moment of awkward silence following this statement and then Bonnie leans forward in her chair and calls for "That's Amore." Nico strikes up the first few notes instantly and Dad, less sure on his feet, catches up a few seconds later.

"He's got a good voice," Bonnie says, speaking quietly in my ear. She doesn't want to disturb the floor show.

I nod. Dad has always been musical. When my brothers and I were little, we used to sing Christmas songs while he played the accordion. The results were never particularly elegant—listen to the eight-track tapes now and you mostly hear us arguing over who gets to hold the microphone— but it was great fun. Mom never participated. She always hovered in the background with a camera, hesitant, I think, to hone in on Dad's special thing.

"I'm impressed," Bonnie adds. "I'll be honest, I thought this was going to be like karaoke, but your father can really sing."

"Yes," I say. Although Dad can hit the right notes, there's something unrefined about his performance. He needs some training—someone to show him how to breathe from the diaphragm and sustain a note. I've mentioned this a few times, but he's not interested in lessons. My father relishes being a diamond in the rough.

Bonnie bounces her head to the music and tells me yet again how lucky I am to have such a cool father. Robert Easton is a society lawyer with many high-profile clients, most of whom are getting divorces. When he's not taking depositions, he's on the golf course wooing new business and cursing his awful swing. He might not be the most exciting man in the world—he has very rigid notions of what befits his station—but he doesn't tell his daughter stories of his romantic conquests. Bonnie has never heard about the time her father hit on an Australian woman while she was peeing in the stall next to his.

The tempo changes again and Dad transitions smoothly into "Volare." One of the women in the group of six, a brunette in a red skirt, claps happily when she recognizes the song, and Dad, taking this as an invitation—not, of course, that he needs one—glides over to their cramped quarters. He squeezes between two chairs, never once losing the melody, and sidles up against her. The woman laughs and flushes. She's about my age, in her late twenties, and only a little self-conscious.

I play with the ice in my glass and shift my eyes to the front door. I don't want to watch. The exchange is harmless and everyone in the restaurant is having a good time, but something about the scene makes me uncomfortable. There's an odd pressure in my chest—heavy and thick and breathless. I know what it is: sadness and the fear that Mom wouldn't even recognize him if she saw him now.

I'm staring at the door waiting for the song to end when it opens again. Ian steps in. He walks into the restaurant in jeans and a rugby shirt that I bought him for Christmas two years ago. The shirt has seen better days—the collar is worn and the cuffs are frayed and the color has faded to a pale shade of blue—but Ian doesn't care. He always wears everything into the ground.

For a moment his presence seems natural—another sin to lay at the whiskey's door—but only for a moment.

"What's he doing here?" I ask Bonnie. I mean to ask this quietly in her ear but I'm too disconcerted to keep my voice down. Several diners closest to us turn, and Judy, who's pouring vodka into an old-fashioned, pauses a moment to raise her eyebrow. I ignore all the attention and try to figure out why he's here. Maybe it's a coincidence.

"I invited him," Bonnie says. She's calm and assured and not the least put off by my anger.

"What?" I ask. My voice is high and shrill. I'm screeching. I know I'm screeching. "When? *Why?*"

Bonnie doesn't balk. She sees Ian watching my father and raises her hand to get his attention. "Because he called yesterday while you were out and we talked for a long while. The conversation, the first one we've had since you dumped him, reminded me why I like him so much and it got me thinking. What you're doing is wrong. He should be in your life or out of your life, not in some intermediate waiting room," she says, her voice hardening despite the pleasant smile on her face. This is why she's so good at raising money—you can never tell what she's thinking by just looking at her. "He deserves to be with someone who doesn't use him."

"I don't—"

Across the room, Ian turns and sees us. He waves.

Bonnie waves back. "You do. All the time."

"I don't use him," I say vehemently. The idea is so absurd I could almost scream. Who based evil incarnate on whom?

"You do," she insists.

"I don't."

"Do."

"Don't."

We would have gone on like that, batting dos and don'ts across the bar like tennis balls, if Ian hadn't reached us. Bonnie, who's already wearing the best version of her greeting face, stops abruptly and jumps out of her chair to hug him.

It's obvious to anyone watching that she's happy to see him. I understand she misses him, but that doesn't make it okay. When your best friend breaks up with a guy, you support her. You hold her hand and tell her it's the right thing to do, even if you don't understand why. That's the way it works—viscerally and without questions.

Ian wraps his arms around Bonnie and holds her for a moment. Then he steps back and turns to me. "Hey," he says, kissing me on the cheek.

I give him a "hey" back, feeling awkward and ill at ease.

He doesn't notice. He leans against the bar, gets Judy's attention and orders a Peroni. While he waits, he catches up with Bonnie. Ian is relaxed and affable and unruffled as always. He's not at all self-conscious. And why should he be? He didn't just spend the last thirty seconds volleying dos and don'ts with his supposed best friend.

My father winds up his set with a flourish and joins us at the bar. He greets Ian as enthusiastically as Bonnie did and makes eye contact with the hostess, who seats us at a table for four in the back, away from the piano.

"Are you all right here?" I ask my dad.

He looks at me quizzically as he unfolds his napkin.

"We're several tables away from Nico."

Dad laughs and assures me it's not a problem. He doesn't perform in between courses. "Only before and after dinner. Although, sometimes, if there's a bachelorette party here or a couple celebrating an anniversary, I'll do an intermezzo medley."

Ian is fascinated by my father's incipient singing career. When we broke up a year ago, Dad had still been dating Sarah. They went out to fancy restaurants and saw a fair number of Broadway shows, but there were no midweek gigs and practice sessions. I don't pretend to know what it's like—finding yourself aging and alone—but I get how the communal vivacity of singing can mitigate the condition.

While Ian is engrossed in conversation with Dad, I glare at Bonnie, who pretends to be blithely unaware. She takes another piece of bread and examines the menu with intense interest as if all the choices are fascinating and she can't quite decide what to get. I know it's an act. Bonnie doesn't like Italian food and always orders the dish with the most cream, invariably fettuccine Alfredo.

"I can't believe you did this to me," I say softly in her ear as Ian asks Dad where else he performs.

She doesn't look up from the menu but she smiles tightly. "And I can't believe how you treat him like shit." Her tone is smooth and unconcerned. She might as well be asking me how the chicken is prepared for all the inflection in it. "The only reason you're still interested in him is you haven't met anyone new. That's not fair."

"I'm not using him," I say again, my voice rising despite the fact that the person in question is less than two feet away. We shouldn't be doing this here—fighting in the middle of Dad's favorite restaurant. We should save this argument for the apartment, where we can holler at each other at the top of our lungs. But Dad and Ian are oblivious to our enmity. They're eating and drinking and talking about Neva, a little club on the Upper East Side that has a piano bar in the front room.

"Really?" she says, flipping the page of the menu. Now she's staring at the wine list with equal, feigned interest. "What do you call going around whenever you're drunk and lonely and sleeping with him?"

"I don't go around when I'm drunk and lonely," I snarl, glancing quickly at Dad and Ian. They still haven't noticed anything amiss.

Bonnie finally closes her menu and looks me in the eye. She's wearing her cynical face but doesn't say anything. She doesn't have to. The look speaks volumes. It always has.

"It's true," I mutter, picking up my drink. I'm trying to use it as a prop to hide my discomfort, but it doesn't work. The glass is empty. I put it down and look for a waiter, feeling mildly ridiculous and annoyed that I even have to ask for more whiskey. Isn't this what waiters do—keep the alcohol coming to inflate the bill? My timing is awful. Every single staff member is busy with a table—taking orders, opening wine bottles, grating Parmesan cheese—and I consider going up to the bar, but I don't. That would be running away. Worse, that would be admitting to Bonnie that she had backed me into a corner. I turn around, determined not to be cowered and ruffled by her cynical expression, and tell her that I don't go around when I'm drunk and lonely.

But my calm delivery doesn't sway her. "Whatever," she says, before tearing off a piece of bread and dipping it in olive oil.

The patent disbelief, the emphatic implication that the idea is so ridiculous it isn't even worth considering, makes me so angry I have to hold my hands in my lap to stop them from shaking. The way she thinks she knows everything—it's maddening. "For your information," I hiss into her ear, "I go around when I'm drunk and bored. Bored, not lonely. There's a huge difference." Lonely is easy and manageable. It's spaghetti with jarred sauce on a Saturday night. But boredom, with its cargo hold brimming with air and emptiness, breaks me.

Bonnie stares at me for several seconds. Her mouth is open and her eyes are unblinking and she looks as if she's doing some swift, complicated calculation—the square root of pi—in her head. Then, just as I begin to feel painfully self-conscious, she looks away. She opens her menu, quickly confirms the presence of fettuccine Alfredo and asks if someone would like to split a salad. My dad immediately attests to the superior quality of the Caesar, but he doesn't volunteer his portion. He likes Caesar salad too much to settle for half.

"I'm game," I say, determined to make a conciliating gesture. I want to be the bigger person. "The Caesar or the caprese. Either one's cool with me."

"Let's try the Caesar, then," she says with a bright smile. Bonnie's manner is breezy and relaxed, without any evidence that she was recently arguing sotto voce at the dinner table. Despite my gestures of conciliation, she's one step ahead of me. My hands are still clenched in my lap.

The waiter comes by to take our order a few minutes later, and when he leaves, Dad asks Ian about the book. He starts at the beginning, asking about plot, and works his way up to the present. Dad knows some general information— name, rank and serial number stuff—but I broke up with Ian before he could learn the details. Nobody saw the end coming, least of all my father, and when he called to congratulate Ian on the sale, he had no idea it'd be the last time they'd speak for almost a year.

I sit quietly while Ian handles the interrogation with grace. He shares only the good stuff, keeping his PR problems out of the conversation. This isn't a surprise. Ian is a Stoic. He doesn't complain and he doesn't whine. Even when he's telling you awful, painful things—that he hasn't spoken to his father in ten years, that his mother auctioned off his silver baby spoon at Christie's—his tone is so ironic and wry that you're not quite sure if he's talking about real life or a movie he saw the night before.

Jawbones carries us through salad, despite Ian's attempts to deflect attention. When he asks Bonnie about Stage Left, she sums up last week's fund-raiser in five words and brings the conversation back to him with a question about book readings.

Bones McGraw's exploits remind my father of his childhood in South Philly—on a street so narrow that delivery trucks could not turn down it without scraping against the brick building on the corner—and Dad starts telling tales about the roughs in the old neighborhood.

"Tell them about Roy Rogers," I say, calling for my favorite story as the waiter takes away our salad plates.

Ian laughs. "Hate to break it to you, Meg, but Roy Rogers wasn't considered a rough in any neighborhood."

Dad orders another round of drinks and leans back in his chair. "I lived in South Philly, and the guys and I used to wander around the streets. That's what we did for entertainment, walk around. We'd follow Broad Street for miles, past Center City. One day we've got nothing going on and Mikey suggests we go uptown. Somehow we wind up inside Wannamakers department store. I don't remember why we were there but there probably wasn't a reason. Like I said, we just wandered around. It must have been winter, around Christmas. So we're wandering around the store and we walk into a room and they're having a party. On a table in the middle of the room are free hot dogs and soda. And there, on a stage, is Roy Rogers, Dale Evans and Trigger." Dad laughs and shakes his head as the memory becomes clearer. "No, it wasn't even a stage. They were walking around. They walked right by us and shook our hands. Can you imagine? Being ten years old and there's Roy Rogers, Dale Evans, Trigger *and* hot dogs. It was a fantasy."

"Why were they there?" Bonnie asks. "Was it some kid's birthday or a store promotion?"

Bonnie's trying to find an explanation, but there isn't one and Dad shrugs. He never knew why they were there. He ate his hot dog, met Roy Rogers, pet Trigger and went home without questioning any of it. He didn't have to—it all made a sort of ten-year-old-boy sense. It's this inexplicable randomness, this insane arbitrariness and beautiful unpredictability, that I love so much about the story. It's a moral I cling to—that sometimes you can walk into a room and there's everything you've ever wanted.

The waiter returns to the table to deliver fresh drinks, and just as he's putting a glass of pinot grigio in front of Dad, the woman from earlier, the brunette in the red skirt, comes over to request a song. She and her party are about to settle the bill and before they leave they'd like to hear "New York, New York." Typically, they are out-of-towners.

Dad submits to the demands of his public happily and follows the woman to the piano. Her friends, only a little worse for drink, cheer enthusiastically. Dad nods solemnly, accepting the praise with a touch of gravitas, and turns to Nico, who plays a quick intro. The acoustics in the restaurant are not made for talent shows and well-heeled extroverts, and we can barely hear him over the din of dinner chatter. After "start spreading the news," Bonnie excuses herself to go to the bathroom, leaving me and Ian alone for the first time all evening. Before she disappears, she looks at me meaningfully. She tilts her head and indicates with fluttering eyelashes that I should talk to Ian now. She wants me to resolve our relationship problems while my father is singing and she's washing her hands. I won't. I can't. Conflict resolution isn't something that happens while the waiter is laying fish knives for the next course. As soon as she's out of earshot I ask Ian if he's enjoying the freakishly nice weather.

Ian says yes. He spent the day reading in Washington Square Park with pigeons and tourists and college students who play too many James Taylor songs over and over again on their guitars. "There was this magic circus dog who did amazing feats of perception. His owner would pick an audience member and have them think of a number from one to ten. Then the dog would lay that number of sticks at the person's feet."

"Sounds impressive," I say, thinking about the large crowd a spectacle like that would draw. Tourists love animal acts. "Was the dog ever right?"

"That was the truly amazing part. The dog got it right ninety percent of the time. This, despite the fact that his owner forced him to wear a huge, humiliating, red nose," he says, not a small amount of awe in his voice. "I don't know how he did it. If I were forced to wear a clown nose, I wouldn't be able to count to ten, let alone guess a number in front of a large crowd. I'd just sit in my little doggie bed staring at it cross-eyed all day wondering why the other dogs in the park didn't have to wear red noses. But then I've always been too preoccupied with what other people are doing."

This isn't exactly true. Over the years Ian has cultivated a wonderful indifference to other people. It was another thing that attracted me to him in the first place—the way he can be in the middle of a noisy crowd and stay focused. "So what were you reading while all this mayhem was going on?"

Ian smiles. It's an oddly self-deprecating one and to the casual diner he seems a little abashed. To a former girlfriend he seems a lot abashed. *"The Ballad of Butcher Kane."*

I take a moment to digest this. *"The Ballad of Butcher Kane?"*

He looks down at his plate and plays with his knife. He's running it through the tines of his fork, one after the other. "I know."

He seems so uncomfortable that I don't want to tease him, but I'm too surprised to politely change the subject. "You mean rereading it, don't you?"

Ian looks up. He stops playing with the knife and fork and straightens his shoulders. "Nope. This is my first go-around. I've read other books in the genre—*The Last Cavanaugh, The Black Stain, Twisted City*—but never *Butcher Kane*. I figured it was time. *Publishers Weekly* called Bones McGraw the typical magical nihilism antihero, and I thought I should know exactly what makes the antihero typically nihilistic or magical," he says calmly. There's a trace of something new in his voice—acceptance.

When Ian started writing about a bartender who gets sucked into the underlife of New York, he didn't know he was participating in a mass literary movement. He was simply taking life as he knew it—the late nights, the bathroom drug deals, the bored-looking prostitutes at the end of the bar—and exaggerating it. When he turned reality into a carnival of sights and sounds, with bright neon swirls of color and screaming music and long monologues about meaninglessness, he wasn't complying with a magical nihilism checklist. But that doesn't matter now. Slap on the requisite black and navy blue cover with a violent slash of yellow—because, yes, every one of these book jackets has yellow on it somewhere—put it on the bookshelf and watch it disappear into the midnight sea of magical nihilism.

"What do you think?" I ask, trying to recall what I'd

liked most about the book. I'd read *Butcher Kane* more than
four years ago, when it first took the publishing world by
storm. But there have been other books since then, less
flashy ones with more endurance, that have supplanted it
in my memory.

He sighs. "I think it's good. I think it's significantly better written than its knockoffs and imitators, which I didn't
expect," he says honestly. "I'm not sure why Butcher struck
a chord with so many men, though. He's entertaining and
he tells a good story, but he seems more like a caricature or
a symbol—all the worst traits piled on the back of one
human being to serve a function—than a fully developed
character."

I nod emphatically, my head bobbing up and down with
too much enthusiasm in my rush to agree with him. I, too,
was amazed by the number of men who stood up and said,
"Oh, my God, *I'm* Butcher Kane."

"The nice thing is, I feel much better about *Jawbones*
now," he says as my father launches into another song. I can't
hear the lyrics but the piano is crystal clear. "I think it can
stand up to comparisons."

I reach across the table and take his hand. Out of the corner of my eye, I see Bonnie perk up at the gesture. She's
standing by the bathroom door waiting patiently for her
turn. Or at least that's what she wants me to think she's
doing. But I know better—I've already seen her wave one
woman in before her. "That's fabulous, Ian. That's really
good news," I say sincerely, squeezing his hand in assurance.
And the truth is, this *is* good news. Despite his individual-
ity and his wildly independent streak, Bones McGraw owes
a debt to Butcher Kane. The renewed attention to thirty-
something males, the huge proliferation of gritty urban lit,
the sudden interest in the consequences of the solitary

life—all these owe their black-tinged existence to Butcher Kane. Ian might not be able to say it out loud. He probably can't admit it to me or his sister or his agent, but he knows it. Deep inside, he's keenly aware of who holds his IOUs.

On the other side of the room, Dad stops singing for a moment—it's the interlude between verses—and takes the tourist in the red skirt into his arms. There isn't a lot of room to dance, only a few unobstructed feet between the front door and the piano, but Dad makes do. He whirls her around in a loosely sketched waltz before dipping her dramatically over the umbrella stand. The diners eat it up. They cheer loudly and call for more and someone at the table next to ours whistles. I'm fascinated by this—fascinated, appalled and oddly happy.

After a moment, the verse picks up again and Dad resumes singing. His dancing partner returns to her seat, flushed and glowing.

I turn to Ian to get his take on the events. "It's wild, isn't it? The singing, the dancing."

He shrugs. "Your father has always been outgoing and friendly."

As far as Ian knows this is true. He's never met the other George Resnick—the cornerstone of middle-class normalcy who worked nine to six and mowed the lawn on Saturdays. He doesn't know the comforting, sullen silences I grew up with. It was Mom who was the whirlwind, who was always darting from one thing to the next. That I can't say what kept her so busy—she never had a job and rarely did happy homemaker stuff like cook dinner from scratch—bothers me. Because I'm not sure if I never knew or if I've forgotten.

"I have this theory," I say. "When one spouse dies, the

surviving partner reverts to the mental age they were when they met. I've seen it happen again and again. A friend is going through the same thing with her mother right now. And it makes it harder. Because in some ways you've lost both parents."

"I don't think anyone could tell if my father reverted to the mental age he was when he met my mom," he says, only a hint of wryness in his tone, "and they were both fourteen at the time. Consider yourself lucky."

Ian has always envied the reliable ordinariness of my upbringing. He's as fascinated with my childhood stories—the broken bones at summer camp, the weekend skiing trips to Hunter mountain, the car rides into Manhattan with three squabbling kids in the back seat—as I am with his.

Dad finishes the song and graciously accepts the appreciative cheers of his audience. The women at the table give him a standing ovation, and he blows them kisses across the room.

"Okay," I say, because I know he has a point, "but this aggressive joie de vivre—it doesn't seem a little bipolar to you?"

Ian refuses to state an opinion. He simply shrugs again and glances down at the table, where his hand is still grasped in mine. Then he looks at me with a pointed expression. The second I realize I'm still holding on, I drop his hand and look toward the bathrooms. The hallway is empty. At least Bonnie isn't still standing there.

Feeling awkward and embarrassed, I sit back in my chair and wait for Dad and Bonnie to return to the table. I'm not sure what just happened. I can't explain his pointed look or make sense of the uneasiness on his face, but I know one thing: Bonnie is wrong. Her tidy little assumption—that I'm still interested in Ian because I haven't met anyone new—is wide off the mark. The truth is, I haven't met any-one new because I'm still interested in Ian.

Nico starts another song, and Dad follows enthusiasti-cally. He stumbles over the first few notes—more diamond-in-the-rough authenticity—and watches his accompanist to get a better sense of the tempo. It's obvious that he's not returning to the table anytime soon. Bonnie, meanwhile, seems to have decamped permanently to the women's room. I wouldn't be surprised to find her sitting on the toi-let reading this week's *New Yorker.* I take a sip of whiskey, sigh loudly and submit to the inevitable.

Leaning forward, I look at Ian. "How's the marketing going? Did you find someone to do PR?" I ask, extremely reluctant to bring the topic up but perfectly aware that it can't be avoided forever. Sooner or later we have to talk about the fact that I haven't done anything to help advance *Jawbones,* and it's better that we do it here, surrounded by singing Dad and overly concerned friend who can return at any moment. I'm taking the easy way out—if I really wanted to have this discussion I'd stop by the bar on a slow night—but sometimes the easy way out is the only exit.

Ian is watching my father sing, and he turns to me with a distracted smile. "Hmm?" he asks.

I repeat the question, feeling the impulse to apologize again for not being able to help. But I squelch it. Even with several shots of whiskey in me, I know it's not my fault. I chart trends. I don't invent them.

"Yeah, I found someone," he says brightly.

"Excellent," I say with a little too much enthusiasm—but that's only because I'm so relieved to be off the hook. "Who?"

He shrugs. "A friend of a friend."

I nod. Getting recommendations is the only way to find

someone reliable. "I hope they're not charging you too much."

"Nothing at all, actually. She's intrigued by the challenge," he explains.

That Ian is getting publicity support for free is the best possible news. Even if we were still together, I couldn't have been any happier for him. "Yay, Ian. That's wonderful," I say, the urge to touch him coming over me again, but I ignore it. There's no reason to embarrass myself twice during one short musical interlude.

"Yeah, it's cool." He turns his eyes toward the piano, where Dad is busy taking his bow. It's only then that I realize he's done performing and belatedly start to clap.

"What's the plan?" I ask, eager to hear about ideas I could never have. That he found someone—a PR professional—appeases my conscience. I was right to say no.

"There are a few things in the works. I haven't heard the details yet but I've been told not to worry, things are firmly in hand." He smiles somewhat deprecatingly. "I'm *trying* to follow orders."

Just as Dad sits down at the table, the waiter brings our dinner. He puts seafood risotto in front of Ian and a heaping plate of pappardelle with mushrooms in front of my father. A second later Bonnie returns from the ladies' room. Her timing is precise and accurate, and I don't doubt that she's been watching us through a tiny crack in the bathroom door.

The waiter puts Bonnie's fettuccine down in front of her as she looks around the table. "So," she says, "what'd I miss?"

The subtext is clear to me but blurry to everyone else, and Ian launches into a five-minute speech about Dad's performance. He spends an especially long time on the dance portion. Bonnie nods as if she's paying attention but she keeps looking coyly in my direction. It's obvious that she still thinks she knows something I don't, but that's impossible. The ladies' room at Cappellini's has a toilet and a sink and a garbage can frequently overstuffed with brown paper towels. It's not outfitted with sophisticated surveillance equipment. It doesn't have radar or satellite hook-up or a crack team of undercover agents who can decipher complex codes.

I ignore Bonnie, dig into my Chilean sea bass and listen to the couple at the next table argue over which movie they're going to see—overrated comedy or overwrought drama. Movie tickets are always hard to come by in New York, and it seems likely to me that if they continue to linger over cappuccino they'll be shut out of both flicks. I consider pointing this out but then Ian, at the urging of Bonnie, insists that Dad take another twirl around the floor, and I decide to keep my mouth shut. I have enough problems at my own table.

TEN

On Tuesday morning I don't make it into the office until after twelve. I've spent the morning in Williamsburg, showing sunglasses to teenyboppers eating supersized fries at McDonald's. The Mutants went over well, although the kids with their homegrown version were understandably unimpressed. Girls were again hesitant. The visual cacophony of the mismatched arms and frames made them uncomfortable; the imperfection, though part of the design, seemed too much like an unintended flaw.

When I get to Pravda, Helen is waiting for me. I'm allowed to turn on my computer and fetch a cup of coffee before she orders me into her office.

Helen's office is large and comfortable, with beautiful curios and elegant fabrics. The room looks exotic—the objets d'art seem express-mailed from the four corners of the globe—but everything is either a suburban flea-market find or a Sears special. The most foreign item in the room is a bonsai tree she bought at Pearl River Trading on Canal

Street. The tree looks real but it's made of a space-age poly-
mer that feels like rubber. All the plants—the fern by the
door, the African violet on top of the filing cabinet, the am-
aryllis in the window—are fake. Helen can't stand the inef-
ficiency of cultivation. She hates the way plants need water
and light to grow.

"You're late," she says, shutting the door.

This is true—my Mim report was scheduled for eleven-
fifteen—but I don't apologize or hang my head in shame.
I left a message on her voice mail this morning letting her
know what I was up to and when I'd be in.

Helen looks at me expectantly and I take out my Filofax. I came to the first meeting empty-handed, which didn't
go over well. She was skeptical of my details because they
weren't marked down in a log. Now I bring props. "Nothing major to report," I say, running quickly through a made-
up list of things I watched Mim do. Giving the Mim report
to Helen is a bit like making confession. You sit outside the
door coming up with a believable combination of impure
thoughts and parental disrespect.

"That's all?" she asks. "Coffee, shopping, eating?"

"Don't forget working. A lot of the time she was in her
office." I feel compelled to draw attention to the one thing
I actually witnessed.

She nods slowly, makes a notation and smiles. Her belief
in the system amazes me. Helen sees only what's directly in
front of her—me at the beginning of her shift, Wendy at
the end—and assumes the rest. Her failure is one of imagination: She can't conceive of her employees not obeying.

"That's all good. You see, I knew my system would
work," she says, satisfied. It's been almost two weeks since
the *USA TODAY* quote, and I feel like she should have one
of those on-the-job-injuries signs you see in factories: 12

Days Without a Mim Incident. "The new office will be ready a week from Monday. They're just giving it a fresh coat of paint and refinishing the floors. I'm going down tomorrow to take a look."

With the implementation of Mim containment, Helen has found it necessary to come in every day. Even Fridays, which used to be sacrosanct, are now part of her regular workweek. What she did with the other half of her life—the test-prep publishing company whose accounts she manages—I have no idea.

"All right," I say.

My tepid response gets her hackles up. Even though I've never been a full-throated follower of the Helen camp, my lukewarm interest is a continual surprise. "I have a new recruit, someone who is as interested in Mim's well-being as I am," she says intriguingly, trying to excite enthusiasm.

"Oh?" It's only a vowel sound but I raise an eyebrow. I'm making an effort.

"Yes, I've asked Mim's husband to help me out. He said he *has* noticed a change in her recently."

I gape at Helen. For fifteen seconds, I stare at her in absolute shock. Then I sputter and finally force out a word. "What?"

"I've asked Mim's husband to help," she says, pleased with my reaction. Gaping and sputtering—it means I'm finally bowled over by her genius. "He spends as much time with her as I do. I can't believe I didn't think of calling him sooner. It's our careers. We're both so busy we're not as close as we used to be. But he's an obvious answer to finding out what's going on with Mim. I'm sorry to report that he doesn't know either." But she's not sorry at all. Her vanity is appeased by his matching ignorance. That there is something vaguely curious about this arrangement—a wife not confiding in her husband—doesn't strike Helen. She doesn't stop to wonder if perhaps Mim's problem isn't Peter.

She pauses here for me to make some appreciative comment but I can't. I'm too appalled by her—her gall and her spite—to say anything. The shiny friendship veneer, previously cracked, is gone completely. There's nothing left of it but the seething underbelly: She *will* cement Mim in the basement with a cask of Amontillado.

"It's not my fault it's come to this. If only Mim handled things better," Helen continues, when I don't jump in. "She should be careful. Secrecy isn't good for her marriage. And I told Peter that. He agreed completely. He said marriage is a difficult thing to make work and partners shouldn't keep things from partners."

Although I don't know what exactly is going on in the Warner-Kreisky marriage, I do have two solid facts: that Peter is sleeping with a sexy redhead and that Mim is wearing a Burberry coat to crime scenes. It's easy to draw some conclusions. "So what has he agreed to do?"

"Keeping an eye on her at home, checking her mail for important-looking information, screening telephone calls. You know, the usual stuff," she says.

I don't know how she can pull it off—this seemingly sincere obliviousness to the horror of her own behavior. Even if the couple weren't already having problems, Helen's request would have been completely out of line. "Aren't you worried that he'll tell his wife that you're spying on her?"

She scowls. "It's not spying. It's like a receivership. I'm just holding the reins of the company until Mim is well enough to resume running it. And, no, I'm not worried. Peter's completely trustworthy. I know him pretty well. Actually, I met him first. We took photography together freshman year. He was interested in me for a while, before he met

Mim. It was at the spring formal. I remember Mim was wearing tiny daisies in her hair. We'd gone together, but when he saw her it was all over for me."

Helen tries for a light tone—as if this were lovely water under the bridge—but the tinge of waspishness undermines it: She's not so much recruiting Peter in the Mim cause as bringing him back to her side.

While Helen rambles on about Peter ("It had been so long since we talked. We won't let that happen again.") I stare at the clock, feeling particularly helpless. There's nothing I can do with this new information. I can't tell Mim that her husband knows she's coming unglued. I can't tell Peter to stop humiliating his wife. I can't tell Helen to mind her own damn business. All I can do is watch the second hand and wait to be released.

On Friday Ian drops by around lunchtime and asks me to go to the bookstore with him. It's been almost a week since we had dinner with my father, and he greets me as if none of the awkwardness had ever occurred. Although I'm sitting at my desk waiting for a client to call back, I grab my handbag and jump to my feet. Ian's seeking me out is still too novel and surprising—it's always the other way around—for me to refuse.

"What's the deal?" I ask, wrapping a red scarf around my neck as we wait for the elevator. "Do you need my opinion on something?"

He answers vaguely with a shrug and compliments me on my scarf. "Is it new?"

I'm telling him about the store on St. Mark's where I got it when the elevator doors open. Mim steps out. Her cheeks are red from the brisk air.

She greets us quickly—"Hi, Meghan, hi, Ian."—as we

brush by her. We only have time for a wave before the doors close.

"So what's up?" I ask on the way to the bookstore, which is less than five minutes away. The air's cold but the sun is shining between the buildings and I take a deep breath, suddenly happy just to be outside.

"Nothing. I just wanted to check out the book," he explains.

"Which book?"

"My book."

"I don't understand," I say as he holds the door for me. "It's been out for almost two weeks and you're only going to the bookstore now?"

He smiles sheepishly. "Yeah, well."

I know exactly where the book is—on the new trade paperback table in the front of the store—and I lead him right to it. Ten copies of *Jawbones* are front and center, and I feel a tingle of pride at the sight. Despite the book's Delilah Quick-infested pages, I want to hold it up and tell everyone in the store that my ex-boyfriend wrote it. When I bought my copy last week, I raved about it to an indifferent cashier.

For a moment I think Ian is equally overwhelmed. He's standing by the table and staring at it silently. But then he turns to me and asks if I'm ready to go.

"That's it?" I ask.

He shrugs. "What else is there?"

I open my mouth to answer but I don't know what to say. If it were my book, I'd want to stand there for hours and absorb. "I'm going to buy a copy," I say, even though I know this probably won't give him a thrill either. Ian isn't the sentimental type. "You must sign it. Make it out to my father."

Outside, I offer to treat him to lunch. We have to do something celebratory to mark the occasion. Ian agrees but only if we go dutch.

We head to the diner across the street. Ian gives his order to the waitress and then broods quietly. I look around the restaurant and wait. Ordinarily I'd jump into the void and babble inconsequentially, but today I don't say a word. He's the one who sought me out.

"I can't explain it, the weird sort of nothing I felt seeing the book in a bookstore. I thought it'd be exciting but it was just nothing," he says, after the food arrives, surprising me with his willingness to talk about it. Perhaps I played all our conversations wrong. My eagerness to leap into chasms of silence—maybe I just never gave him a chance to speak.

He pauses to take a bite of his burger and then continues. "The book itself is so familiar that it was like…I don't know…seeing my mother's face in a crowd. You don't think, There's my mother. The recognition happens on a level so deep, it almost doesn't happen."

I nod. Despite his disclaimer, he's managed to explain it very well. I'm about to say something comforting when he continues. "The nothingness lasted for about fifteen seconds, and then it was supplanted by this extreme sense of dread. Seeing it there, engulfed entirely by all the other magical nihilism books, freaked me out."

It didn't affect me as strongly but I'd noticed it, too—all the yellow-and-navy-blue covers, each one almost identical to the next.

I understand Ian's dread because I see it all the time—the terror of being subject to something completely arbitrary. People like Mim don't create trends, they just identify them. And that's the scary part—no matter what you do, you can't invent a trend. Not really. Not in the way marketers and magazines and advertising agencies would like. You can exploit it and suck it dry, but you can't whip one up in your test kitchen. In some ways, they're giant cultural coincidences, and no matter what you do, you can't dictate what's going to capture the popular imagination. What's more, you can't stop the public from moving on to the next thing. All you can do is ride it out and steel yourself for the backlash. Because there will be a backlash. It's unavoidable. Once a craze passes, people inevitably feel taken in. It's the emperor's new clothes over and over again.

I study Ian thoughtfully as he waves down a waitress, and I realize in a flash that I can help. The last time he came to me with a problem, I was useless. I couldn't do anything but shrug my shoulders and make vague promises. But this is different. Thanks to eight years of coolhunting, I know exactly what to do next. "Start the backlash," I say.

Ian looks up abruptly. He's in the middle of pouring ketchup onto his plate and half the bottle spills out before he realizes it. "What?"

"Start the backlash. Magical nihilism has, like, ten minutes left. Don't get caught in the recoil. Your next novel, make it post-magical nihilism. Deconstruct magical nihilism or make fun of it or exploit its clichés to demonstrate a point," I say excitedly. "Do something to call attention to the conventions. Don't write another straight MN text. It's the only way. Only a certain number of magical nihilism writers will make the transition to straight fiction. Make sure you're one of them—distance yourself."

During my manic little speech, Ian sits up straight and leans forward. "It's a good idea."

"I know."

He's silent for a few moments, thinking. "Like, a really, really good idea."

"I know."

Then he smiles widely. "Meg, you're a fucking genius."

I shrug.

"Post-MN." He laughs. "I could do that."

"You'll have to get started straight away. Trust me, someone is sitting at a computer at this very moment writing just that kind of book," I say, recalling the first time I met Mim, when I'd asked her about the spate of fashion-magazine-industry-insider novels that had just been released. Mim couldn't explain why. She made a few guesses—the way fashion editors are notoriously easy targets for satirizing, the way fashion morphed into entertainment about five years before—but in the end she really didn't have an answer. The zeitgeist is a strange animal. Sometimes I'm convinced it doesn't exist, but then something truly inexplicable happens—Isaac Mizrahi and Jean-Paul Gaultier showing *Nanook of the North*-inspired collections in the same season—and I realize it's there. It's always there.

But this word of caution doesn't dull his enthusiasm, and, taking me at my word, Ian starts gobbling his fries two at a time—the faster he finishes his meal, the faster he can start writing. I keep up as best I can and try to snag the check as soon as it arrives. Ian beats me to it. I remind him that we're supposed to go dutch, but he insists on paying.

It's not until I'm back at my desk waiting for the British sportswear executive to call that it hits me: Mim said hello to Ian. She looked him in the eye and addressed him by name and seemed to be on friendly terms. But how could that be? I've never introduced them.

ELEVEN

On Monday Mim starts packing for her big move downstairs. Helen told her the building maintenance crew needed to do major construction in her office—it was a convoluted story about water mains and fire hazards—and she had to temporarily switch offices. Mim agreed to the relocation without a peep and even seems to be looking forward to it. She sometimes talks about her new space as if it's uncharted territory—here there be dragons, like on an old map.

"Hey," I say, knocking gently on her office door, which is partially open.

Mim looks up. She's wearing thick-rimmed black frames and a crisp white shirt. There it is again—prototypical Mimness. "Hi, Meghan." She takes off her glasses, which she only needs for reading, and waves me in. "How can I help you?"

Mim's ordinarily neat office is littered with boxes and bubble wrap. The usually comforting space is sparse and empty. Her lithographs have already been carried down-stairs, and there are large rectangular patches of light cream on her otherwise discolored walls.

"Who should I speak to at Stellar?" I ask. "Vivian is on vacation and I have some questions about the project."

"Try Addity Fadden. She's the head of marketing. I have her number in my Rolodex." She looks at her desk buried under paper and boxes. "Now, let me just remember where I put it."

Mim gestures for me to have a seat and I push several folders aside to make room on the chair. "How's the pack-ing going?" I ask, feeling like a traitor. I shouldn't be doing this—pretending this move is a run-of-the-mill business de-cision and not part of a sinister plot. A better person would warn her. A brave person would look her in the eye and tell her the truth. But that's not me. I watch things happen and wonder why I'm not more proactive.

"Good, thanks. I'm pretty much done. Helen's been a great help," she says, without a trace of irony. "I'd still be emptying my bookshelves if it weren't for her. There are a ton of things that have to be boxed up." She gestures to her desk, which is covered with folders and envelopes and thick black binders. "It seemed like the perfect opportunity to throw out some stuff. Like this"—Mim holds up a gray vinyl checkbook—"why am I keeping this? I closed that account three years ago." But rather than throw it away, she drops it on the desk. It lands next to a well-thumbed book that also looks ready for the trash. It's half-hidden under an old memo from Helen but I can read half the title: *Codes for Police.*

It only takes a second for me to put it together—the po-lice scanner, Mim's excited behavior, the book she was holding. Mim notices right away that my attention is elsewhere, and she follows my gaze until she, too, is looking at the book. It's harmless enough but I feel like I've stumbled onto some skeleton in the Mim closet, and I try really hard not to make any sudden movements. Slowly, I move my eyes across the desk as if carefully perusing everything on it. Stapler, No. 2 pencil, day planner—all of it is fascinating. Mim also behaves herself. She doesn't rush to hide the book or offer a quickly conceived explanation. She brazens it out, pretending that nothing is wrong. She asks me about my weekend and seems absolutely fascinated as I tell her about the movie I saw.

"Here it is," she says a few minutes later when she finally finds the Rolodex under a black binder. She flips through it quickly. "There you go, Addity Fadden."

I take the card, thank her and walk toward the door, but before I leave the room I look again at her desk. The book of police codes is gone.

Friday night at seven I pretend to leave for the fifth day in a row. I stick my head into Mim's office and wish her a nice evening; then I take the elevator to the ground floor, duck into the stairwell, climb up six flights, open the door to the office a crack, sit on the top stair and wait. About a half hour later, when she's sure nobody is coming back for a forgotten file or umbrella, Mim turns on the police scanner and settles in for a long night of listening. Out in the stairwell, I do the same, although without Mim's enthusiasm. Listening to the dispatcher relay crimes in progress is dull business, and after the first watch I bring a book with me and a little portable reading light. Despite the distraction, I have a difficult time sitting still. The stairwell is hot and dark, and the floor is as hard as stone; my butt always falls asleep after ten pages.

I stand up now to stretch my back and get the blood circulating again in my legs. The effects of stairwell-sitting are accumulative and I'm stiffer today than I was yesterday. Thinking about it makes me cringe. I don't want to do this again tomorrow and the next day and the day after that. The weekend is finally here and I want to do fun things, not stalk my boss. Not that this is stalking. Stalking requires accoutrements—binoculars and grease paint and bugging equipment. No, this is curiosity tempered by boredom. I glance at the time: nine o'clock. Only two more hours until Mim turns off the scanner, waves down a cab and goes home.

My stomach rumbles loudly—it's been seven hours since lunch—and I take a bag of potato chips out of my backpack. As the Mim siege drags on, my list of provisions becomes increasingly extensive. On day one I had a half a Snicker's bar and a stick of unwrapped gum. On day five, an eight-ounce container of yogurt, a fudge brownie, a quarter pound of roasted asparagus, breath mints and, of course, the aforementioned potato chips.

When I finish eating, I throw the empty bag into my backpack, sit down against the far wall and try to find a position in which I don't feel my tailbone. I'm unsuccessful, but I open my book and start reading as if this aching pain isn't a problem. A few minutes later, bored and irritated and miserably uncomfortable, I throw the book across the floor. I should go home. I should pack up my provisions and run down the stairs and go back to my apartment, where the couch is soft and cushy. But I don't. I have too many hours invested in strange Mim behavior to abandon the field now.

Sighing resignedly, I pick up the book, find the correct page and continue reading. After a while, I look at my watch. Only four minutes have passed.

At its core, Mim watching is like baby-sitting. It slows down time; seconds tick by as sluggishly as frames of a slow-motion replay on a sports highlight reel. And it plays with your mind. Activities you enjoy doing at home—reading, watching television, eating potato chips and letting the crumbs fall onto the floor for someone else to clean up—suddenly seem unendurable. The only thing you can do is watch the clock. Even when you're not staring it straight in the face, you have one eye on it.

My pocket reading light flickers and I put the book on my lap so I can tighten the lightbulb. The police scanner drones on in the background. These days the police scanner is always droning on, whether I'm here or not. The sound has invaded my subconscious and planted itself like a tree in my mental landscape. Some nights I hear it while I'm sleeping.

This is why I'm so surprised when it stops a few minutes later. It's only nine-thirty but Mim turns the scanner off. The silence is loud but preferable and I listen with my ear against the opening to hear what happens next. Nothing for a minute and then ding—the elevator.

I grab my bag and run down the six flights. I'm not faster than the elevator but the timing works out perfectly each night. I always reach the ground floor just as Mim is exiting the building. She waves down a cab. I watch from the lobby and then follow. Usually the cab goes a mile, dropping Mim in front of her building on Waverly. Today it zooms past the Village. It flies down Hudson and makes a left onto Houston.

The traffic is surprisingly light for a Friday evening—the bridge-and-tunnel set haven't begun their invasion yet—and a few minutes later she turns left onto Avenue A. The streets are crowded and bright, and I lose sight of Mim when my cab gets stuck behind a double-parked station wagon. The driver maneuvers around the car, at some risk to his safety and mine, and catches up to her car just as it's stopping in front of a little French restaurant. Something about the bistro is familiar—the red awning, the antique windows, the worn sign—and I stare at it, trying to figure out why I know this place. Then it hits me, and my enthusiasm dips, drops and disappears. This isn't an adventure. This isn't Mim on her way to some classified destination in her secret-agent overcoat. No, this is her going to dinner at her favorite East Village restaurant.

Feeling foolish and stupid, I lean my head against the back of the seat. A clever person would have anticipated this. It's Friday night—of course Mim is meeting people for dinner. A really clever person would have left the office at six o'clock, instead of torturing her tailbone, and gone out with her own friends.

The cab driver asks if I want to get out here and I tell him no. I'm too disheartened to walk home. I give him my address and take out my cell phone to call Bonnie, who is supposed to be meeting up with some college friends for drinks tonight. Perhaps if they're going somewhere local I'll tag along.

The cab pulls away from the curb and does an illegal U-turn while I'm dialing Bonnie's number. Several drivers honk loudly, and a jaywalking pedestrian—whose crime is admittedly the lesser—smacks the hood with his fist and curses. The cabbie rolls down his window and tells the guy to fuck off as we drive pass. The guy gives us the finger and stands there in the middle of the street for a moment. I see this when I turn around. I also see Mim crossing the street.

"Stop the car," I screech. "Stop the car." There's more

vehemence in my tone than the situation calls for—Mim is only a few yards away—but I can't help myself. I'm too surprised by her don't-worry-about-me-I'm-just-having-dinner-with-friends trick to do anything but shriek at the top of my lungs.

The driver takes me literally and stops the car right where we are—in the middle of the street. The car behind us honks obnoxiously as I dig through my bag for money. It takes me a while to find my wallet, which is buried under greasy potato chip wrappers and several mass-market paperbacks. The persistent honking isn't helping—damn it, why can't the driver just pull over?—and I try to tune it out as I count singles.

"Here," I say, handing him a fistful of dollars and opening the door. "Keep the change."

I jump out of the car and walk quickly to the sidewalk. Mim is still in sight. She's in Tompkins Square Park now, walking toward the north end. I follow at a discreet distance and look around for Forty-fifth-Street-type clues—milling crowds, flashing lights, police officers with yellow tape—but there aren't any. This isn't a crime scene.

Mim slows her pace as she nears a brick building in front of the basketball courts. Her steps are less confident and she doesn't seem quite sure what to do. Finally, she stops by a concrete square column that holds the flagpole and peers carefully around it. I'm too far away to see what she's looking at, but when Mim proceeds to her next stop—a green park maintenance truck a few yards closer to the building—I duck behind the flagpole. The night is calm and I hear the cop's radio before I see him. He's standing in front of the men's toilets, directly beneath a lamppost. Another person—male, white, eighteen-to-thirty-four—is there but he's lying on the ground, his legs brushing against an overflowing garbage can. At first I think he's sleeping or passed out but there's something about the way his head is positioned—the strange, sharp angle—that makes me realize he's not unconscious. He's dead.

The lamplight flickers as I try to understand what's happening.

It's only when I hear the siren in the distance that it hits me—this isn't a crime scene *yet*. It's just Mim and the dead man and the officer who found the body. Everyone else is still on their way.

Mim doesn't react visibly to the approaching sirens. She keeps her eyes trained on the scene in front of her—on the brick building and the policeman and the gravel sidewalk. Mim is waiting for something. I can't figure out what, but she has an air of expectation, like a cat ready to pounce. All she needs now is a mouse to cross her path.

And then it happens. I turn my eyes away for only a second—a fly is buzzing loudly around my head—and Mim is gone. By the time I swat away the bug, she's three paces away from the dead body and getting closer. The policeman is still standing guard but he's distracted. A posse of teenage boys has wandered over to the building. They don't know anything is wrong—they just want to play basketball—and the policeman is trying to discourage them without tripping the alarm. His efforts take him several feet away from his post and Mim slips in. She's moves silently and quickly and with Navy-SEAL stealth, achieving her goal with a minimum of movement. One second she's leaning over the body; the next second she's putting something in his coat; the following second she's walking away as if nothing happened. Her timing is impeccable. Just as she disappears behind a bend, the policeman turns around.

The scene looks exactly as it did thirty-two seconds before. Mim has left nothing behind to raise eyebrows.

While I'm trying to convince myself that this just happened, that Mim had, in fact, tampered with a crime scene, she leaves. She takes her tote bag and her Burberry coat and her flawless sense of timing and exits the park through one of the side gates. I don't watch her leave. I'm too distracted by recent events to even notice which direction she goes in.

I'm still standing there when the cavalry arrives. Cars filled with medical examiners and crime-scene experts and plainclothes detectives pull up against the north side of the park and screech to a halt. Within seconds the police are everywhere, like ants at a picnic, and I become keenly aware of my situation. I shouldn't be here—hiding suspiciously behind a flagpole just feet away from a dead body. It looks bad. It look worse than bad. It looks guilty.

My movements aren't as smooth as Mim's but I manage to get away before anyone notices me. The flagpole is outside the perimeter of the crime scene and I walk in the opposite direction as quickly as possible. I want to run but I don't. Running implies guilt.

I leave the park on the Avenue A side and stop at the first bar I pass, a rough-looking place with two-dollar Pabst and faded Halloween decorations in the window. I sit down on a stool, order a whiskey and lay my head on the bar. I'm trying to think of other things—the Potter account, my father, how to get Ian's book on the best-seller list—but it's impossible. Mim's actions are too extraordinary to be pushed aside. They're pop-up ads that won't close no matter how many times you click "no thanks."

The bartender brings my whiskey, forcing me to lift up my head and look at the world. The drink is reasonably priced—in my Mim haze I've managed to stumble into the only bar in the East Village that's not expensive and self-consciously hip—and I put a ten on the bar, wondering if I can add this to my expense account. That I'm here at all is Mim's fault. If she weren't slowly unraveling in a profoundly disturbing and dangerous way, I'd be home right now listening to Bonnie nix her friends' dinner suggestions ("No, not Euzkadi, it's way too loud. No, not Wild Ginger, I was just there on Sunday.").

It's still early for a Friday night and the crowd is thin. A couple enters the bar together and immediately splits up. The man takes the barstool next to mine, even though half of them are empty and we could spread ourselves out nicely if we were all willing to, and the woman disappears into the back. When she returns a few minutes later, he's still waiting for the bartender to notice him. She flags down the guy with little trouble and orders two margaritas. While they wait to be served, she asks him about his family. I'm listening with only half an ear, but it's obvious that the two are suffering from first-date-icitis. I know the symptoms well: stilted conversation, awkward pauses, inordinate interest in the number of siblings the other person has.

Their date is only marginally more interesting than my Mim troubles and I try to give it my full attention. I'm here at the bar to take my mind off things. But it's hard and I have to force myself to concentrate on their words. Still, I keep drifting back to the scene of the crime—Mim leaning over the body, Mim dropping something into the jacket, Mim walking away.

I finish my drink and order another, a single this time because I'm calmer now. I stay for an hour, drinking slowly and eavesdropping discreetly—all the while painfully aware of the fact that if I had just taken Bonnie's damn camera, I'd know what exactly Mim is planting on dead people.

TWELVE

Saturday morning I go clothes shopping. I throw on sneakers, take out cash from the ATM and head over to Broadway to spend money irresponsibly. Shopping isn't therapy. It doesn't make me happy or keep me sane. Within minutes of stepping into a store, I'm always frustrated and angry and ready to go home. Nothing is ever right. Either the hem is too wide or the waist is too high or the shade of magenta is too red. I hate trying things on. Dressing rooms are inevitably too hot from the glaring floodlights, and you stand there in clothing that doesn't quite fit, sweating and wondering if the overeager teenager who hung the number six on your door is waiting, ready to pounce when you step outside to glare at yourself in the three-way mirror along the back wall. Still, I do it because I like clothes. Or at least I used to.

I start at Banana Republic, whose oversolicitous sales help always make me want to scream. No, I don't want this in another color. No, I don't need you to fetch me another size. I usually avoid the mainstream chains. I spend too much time noticing what everyone in New York is wearing to want to look like everyone in New York. But today the Banana's uniformity is a tonic. The petite saleswoman with her sleek brown bob is just what I need, and the moment I clench my teeth and assure her quite emphatically that I don't need help, I start to feel better. This is working. Forcing myself to do a much-despised activity—this is pushing Mim to the corners of my mind.

I linger over a gray A-line skirt. The material is funky, a smooth mix of cotton and nylon, and I run my hand over it consideringly. The A-line skirt is already over—after a five-year absence, pleats are on the rise—but I don't care. I like the fabric and the cut, and my sediment-rock closet has documented enough clothing periods to last a lifetime. I locate my size and wander over to the sale rack in the back of the store. The selection is pretty thin—odds and ends that they couldn't unload during the postholiday sale frenzy, even at dramatically marked-down prices—and I take the skirt to the dressing room. It almost fits perfectly. The waist and length are good, but there's an odd bulge by the hips where the pockets are, which makes me look like a camel with misplaced humps. Despite these imperfections, I take it to the cash register. I hand over an exorbitant amount of money for an ill-fitting skirt that will have to be tailored and leave the store feeling almost lighthearted. Mim's insane and most likely criminal behavior pales in comparison to this—the buyer's remorse that comes from purchasing something you don't need at a price you can't afford.

I go into Club Monaco next. Almost everything in the store is black or white, even the spring collection, and I take two monochromatic shirts with French cuffs into the dressing room. They're not quite my usual style—I'm incapable of keeping track of cuff links and have finally stopped trying—but I take the black shirt because it goes so well with the new gray skirt. This is even better—an entire outfit I don't need.

The shopping solution works for a little while. It keeps my thoughts Mim-free for almost five hours, but then I stop at the New Era Café to get a cup of coffee, and a burst of energy and memories from last night return as soon as I sit down. With my shopping bags on the chair next to me, I sip French roast and flip through the *Village Voice* and try to make sense of Mim's strange behavior. But it defies sense. It stands up on its tippy toes and sticks its tongue out at reason and logic.

Something has to be done. Someone with a degree in psychology and a soothing voice has to intercede. Mim needs help—real help, serious help, the climb-out-onto-a-ledge-and-offer-your-hand help that Helen, with her isolate-and-infantalize tactics, can't provide. Otherwise she's going to get into trouble. You can't do this—hang out at crime scenes, make guest appearances at murder sites—and expect no one to notice. Sooner or later a police officer will catch on. He'll see her loitering on the fringe, ask a series of leading questions and take her downtown to central booking to charge her with murder. That would be the deathblow for Pravda.

Maybe I *should* tell Helen. The thought alone seems like a betrayal, but I can't stop from thinking it. When the Mim crisis was only a few ridiculous statements on the morning news, Helen's tailored Josh response seemed extreme. With the redirected telephone calls and the second office space, she was extinguishing a tea light with a garden hose. But suddenly her overzealousness has an air of legitimacy. Mim must be contained. For her own sake and the sake of Pravda, she has to be stopped. And Helen can do it. Not in the nicest way or the most gracious, but she can save Mim.

This—deciding the fate of Mim and Helen and Pravda and myself—is precisely what I didn't want to do today, and I finish my coffee in a single gulp, gather my bags and leave. I've already hit all the reasonably priced stores so I duck my head into Dolce & Gabbana to have a look. The clothes are lovely and eye-catching, but they're too expensive to be successful Mim distractions. Even in circumstances like these, I can't spend half a month's rent on a shirt. When it comes to haute couture, I only buy at sample sales or Century 21.

I take my purchases and head home. Bonnie's not there when I arrive, and I drop my bags in the middle of the kitchen floor before throwing myself onto the couch. I'm tired and cranky and annoyed that I didn't pick up something to eat on the way home. The fridge is fully stocked but it's all Bonnie food—organic graham crackers and soy milk and frozen vegetarian dinners with wheat gluten and tofu.

While my stomach grumbles, I lie on the couch, staring at the cracks in the ceiling and wondering if Ian is home. We haven't spoken since lunch at the diner. I've been tempted several times to check in with him, but I keep holding back. I'm trying something new, a sort of telephone austerity, to see if he'll do it again—step into the conversational void.

But this is an extraordinary circumstance. Mim's behavior is puzzling and frightening and I need to hash it out with someone. Ian is good at hashing. He has the unique ability to break everything down to its barest components. To him, problems are chemical compounds and at a glance he can identify the elements. This is what I covet—his analytical distance, his highly developed sense of detachment, the way he can shake conflict off his shoes like it's mud. I can't do that. I tried. With Delilah Quick, I shrugged my shoulders and left. I didn't make a scene or pick a fight, I just saw what was happening—tears: hydrogen and oxygen—and walked away. But it was only a gesture. Despite the truth that started to sink in during those five humiliating minutes in his hallway, I keep expecting him to come after me.

The phone isn't within easy stretching distance from the couch—for some inexplicable reason, Bonnie keeps leaving it in the bathroom on the ledge next to the window—and I think about getting up for several moments before I actually do. I fetch the phone from the bathroom, dial Ian's number and open the refrigerator to reassure myself there's nothing to eat. I open the box of organic graham crackers and stick my nose inside while I wait for him to answer. Ian's phone rings three times and then the machine picks up. I listen to his voice but hang up before the beep. I don't want to leave a message. We don't do that anymore. Our relationship now is based on the notion of spontaneity. We never plan to meet up—that's what dating is. We just happen to sometimes be in the same place at the same time.

The graham crackers smell normal enough, so I take them, along with a glass of water, to the couch. I put my feet up, turn on the television—the ceiling cracks aren't that fascinating—and wait for Bonnie to get home. Bonnie is another good person to talk to. She doesn't have Ian's analytical bent or his detached clear-sightedness, but she's an enthusiastic listener who embraces the minute-by-minute replay and the you-are-there aesthetic of early television dramas. Bonnie needs to see the scene in her head—the color of the leaves, the smell of the wind, the timbre of the rude bank teller's voice as she tells you for the fifth time that your checking account is overdrawn.

More from habit than interest, I flip through the channels, trying to remember the color of Mim's bag. It was black, wasn't it? Or maybe it was dark blue. And there was stitching along the side but I don't know what kind. How could I? The only stitch I'm acquainted with is the one that keeps buttons from falling off. Not that it matters. The point is that Mim is visiting crime scenes, that she's sneaking under the yellow tape, that she's slipping something into the front pockets of dead men. The details don't matter. With the Mim stories, it's only the broad strokes that count.

But I'm not one hundred percent sure that Bonnie will understand that, so I pick up the phone to try Ian again. It's been twenty-two minutes. Maybe he's home now.

I dial quickly and listen as the phone rings and rings and rings. Ian's still not there, but this time I consider leaving a message. It wouldn't hurt, would it, to just say call me. I open my mouth to utter something harmless and casual, but I can't do it. It's too much like the old days and I hang up. It's easier and simpler and less rife with relationship implications to just drop by the bar later. I'll go early in his shift. The bar won't be too crowded yet and we could have a nice, quiet, conversation. It would be totally innocuous. I go around to the bar all the time.

I'm happy with this plan for five minutes. Then I remember Bonnie's accusation that I use Ian. I don't use Ian—I know for a fact that I don't—but the charge sticks and makes me annoyed with her. And with him. I get up from the couch and retrieve my Filofax from my shoulder bag. I know more people in the world than Bonnie and Ian. I have many other friends. I call one of them. It only takes three tries to find someone who is free for dinner and we arrange to meet at eight o'clock at a Korean restaurant on Carmine Street.

I hop into the shower and throw on my new black-and-gray outfit. I'm tempted to leave the tags on but the only way to truly regret a purchase is to make it unreturnable. As soon as I cut the tag off the shirt, I notice that the collar is a little too wide. The seventies vibe is subtle but it's enough to keep my mind off Mim, and by the time Clarissa and I sit down at a barbecue table and order *bulgolgi,* I'm tipsy and giddy and enthralled by her recent adventures in catering. After several years of bouncing around from job to job, Clarissa had lately discovered that she had a talent for organizing huge affairs.

"It was a gigantic mansion in Montauk. Like the size of Buckingham Palace with maybe one less wing," she says as the waiter brings another round of cocktails. Clarissa is drinking a lime-green concoction that tastes like cotton candy. My drink is considerably less froufrou—whiskey on the rocks—but is equally potent. We both need to get some food in us, stat. "The wedding was in the ballroom, because, yes, the mansion actually had a room for balls, and there must have been a thousand guests there. I had to hire seventy-five people for the day, which wasn't easy to do. Nobody wants to work on Christmas. They say they do because they hate their dysfunctional families or it costs too much to fly home but when push comes to shove, everyone hops on that plane to Idaho to see Ma and Pa Kettle." She pauses to take a sip of her drink. "I still can't believe I found enough people to work the wedding. And after all that, the cheapskate stiffed us."

Clarissa has only been a site manager for Fifth Avenue Catering for four months, but already she's been appalled by the behavior of New York's upper crust. She's no longer impressed by society dames and celebrities. They're just the folks who hire you to serve a five-course meal on Christmas Day and don't bother to tip your staff.

"You should call Liz Smith," I say, watching a hot pot of sizzling *bibim bop* go by. Maybe I should have ordered that. "The highest-paid sitcom star in television history stiffs catering staff on Christmas—they eat that kind of thing up with a spoon. Plus, the woman he was marrying was barely divorced, which makes it even more salacious. She signed the papers like five minutes before the service."

Clarissa picks up her glass. "Actually, it was ten minutes."

I smile at the pedantry until I realize she's serious. "Really?"

"Her lawyer almost ran me over in his enthusiasm to deliver the papers," she explains. "Apparently there was a tie-up on the L.I.E."

A few minutes later a waiter comes by with our spring rolls. His timing is perfect. The whiskey has made me warm and relaxed. Perhaps too relaxed; I'm about to tip over from lack of sustenance.

While we eat, Clarissa talks more about work. Since she's still relatively new to the job, she makes lots of fun observations that are only obvious to an outsider. In a few months, the blanketed sweep, in which waiters fan out around a table in one smooth choreographed move, won't seem so odd to her.

At one point she breaks off her monologue in midsentence. Looking very self-conscious and embarrassed by her extended self-involved speech, she asks me about work. Since I don't want to discuss it, I try to think of a different topic. Mim, Ian, my father—nothing is acceptable. I divert her with another question. A sober Clarissa would have recognized the conversational dodge and returned it with equal skill, but the cotton-candy-soaked one simply launches into one more long answer.

Dinner passes quickly. Neither one of us has the cooking skills needed to turn out medium-rare beef on the barbecue at the center of the table, but nor do we burn it to a crisp. Oblivious to the charcoal edges, we wrap the well-done meat in lettuce leaves and munch away happily. I only self-consciously play with my extra-wide collar twice.

After dinner I want to go to a bar, but Clarissa has an early-morning event. "Ordinarily I'd be game but I was up at five this morning as well. That's the one thing that sucks about catering—the hours. The holidays were brutal, then things slowed down for January and early February. But they're getting in gear again. This is the last Saturday night I have off for two months."

The one and nine trains are a few steps away on Varick Street, but Clarissa wants to clear her head a little before hopping onto the subway, so we walk to the Christopher Street stop. It's a quick walk—only ten minutes away—but it takes us into another neighborhood, the West Village. She gives me a hug, promises to call soon and descends the stairs quickly. I wave goodbye, watching her disappear into the well-lit platform. Then I stand on the corner. The smartest thing to do would be to go home and sleep off the whiskey. I've had an exhausting day and could use the rest. But I'm around the block from Ian's bar and I'm not that wise. Maybe if I had left Clarissa on the corner of Varick and Houston, I would be able to walk away. But I didn't. And I can't.

The Cardinal Rule is mobbed when I arrive. The usual Saturday night crowd of drunken suburbanites and annoyed locals has set up camp at the bar and I have to wait fifteen minutes before a stool opens up. I hover near the wall, behind a group of overage frat boys drinking shots of Jaegermeister. One of them goes to the bathroom to throw up or pee—from his body language both seem possible—and I slide into his seat. His friends don't notice.

Ian is at the other end of the bar. He's pouring Stoli into a highball glass and scooping ice, but his attention is focused entirely on a cute blonde sitting across from him. He puts the drink on the bar and takes a ten-dollar bill from a thirty-something man. He counts out change without looking and leans in to hear what the blonde is saying. This is Ian's special trick—being completely drawn into a conversation while there are a million things happening around him—and it's persuasive. I was certainly persuaded by it. All bartenders are congenial and good-looking, and they all banter with you because they want a nice tip. But Ian's the only one who keeps his eyes on you all night long.

I watch him flirt with the pretty blonde, wondering if he's already asked her out for brunch tomorrow. That's how he got me—not asking me to hang around until after closing but suggesting a midday outing to a quiet place where we could talk.

Ian leans in to say something and the woman laughs and bats her eyelashes at him. I'm several yards away on the other side of the bar but I'm still close enough to be disgusted by the come-hither frankness of her look. I turn away, angry at myself for being here. Even though Ian and I lasted a year, there's something about the display—the familiar way he's chatting her up as if following a blueprint—that makes me feel like a cheap one-night stand. I fell for that smile, the one he takes out of his pocket every Saturday night.

Leaving now would be the wisest thing to do but there's

something oddly satisfying about sitting on this stool and glaring at him. My dependence—or his independence—isn't Ian's fault but I'm happy enough to take it out on him anyway.

Ten minutes later, Ian puts a whiskey down in front of me. He does this without any warning—no glance in my direction, no discreet nod, no flickering interest—and I have no idea how long he's known I was here. Maybe the entire time he was talking to the next Delilah Quick.

"Hey," he says while the frat boys next to me order another round of Jaeger. He nods, reaches for five shot glasses and lines them up on the bar.

"Hey," I say. Even while deep in a mood, I can comply with the most basic social requirements.

Ian fills the glasses and takes another order. He stays at my end of the bar for almost five minutes. I don't say anything else. I just sit there and watch him work and glare angrily. He doesn't ask any questions. His eyes flicker once in confusion but he doesn't follow it up. Ian isn't the sort who goes after trouble. He lets it come to his doorstep and ring the bell.

A half hour later, a busload of Irish tourists enters and the space becomes even tighter. Behind the bar, Ian doesn't notice. He's so involved with serving patrons that he barely notices anything, not even the pretty blonde who had so successfully engaged him in conversation less than an hour before. After another few tries, she realizes it's hopeless and starts chatting with a ruddy-faced Irishman.

It's my intention to leave after the one drink but I don't go anywhere. I'm disgusted with myself for having so little self-control and annoyed at Ian for not asking me what's wrong, but I stay firmly affixed to the stool. A bachelorette party enters and sidles up next to me. The bride-to-be, who is decked out in full regalia—veil, glow-in-the-dark penis earrings, two-foot inflatable man handcuffed to her wrist—elbows me in the ribs. She apologizes drunkenly before doing it a second time. But I still don't move. Despite the bruises, I'm not ready to leave.

I don't know why I always wind up here—on a barstool across from Ian at one o'clock in the morning. I have no idea what pulls me to him. I'm the one who ended the relationship. I should be the one who's flirting with pretty blondes. But I'm not. I'm sitting in his bar trying to figure out why I can't leave and coming up empty.

Still, I know one thing for sure: I'm not using him. Despite Bonnie's claims, Ian isn't convenient. Whatever it is I feel—this missing, this sadness, this compulsion to be near him—is far too strong to be something as innocuous as convenience.

THIRTEEN

By the time I arrive at Pravda Monday morning, Mim is firmly ensconced in her new office. She's sitting at her desk typing quickly and unselfconsciously on the keyboard as if this—the cavernous white space, the isolation, the unscuffed gleaming wood floors—were normal. At her elbow is the requisite mug of steaming coffee and she even has a famil-iar bouquet of gerbera daisies on the black filing cabinet next to her. There is nothing un-Mim-like about the presentation, but for some reason the scene is disconcert-ing. There is something about the arrangement of objects, the way she put all the furniture in the center of the room—bookshelves to the right of the desk, filing cabinet to the left, couch and coffee table a few feet in front—that's almost surreal. Sitting there in the middle of all this empti-ness, Mim looks like an advertisement for Ikea or an art in-stallation in the Whitney Biennial.

I duck my head inside to say hello, but Mim doesn't no-tice me. She's too deeply engrossed in her typing to detect discreet visitors hovering by the doorway, and I stand there for a moment watching her. Mim seems fine. Here in the sunlit glare of two wide eastern exposures, she seems completely okay. The stress and worry of the past two days suddenly feels ridiculous and I begin to believe that I've lain awake at night for no reason at all. I walk away without interrupting.

Norah greets me as soon as I step off the elevator into Pravda proper. She's sitting at the reception desk flipping through the Yellow Pages.

"Hey, Meghan, how was your weekend?" she asks as she looks up. The phone book is open to the *P*'s, from physicians to pianos.

I shrug. "Uneventful," I say honestly, with little enthusiasm. Worry and stress don't count as pastimes. They're draining and exhausting and they keep your eyes open at three in the morning but they can't be distilled into two-minute anecdotes. "Yours?"

"Pretty darn cool. A friend of mine just moved out to a huge loft in Williamsburg—we're talking like landing-strip huge—and had a big house-warming blowout. The band he hired was fab. I still can't hear out of my left ear but it's a small price to pay."

I smile politely because it seems the only appropriate response to temporary hearing loss and proceed to my desk. Josh is standing in front of the open refrigerator listing the merits of the mega-annotated database to Liz while they consider the drinking selections. Snapple or Diet Coke? Snapple or Diet Coke? I wave hello as I turn on my computer.

"Isn't it great?" Josh asks, approaching me with a bottle of raspberry ice tea in his grasp.

My wave was only a polite gesture—it's what co-workers do on Monday mornings—but Josh has read into it. He thinks I'm being friendly. I'm not. I'm too tired from Mim insomnia to indulge the usual social graces. "What?" I ask, biting back a sigh. Sometimes Josh is exhausting to talk to even with the usual eight hours.

"How productive the office is without Mim here," he explains. There is a smug smile on his face, as if he himself were responsible for the Mim-free environment. I suppose in a way he is. "I've gotten so much work done already."

Josh's computer isn't on yet. I'm several feet away from his desk, but I know this for a fact. He's a creature of habit. His routine is regular and ingrained and strictly followed: office small talk, morning refreshment, voice mail, newspaper, computer. Given his placement on the Josh movement chart, he's still a good thirty minutes away from actual productivity. But I don't say anything. I just smile blandly and sit down.

A little while later, Norah drops by to ask for the name of my GP. I have been staring unfocused at my computer screen for several minutes and it takes me a second to concentrate. "My what?"

"Your doctor, your general practitioner, your go-to guy for all the aches and pains that weigh you down," she says, leaning against my desk. "The ringing in my ear won't go away and I'm starting to wonder if it's tinnitus."

"Tinnitus?" I repeat, my thoughts still scattered.

"Yeah, you know, that thing rock stars and jackhammer operators get all the time."

"There's ringing in your left ear?"

Norah shakes her head. "Nah, I'm completely deaf in my left ear. It's the right one that I'm worried about. The ringing won't stop."

There's something wrong with this reasoning but I'm too

tired to embroil myself in a debate. I dig Dr. Walden's card out of my Rolodex and hand it to her. "He's nice but be careful—he likes to push pills."

Norah perks up at this and winks. "Don't worry about me. I'm a woman of the world." Then she takes the card back to her desk. She walks past Josh, who is, contrary to habit, getting a second drink from the fridge. Obviously I've underestimated him. He can vary from the routine upon occasion.

"Here," Norah says a few minutes later, dropping Dr. Walden's card on my desk. "I set up an appointment for two o'clock today." She shakes her head consideringly. "Man, it is *so* weird. It's like without Mim here, I am more productive. What are the odds?"

I roll my eyes at this statement—she's Mim's assistant; of course she has more time for personal stuff with her boss banished to another floor—but Norah doesn't notice. She's already moved on to bigger and better things: borrowing Liz's stack of lunch menus. Liz hesitates for a second as if not quite trusting this request; then the suspicion lifts and she smiles.

"What an excellent idea," she says as she retrieves the rubber-banded pile from her top drawer. "Let's put in our orders now. I'd get so much more done if I didn't have to stress about lunch. I usually spend half the morning trying to decide what I want."

Liz's comment is the last straw, and I get up from my desk, grab my bag and run down the back stairs to the first floor. It's rainy and cold outside, but I need fresh air and distance. This collective hallucination—that Mim is a siphon, that she's an albatross, that her presence is a toxin in their bloodstream—is so absurd that I have to literally step away from it. I walk across the street to the greasy spoon on the corner and order a cup of coffee. The restaurant is small and still crowded with the break-fast rush, but I find a seat at the counter and watch the cook make omelets. His movements are swift and grace-ful and even though the orders keep coming—cheese omelet, western omelet, egg-white omelet with mush-rooms and onions—he never falls behind. Now, *that* is productivity.

I drink my coffee slowly and motion to the waitress for a refill as soon as I'm done. She swings by with the coffeepot a few seconds later and smiles pleasantly. I sink deeper into my stool and consider not returning to work at all today. I shouldn't have come in anyway. My eyelids are heavy and my mind is sluggish and I probably won't get anything done. Still, my sense of responsibility runs deep and I leave a few dollars on the counter before heading back to the of-fice.

I'm feeling better equipped to deal with Pravda lunacy—and make no mistake, that's exactly what this is: complete and total madness—but I get off on Mim's floor first. I want to make sure that the busy, involved, seemingly sane woman I saw earlier is still present and accounted for. Isolating Mim on the fifth floor is a dangerous move. It means she can lis-ten to the police scanner twenty-four hours a day. But Helen isn't thinking about consequences. Her anger at being shut out of Mim's life—because that's really what her failure to confide adds up to—is too consuming for factoring out-comes.

As before, Mim's door is open. Incandescent yellow light is spilling out of her office and pooling in the fluorescent hallway. I approach quietly and stop a few feet from the en-trance. I hover there, listening to Mim. She's on the telphone with her personal trainer, rescheduling an appointment for later today. This is another good sign. If she intended to drop everything to chase police cars, wouldn't she want to keep her schedule open?

She hangs up and immediately makes another call, this time to her hair salon. This is all the assurance I need, and I turn around to leave. Helen is standing behind me. Her face is only inches from mine. I take a step back.

"What are you doing?" she asks, warily.

"Nothing."

"You're watching her." Her tone is accusatory and snappish.

"I thought that was the plan," I say, only a little bit flippant. Part of me feels guilty for the dodge. Helen's suspicion is completely justified. Her worst fears—that Mim is keeping things from her and risking the future success of Pravda—are on the mark.

"I'm done with that," she says, leaning to the left to peek over my shoulder at Mim.

I step to the side to give her better access. "You're done?"

She looks at me out of the corner of one eye. The other is still trained on her partner. "Yes, I'm done with watching Mim. I just told the others. Now that she's out of the way, I've moved on to a new challenge—implementing MAD B 4.0."

She's talking about the superdatabase as if it's another project entirely, but it's not. It's just the next phase of containment. Helen's managed to lock Mim out of the house, but her fingerprints are still all over the silver.

"Electronic youth-marketing research is the wave of the future," Helen says. "MAD B 4.0 will allow us to gather data that's one hundred percent accurate. Corporations will be begging us to sign them up."

Her outlandish claim unwittingly reveals just how little

she understands what her own company does. Perfect information for perfect products is a pipe dream. No computer, however super-megaintelligent, can fix for the varying tastes of millions of teens. That American youth culture is a variety pack of flavors—it's coolhunting's great weakness.

When I fail to respond, Helen narrows her eyes. "You probably don't know this but you're on the list, Meghan."

The impulse to smile is quick and nearly overwhelming, but I can't tell if I'm amused or uneasy. "The list?"

"I've seen how you've been palling around with her. In recent weeks you've been practically living in her office. I know what that means."

Of course she does. I've kept her apprised of everything. Each time Mim hands off another client to me, I alert Helen, who makes a notation on some unseen flow chart.

"You're like her," she continues. "Against progress. That's why you top the list."

In her office, Mim is still talking on the phone. She's making an appointment to get her highlights done. Her regular colorist, Suzanne, is booked, and she's trying to gauge the qualifications of Georgie, who has an opening tomorrow.

I don't say anything and Helen leans in. "I've got my eye on you."

"All right," I say calmly because I don't know what else to do. "I have to get back to the office."

Mim, finally convinced that Georgie's opening is the result of a last-minute cancellation and not a lack of clients, hangs up the telephone. I turn and leave. Helen stays where she is. She looks at Mim and then she looks at me and then she looks at Mim again. She doesn't know who to keep her eye on. Finally, she jogs briskly up the hall to catch the same elevator as me.

"I have to get back to the office, too," she says defensively as the doors close. She knows I've just witnessed her moment of confusion, her head swinging back and forth like a cartoon character's. "I haven't finished packing my stuff."

Although I don't want to engage in polite conversation after being threatened—and what was that talk of lists if not a warning?—I can't help myself. The elevator is small and quiet. "Why are you packing your stuff?"

"To change offices."

"You're moving?" I ask, genuinely surprised. Helen's office is fabulous. It's almost twice the size of Mim's, has a private bathroom and overlooks the river. In early spring, she gets a wonderful, warm breeze that smells like cherry blossoms.

"Of course. Mim's office is the better one," she says without irony or sarcasm or even a tiny sliver of self-deprecation. There is only the indisputable conviction that Mim's small, airless office is superior to hers.

But that's what it's like to be Helen—everything Mim has is the better one.

On Wednesday evening Helen waylays me as I'm exiting the building. I tell her I have dinner reservations but she waves off my excuses and drags me to a Moroccan-themed lounge around the corner. There, she deposits me in a seat, orders me to stay put and goes to the bar to get drinks.

"Here," she says, pushing a bottle of Budweiser in my face.

Great. I have to suffer Helen's company *and* inferior-quality domestic beer. "Thanks," I say.

Helen sits down in the chair next to me, leans forward and rests her elbows against her knees. She has on her concerned face. "I think we've gotten off on the wrong foot."

I take a sip and blink at her several times. "You think we've gotten off on the wrong foot?" I repeat the sentence just to make sure it sounds as silly coming from me as it did from her.

"Yes." She pauses, takes a breath. "You're not on my list."

Ah, that foot. "I'm not?"

"No, you're not. Of course not. How could anyone say that you of all people are against progress? You're not." It's almost a declarative statement but she ruins it in the end by raising her pitch. "Now, Elizabeth Goring is someone you have to keep your eye on."

Liz is considerate and kind and has no idea that Mim is communing with dead folks; she really doesn't deserve a watch. "Oh?" I say, taking gulping pulls at the Bud. In the absence of quality, I embrace quantity.

"Yeah, she's not like us. You know, checking on Mim periodically."

In the past few days, I've passed Helen several times in the hallway while doing Mim rounds. I sweep by her office three times a day—in the morning, after lunch, on my way home—just to make sure she's behaving. Even though she called off the Mim watch, Helen is doing the same thing, only with more frequency. At least once an hour, she darts down to the fifth floor. She always has an irritated look on her face, as if she's checking on Mim against her will. In her sight, out of her sight—she doesn't know which one she wants more.

I put my empty bottle on the table and wonder how long this interrogation is going to last. "No, she's not."

Helen sees that I'm done with my beer and finishes hers quickly. Then she returns to the bar for another round. She hands me a bottle with orders that I "drink up."

"And we are checking on Mim every so often to

make sure she stays where we put her, right?" she asks. "I mean, there's no other reason to check on her, is there?"

Helen is aiming for subtle but it's out of her range and for the next half hour she tries to pump me for info. I don't know what grand conspiracy she suspects me of, but she plies me with alcohol in hopes of loosening my tongue. It doesn't work. The watery Bud doesn't stand a chance against my whiskey-built tolerance.

Trying to keep up, she matches me beer for beer and in no time at all she's maudlin and drunk and telling me sad stories about her and Mim's relationship. She starts at the beginning with the happy days—nursery school, kinder-garten, first three months of first grade—and ends with a diatribe about the previous summer, when Mim invited two high school friends to the Hamptons for a weekend. Every-thing in between is mumbled and muddled, but the gen-eral theme of jealousy comes through clearly. Helen covets everything: what Mim has, what Mim's friends have, what Mim's friends have with Mim.

When she finally talks herself out, I lead her to the street and flag down a taxi. I don't know where she lives, and rather than try to extract an address from her, I rummage through her bag for her license. Then I put her in the cab, slam the door behind her and watch the car drive away.

Thanks to her inquisition attempt, I have a better under-standing of the Helen pathology—the way she wants to be Mim's best friend and to drown her in the East River at the exact same time—but that doesn't help. There's so much junk floating around in the ocean of her life—so much scrap metal and rubble and debris—that she'd need a bat-talion of therapists to dredge the waters completely. I, with my wistful glances at the second hand, am useless.

★ ★ ★

Before I leave work the next day, I do one last Mim sweep to make sure she's still behaving. I slip down the back stairs, turn left at the end of the corridor and stop in front of her door. Mim has only been here a week, but I'm already intimately acquainted with her hallway.

Her door is open only a crack—this is a first; her door is always open wide—and I have to press my eye against the opening to look inside. The view is limited. Even with my head resting against the door, I can only see the edge of her desk and the file cabinet. Mim is just out of sight.

I consider my options—open the door a smidge, go home, announce my presence—and settle on the first. Another inch or two won't make a difference, not to a woman engrossed in some harmless activity, and I'm too devoted to my routine to diverge from it now. This is only an employee spying on her boss, but it feels like something more significant—like a doctor doing rounds—and I take it very seriously.

Mim is sitting on the couch, and I have to open the door almost four inches to get a look at her. The door squeaks loudly as I push it open, but that doesn't matter. As soon as I see her—yellow book in hand, police scanner on knees—I burst through the door like a platoon of soldiers storming a compound. I've been peeking through cracks and walking on tiptoes for two weeks, but that's over now. All thoughts of stealth and discretion fly out of my head when I see Mim sitting calmly with the police scanner on her lap. The fact that I believed she was getting better—that insanity could indeed be temporary, like a stomach virus—makes me even angrier. I feel like I've been tricked by Mim. But I haven't. I only fooled myself.

Mim looks up at me with wide eyes. My noisy entrance—the way the door slammed against the wall, the way my shoes slapped against the floor, the way I stammered a few high-pitched words that didn't form an actual sentence—has pulled her attention away from the scanner. But only for a moment. Even with my unexpected arrival and its attendant peculiarities—the high color, the incoherence—I'm no competition for the Bearcat. Mim stares at me only long enough to take in the scene; then she waves a hand in my direction and flips through her book. "Shh," she says.

Shh?

This stops me for a second, but then I recover. "I don't care what you're—"

"Shh," she says again. Her tone is more emphatic and I shush. I watch her eyes fly across the pages of the police codes book with increasingly excitement. This can't be good.

"Mim, you have to"—I am shushed for a third time but by now I'm prepared for its disconcerting effect and I talk right through it—"stop this right now. I don't know what you're up to and I don't care. It's going to stop this instant." My tone is sharp and assertive. I will accept nothing less than total compliance.

She throws the book onto the couch and turns off the police scanner. For a moment I think my hard line stance has yielded results, but the delusion is short-lived. Mim isn't listening. She's grabbing her bag and coat and running toward the door. I follow. By the time I reach the elevator—I lost precious seconds backtracking to lock the office door—the doors are sliding shut. I throw out my arm to stop them from closing but it doesn't work and I pull my hand away just as quickly. In the elevator Mim is examining a map of Manhattan. She has perfected obliviousness to such a degree, I'm almost convinced I'm not here.

Rather than wait for another car—God knows how long that could take—I run to the emergency staircase and dash down the five flights as quickly as possible. I'm wearing boots with two-inch heels, which makes the dashing thing a challenge, but Mim's elevator is a local and we hit the ground floor at the same time. I follow her out of the building, insisting that she listen to me. I'm like a little lap puppy yapping at her heels, and several people in the lobby watch us breeze by. Mim doesn't notice the attention. She's too busy patting me on the head and calling me a good dog.

"Be a dear, Meghan, and go home," she says with her familiar, warm smile. There is an air of impenetrability about Mim, an air that's always been there but which I've mistaken for professionalism. Her manners, her good breeding, her reliance on protocol—these are stone walls that keep everyone out. As I watch her hail a cab without any regard to me standing there gape-mouthed and astonished, I find myself in sympathy with Helen for a second time. Mim is a fortress. She's a castle with a moat and a turret, and Helen is tired of the siege.

A taxi stops in front of Mim. She gets in and slams the door. I'm about to climb in behind her—my hand is on the cold metal handle—when she locks the car door. Then she leans over to the other side and does the same. For a moment I'm stymied. I look around Hudson for passing cabs but see nothing promising. Inside the car, Mim is leaning forward. She's giving directions to the driver in the front seat. Ah, the front seat.

I open the front passenger-seat door and get into the car. Mim makes a harrumph sound—finally, a reasonable response from her—and stares at me. Her look is a mix of anger and outrage. Her elegant eyebrows are drawn in an angry frown but her mouth is open. She wants to harrumph

again, but it's beneath her. She contents herself with leaning back in the seat and ignoring me. I do the same, slipping on my seat belt and focusing straight ahead. The driver
pulls away from the curb without acknowledging my presence.

We drive for five minutes in silence. A Honda Civic with
a broken window honks angrily at us after narrowly missing our taillight. I sink lower into the seat. New York cabs
aren't as much fun from the front row. In the back, Mim is
calmly gazing out her window. She's watching pedestrians
cross against the light and vendors pack up their wares and
commuters rush home. The air is frigid and damp, but
Canal Street is mobbed.

I don't say anything during the drive. I watch Mim out
of the corner of my eye, fight the queasiness in my stomach from motion sickness and wonder how this will play
out. I will make another attempt to reason with her, but I
don't think it will work. Mim's radar doesn't pick up logic.
Common sense, with its mass appeal and obvious-to-every-
one implications, flies too close to the ground. Instinct, intuition, the little voice inside her head that reminds her to
bring her sunglasses—these are the squidgy, unreliable
things that blip constantly on her screen. Sometimes her
giant cognitive leaps—the twenties revival based on one
woman in a porkpie hat on the corner of Fifty-seventh and
Park—drive Helen crazy. But Helen is a businesswoman.
She recognizes what makes money and is happy to jump
the Mim chasm if there's a dollar on the other side. This
new scheme of Mim's—opening up a telephone book to
a random page, pointing to an entry and calling it the latest craze to sweep the nation—isn't a reliable business
model.

The car stops at the corner of Lafayette and Worth. Our

driver turns off the meter and immediately the machine starts printing a receipt. Mim hands him a ten-dollar bill and waits for two dollars change. She takes the money, and the receipt, and puts them in her wallet. Then she gets out of the cab. I follow.

Mim's stride is brisk as she crosses Lafayette and I have to run to catch up.

"We need to talk," I say, putting a hand on her elbow. My voice is soft but insistent.

Mim looks at me but she doesn't pause or slow down. I understand her rush: There are no police cars on the block yet and her business will go more smoothly if she completes it before they arrive. "Of course we can talk, Meghan," she says as she turns right onto Pearl. There's a black-and-white in front of an auto repair shop. "How's Monday morning? You can be my first appointment. I'll pencil you in. Let's say 10:30. Now, if you'll excuse me, I have business to attend to." She picks up the pace. One police car is better than two.

I ignore the dismissal and tighten my grip on her arm. "I know what your business is. That's why we have to talk about it right now."

My statement has sufficiently surprised her that she stops in her tracks and looks at me. Her gaze is penetrating and sharp and discomforting. I let go of her arm and fight the urge to turn away. This isn't fair—Mim's the one bestowing gifts on dead people. She should be uncomfortable, not me.

"Then you should know more than anyone else how important this is," she says.

I'm still trying to figure out what she means—why me more than anyone else?—when I realize she's gone. Mim has returned once again to the attendance of her important business and is now approaching the garage. A uniformed police officer is in the driveway talking into a radio and Mim walks right behind him. Her shoes making no sound on the concrete, she enters the garage unaccosted. She's only five feet away from the police officer. My heart pangs in my chest.

The policeman is describing the situation to the dispatcher in a rat-tat-tat series of numbers, and he finishes just as I draw near. He reaches through the car window and replaces the receiver. Then he straightens up, runs his hands through his hair and starts to turn around. Mim is now inches away from the body. Oh, God, I can't look.

But I can't turn away either, and without knowing what I'm doing or why I'm doing it, I wave and call yoo-hoo to get his attention.

The policeman frowns at me. "There's nothing to see here, ma'am. Please disperse." His tone is impersonal but there's a hint of annoyance. He thinks I'm a ghoul chaser.

I open my mouth to tell him to turn around and see what's happening right behind his back but nothing comes out. I can't do this—be responsible for Mim going to jail. She needs help, an intervention of sorts, not a prison sentence. "I'm sorry, officer, I was just…trying to find a…place," I say slowly. It's an awful lie but it's the best I can do under the circumstances. Mim is less than five feet away doing things that are highly illegal and I don't know why. But suddenly I'm an accomplice. Suddenly my hat is in her ring. It makes no sense.

Mim is as calm as ever as she reaches into her shoulder bag. Whatever this is—the bag, the bodies, the object she slips into their coats—it isn't affecting her composure. Mim is still Mim, even in the least Mim-like of circumstances.

The police officer raises an impatient eyebrow—clearly

this is only a ruse to get closer to the body—and waits for me to finish. I open my mouth to say more but I get distracted. Mim is now pulling something from her bag. This is it—the missing puzzle piece—and I can't turn away. The police officer is saying "ma'am?" with increasing irritation and a second cop car is driving down the street with its siren blaring, but all I can do is watch Mim. The object is out of the bag. It's in Mim's left hand, upside down but still very familiar—a hot-off-the-presses copy of *Jawbones*.

FOURTEEN

Mim slides into the booth, orders a glass of chardonnay and tells me to stop staring at her. "You're making me feel like I have two heads. I don't, do I?" Laughing, she reaches up to touch her elegantly groomed head to reassure herself that there's only one there.

The waiter asks me what I want to drink and I order a whiskey on the rocks. He's standing directly in front of me, but I don't look at him. I can't take my eyes off Mim. But I'm afraid if I look away she'll disappear.

"Tell me what's going on," I say as soon as the waiter is gone. My conversation for the past twenty minutes hasn't varied much from this refrain: Mim, tell me what's going on. Mim, *please* tell me what's going on. The only thing that has changed is my level of anxiety. The initial shock I felt—a sort of overwhelming calm as if the world had finally slowed to a standstill—was quickly superseded by an intense agitation. Ian can't be involved in something like this.

Mim takes off her glasses and lays them on the table. She folds her hands in front of her on the table and leans forward. "It's like the Lonely Planet in Cambodia." There's a wide smile on her face. Despite the fact that she's just been caught leaving my ex-boyfriend's book at a crime scene, she's very happy with herself.

A smug Mim isn't a familiar animal—in the office Helen is always the cat who just swallowed the canary—and I'm not sure how to deal with it. "Tell me what's going on," I say after a moment, determined not to be put off anymore by her dodges and evasions. I've had enough of that in the past twenty minutes.

"But that's precisely what's going on—the Lonely Planet in Cambodia." Mim sees my impatience and condescends to explain further. Not everyone is privy to her secret language. "Years ago, the *Times* ran an article about travel in Cambodia and how every American tourist who's killed over there has a Lonely Planet guide in their backpack." Mim is expecting a flash of understanding, a eureka of comprehension, but it doesn't come and I continue to stare at her blankly. She sighs with disappointment—obviously her genius isn't getting the appreciation it deserves—and resumes her explanation. "Think about it, Meghan, is there any better way to promote a book about sudden, violent death than sudden, violent death?"

I feel myself go pale and still. My limbs tighten, my heart contracts and a tsunamilike wave is gaining speed and altitude in my brain. What she's suggesting—no, it's not possible. Nobody would ever do that. It's just not possible.

But I look at Mim. She's sitting there with her smug smile and her eureka-moment anticipation, and I know it's already several stops beyond possible.

The waiter swings by with our drinks and as he puts

them on the table, he asks if we're ready to order. The mundanity of the question—the very banality encapsulated in the common motherly assertion that no matter what happens you still have to eat—strikes me as ridiculously funny and I start giggling.

"Perhaps a few more minutes, please," Mim says, reaching for a menu and opening it. Our waiter, Jimmy, lingers for a moment—he's trying to figure out if I'm laughing at him or near him—and then, deciding that the answer doesn't really matter after all, moves on to the next table.

Mim peruses the menu as she waits patiently for me to stop laughing. When I don't in a reasonable amount of time, her lips purse in a prim disapproving way. There's something about my laughter—its volume, its intensity, its belly-deep glee—that offends her. Diners at neighboring tables are starting to turn around to look. Mim hates drawing this kind of attention to herself and would much rather see than be seen. I'm trying desperately to regain control—my ribs now hurt from the exertion and I can hardly breathe—but her obvious displeasure isn't helping. That she could disapprove of this small hysterical fit in a crowded brasserie when she's out in the world dropping Ian's book on dead bodies is even funnier.

The waiter returns twice before the convulsive giggling stops. He comes by ostensibly to take our order, but he's really here to gawk.

Mim's patience is slipping—with the waiter, with me, with the circumstances she can't control. In a sharp, almost snappish voice, she tells him we're going to need a few more minutes, *please*. I'm slowly regaining control, but her peevishness, the way she's behaving like the injured party at the table, almost sets me off again. I fight it. I swallow my glass of whiskey, close my eyes and breathe deeply.

When I am fully recovered, I open the menu and glance at the choices with a distracted eye. The idea of eating at a time like this still strikes me as absurd, but the laughter is gone. The sobering truth has returned with a vengeance, and all I want is to hear the worst of it from Mim so I can deal with Ian.

"So you were explaining," I say as I play with the ice in my glass. Now that we're ready to order, the waiter isn't interested. He's hanging out by the entrance having a cigarette.

Mim looks up at me from her menu. "Explaining?"

"Yes, you were explaining how there's no better way to promote a book about sudden, violent death than sudden, violent death." Just saying it feels horribly wrong. "Please continue."

Mim shrugs. "There's nothing more to say." Either she's telling the truth or sulking. I've never seen a sullen Mim, so I don't know what one looks like.

"Of course there is. You got the idea from a *New York Times* article about Cambodia?" My tone is condescending in its beseeching encouragement. It's as if I'm trying to pull information out of a reluctant three-year-old, but Mim doesn't notice. She's too pleased with herself to worry about subtext.

Mim nods. "The point of the article was how unsafe Cambodia is for travelers but for some reason all I remember is the Lonely Planet guide. It's the same with John Lennon. The only thing I remember about his assassin is that he had a copy of *The Catcher in the Rye* on him when he killed Lennon. I'm not even sure of his name—David Martin something?—but I remember the title of the book perfectly. I don't know why that is. Maybe it's simply because it was a famous book everyone had heard of. But I believe it's more complicated than that. As trend-forecasters we're part psychologists. We have to look deeper than the obvious. I think it has something to do with the irrevocable link forged between the two in the collective unconscious. And that thought kept playing in my mind as I read the book, and I started to wonder what would happen if *Jawbones* turned up at a couple of crime scenes. Would the police mention it in their reports? Would the local news media pick it up?" Mim tilts her head and studies me carefully. "You don't have to like the idea. You can even find it dreadful and abhorrent—I certainly do—but you have to agree that it's a great way to arouse the interest of a jaded media and reach millions of people at the same time. Society has always been drawn to the seedy side of things. You know that as well as I. What's seedier than murder?" Her voice is confident—she's obviously gone over this argument many times, probably once with Ian—but there's a needling note attached. She wants agreement and affirmation.

I stare at Mim, trying with little success to find evidence of dread or abhorrence. The waiter finally wanders over to our table after his extended absence, and Mim turns her attention to ordering. She asks how the swordfish is prepared—broiled or grilled—and wonders aloud if she shouldn't get something with a little more protein. From across the table, the only thing obvious to the naked eye is hunger.

Mim settles on the pumpkin soup and steak frites, and the waiter turns toward me with a suspicious eye. I haven't laughed for a full ten minutes now but he's not convinced of my sobriety.

While the waiter looks on, I glance down at the menu, realizing belatedly that I have no idea what I want. I've been flipping back and forth between the appetizers and the main dishes for almost ten minutes, but I haven't read a word. The menu is a prop; it's just something to do with my hands while Mim reveals her mad plan for world domination. I look quickly at it now while the waiter taps his foot. His section isn't overrun with diners, but I understand his impatience—cigarettes don't smoke themselves.

The selection is typical bistro fare—French café favorites—and I order a duck confit salad to go with spinach crepes. He jots this down in his pad and leaves, taking my empty whiskey glass with him. He promises to return right away with a refill, but I'm not optimistic. No doubt I'd get drunk faster if I went up to the bar myself.

With food out of the way, Mim returns to the topic at hand. She looks at me and waits for a response to her question: What is seedier than murder? I don't have the answer. I know that exploiting sudden, violent death for commercial gain is a pretty good contender.

Mim is silent as she waits for me to comment. It's obvious that she wants to say something provoking—perhaps "Well, Meghan?" in an impatient, irritated tone—but she holds her tongue. She can't figure out where I stand. My expression is blank—no dread, no abhorrence, no admiration—and it fails to provide any clues as to what I'm thinking. Suddenly I'm the sphinx.

This has never happened before and Mim's not quite sure what to do. She leans forward, as if to say something, and then sits back in the booth and looks down at her hands. Mim's struggling to appear indifferent, but she's not. My approval matters. I don't know why—because she respects me, because I represent Pravda, because I used to date Ian—but it's something she wants and is willing to wait for.

I can't give her an unequivocal endorsement, but nor can

I denounce her plan for all the things it is: immoral, depraved, gruesome. The words, which are on the tip of my tongue, won't come out. Mim is a diminutive woman. She has narrow bones and a petite frame, and she looks smaller than usual in the large booth. Sitting across from me in this dimmed light, she seems engulfed—by the bench, by uncertainty, by her own decisions—and overwhelmed, as if she's put on something too big for her, like her father's overcoat.

"What did Ian say?" I ask, advancing the topic from another side. I want to rip into Mim for her irresponsible and criminal behavior, but I can't help making concessions to her perceived vulnerability. Her sudden schoolgirl air isn't deliberate manipulation. I selected the restaurant and chose where we sat.

Mim looks up and draws her eyebrows together. "Ian?"

I nod. "Yeah, the author of the book, what did he say about all of this?" I ask as I recall the scene in my office more than a month ago. There he was—jittery Ian, nervous Ian, eager Ian—asking for my help and I said no. I knew how important *Jawbones'* success was to him. That *Jawbones* get some attention, that someone other than his mother reads it, that it doesn't just tread water and drown like so many other bottom-shelf magical nihilism books— this is why he came to me. He was desperate and determined and he came to me. But desperation and determination don't excuse this. The lengths Mim has gone to are unacceptable, and nothing Ian's ever done has disappointed me more—not Delilah Quick, not misunderstanding what I do, not letting me walk away.

Mim finishes her wine and gestures for more. Within seconds a waitress in braids and army boots is placing another glass of chardonnay in front of her. Impressed with her quick reflexes, I request a whiskey on the rocks. She happily complies and I'm back in the sauce in no time.

"Ian doesn't know," Mim says.

I'm in the middle of taking a sip when Mim clears Ian of any wrongdoing, and the relief I feel is so swift and intense I have to put down the glass. Success might be one of the few things that Ian's willing to go after with both hands, but he wouldn't stoop to this—turning a gravesite into an advertisement. Of course he wouldn't. "You didn't tell him?"

Mim hears the disapproval in my voice and reacts to it. She straightens up in her seat and looks me in the eye. It's a good effort—the extra two inches make her look a little more like a full-grown adult—but the aggressive defensiveness of her stance only heightens the schoolgirl resemblance. "There was no need to tell him."

I laugh again. It's not the uncontrolled hysteria of before, but Mim doesn't know that and visibly stiffens. After a brief pause, I'm fully capable of speech. "You took his book to murder sites and left it on corpses," I say. I'm speaking slowly and pronouncing each word carefully. Maybe hearing it said aloud will give her new perspective. "And you didn't think there was any reason to tell him?"

"I didn't want him to worry," she says calmly.

Her reasoning is so cool and unsound, it makes me stop and put down my glass yet again. I might have finally gotten a refill, but Mim's revelations are going to keep me in such a state of perpetual amazement that I'll never get to drink it. "About his own book?"

Mim blinks a few times. "About me."

A moment of silence follows this statement. Mim's waiting for me to say something, but I don't know what's appropriate so I remain quiet.

"I didn't want him to feel obligated to reject the idea solely because he was concerned for my safety," she says, elaborating. "Considering the risk involved, I thought it was better to present him with a fait accompli to absolve him of any guilt."

This argument is good. It's certainly better than the stuff she lead with—the Lonely Planet, police reports, the American love of seediness—but it doesn't make her behavior moral. You don't get points for protecting someone's soul after you've endangered it. "But it's his book."

"Yes, it is," she says. Her tone is a little sharp and has a tell-me-something-I-don't-know impatience to it. What she doesn't seem to realize is that I *am* telling her something she doesn't know.

"It's his *book,*" I say again.

Mim still doesn't get it. "It's his book" has only one meaning to her, the literal one, and she's not going to dig deeper. She won't even try to understand that *Jawbones* is more than a sheath of pages bound together by glue. It's Ian's heart and his hope and everything he's wanted for ten years. No matter how well it does, it'll never fulfill his expectations.

I look across the table at Mim. She's holding the stem of her wineglass loosely in her left hand and gently tapping the table with her right. There's a wonderful obliviousness about her. Mim thinks she's in possession of all the facts. She believes she has every particular firmly in hand. And maybe she does. Her plan for Ian's success—the loose-fingered sketch on a piece of scrap paper—makes sense. Her supposition that leaving *Jawbones* on murder victims will draw attention to it is well reasoned and logical. But a blueprint is more than the jotting down of a few pertinent facts. It's measurements, dimensions and projected repercussions.

It's a long list of tangibles that Mim doesn't understand. But perhaps it's not her fault. She's been chasing chimeras for fifteen years.

"He had a right to know what you were planning," I say.

Mim reacts to the recrimination in my tone. She tightens her grip on the wineglass and draws her eyebrows together. "I did what I thought was best. I was *helping* him," she says with quiet certainty, "which is more than I can say for you." Mim has seized new territory—the high ground—and isn't going to surrender it without a fight.

The charge against me is no less than fair and I drop my eyes in embarrassment. If I had stepped in when asked, none of this would have happened. "It's just that he had the right to say no," I explain softly. I don't want to browbeat Mim or put her on the defensive, I just want her to understand.

Showing no signs of increased comprehension, Mim swallows the last of her wine, catches the waitress's eye and discreetly waves her empty glass. I'm only halfway through my whiskey, but I do the same. By the time the waitress swings by, I'm ready for another. Mim has driven me to drink. Trying to reason with her is a losing proposition and I stop. I abandon all effort and sit across from her silently. I don't know what Mim is thinking—I'm not sure she's capable of thought at all—but I'm preoccupied with Ian. I'm wondering how he's going to react and what he's going to say. I have to tell him. As soon as I leave here, I have to go straight to his apartment and fill him in on Mim's recent activities. It's not something I relish.

The food arrives a few minutes later. Mim's soup is steaming hot, but she starts eating it immediately. Finally we have something to do other than stare at each other angrily. My failure to admire her plan and her failure to understand why have created tension. The table is thick with it.

The duck salad is lovely—luscious, soft, tangy—but I'm not enjoying it. My appetite is meager and I'm distracted. Too much has happened tonight for the simple enjoyment of well-prepared French food. I put down my fork. "How did you get involved?" I ask.

Mim looks up from her soup, which she seems to be genuinely enjoying. Her digestion is unaffected by her schoolgirl pranks. "With what?"

"Ian. I never introduced you. How did you meet?"

She shrugs. "I introduced myself."

Her answer is pedantic—obviously I want to know more than who said hello first—and I struggle to hold on to my temper. I've come too far to snap now. "When did you introduce yourself? How did you find out about *Jawbones?* Why did Ian ask you for help?" This last question interests me the most. I can't imagine Ian approaching Mim. It's not his style to run through a list of names. He never persists.

Mim eats another spoonful of soup. "Mmm. This is so fabulous. Here"—she holds out her spoon—"have some."

I try to decline politely but she insists, and before I know it I'm swallowing creamy, delicious soup. This seems like a delaying tactic or a full-out distraction but it's neither. Mim's enthusiasm for the soup is genuine. "I introduced myself after your conversation in the reception area," she says. "Remember that day? He came to the office to get your help. You refused. I overheard what he said and thought I could be of some use, so I offered my services. He was a bit reluctant at first. He thought he should run it by you before getting involved with your boss—he has very noble instincts—but I overcame his scruples easily enough." Mim pauses for another spoonful. "Ian's great. Why did you kids break up?"

"You knew he had scruples," I say, seizing on the only

thing that matters. "You knew he'd say no. That's why you didn't tell him."

Mim shrugs again. Her calm indifference is infuriating. "It doesn't matter, Meghan. All these details you insist upon pursuing, they don't really matter. All that matters is the book and if what I've done is wrong, then let it be on my head. If someone's going to hell for it, let it be me." She mops up the last remaining dollops of soup with bread, not at all concerned about eternal damnation. "God, this is so good." She offers the soup-soaked piece to me. I shake my head. "Are you sure?" she asks before throwing it into her mouth. She chews, then swallows. "Pumpkin is having a moment."

The change in topic is so dizzying I can't help but go along. "Pumpkin is having a moment?"

"Think about it. Mario Batali is putting it on pizza, Todd English is serving a to-die-for crème brûlée dished up in pumpkin shells, *Better Homes and Gardens* just put out an all-pumpkin cookbook, *Martha Stewart Living* listed it as the new mushroom and Al Roker wore a pumpkin costume on Halloween," she says.

Citing sources, providing proof, listing examples—this is the old Mim. Once upon a time she did this for everything.

"Pumpkin is definitely having a moment," she says again. A busboy drops by our table and takes our plates. She watches the bowl disappear with something resembling sadness. "But it's just a moment. In a second, it will be shunted to the side and forgotten." She picks up her wine and drinks half a glass in two gulps. "Because that's the way it happens."

"With pumpkin?"

"With people."

Suddenly I realize we're in deep waters. Mim isn't pining for pumpkin soup. "Is this about Peter?" I ask hesitantly. I've been avoiding this conversation for almost two weeks—to preserve her dignity, to respect her privacy, to spare her embarrassment—but it's no longer possible. Mim has brought Peter to the table and unpacked him from her briefcase.

She looks up at me sharply. Her brain is fuzzy from wine, but she knows she hasn't mentioned her husband to me. It's unlikely that she has mentioned him to anyone. "How do you know about Peter?" she asks. Then she takes a deep breath and backtracks. "I mean, what do you know about Peter?" She's trying to sound casual, but it's not working. Her voice is tense and suspicious.

For a moment I consider doing the same. A shrug, a dodged look, an offhand explanation—I could make this all go away in a matter of seconds. But I don't. I'm submerged in Mim's life up to my shoulders. There's no point in pretending only my feet are damp. "I saw him at an Exit Stage Left fund-raiser a few weeks ago."

Mim opens her mouth to say something and closes it immediately. She's thinking carefully now before speaking. This conversation isn't something she's mapped out, like her *Jawbones* publicity strategy. "At the Exit Stage Left fund-raiser? Yes, let me think. I had another engagement."

Again I want to let it go but I can't. It's wrong to get this close to a landmine and not detonate it. "He was with another woman."

"His cousin, I know. They've always been particularly—"

"Mim," I say quietly.

Mim looks away. She's biting her lip and tightening her face and doing everything possible not to cry. But it isn't enough. The tears are stronger than she is, and in seconds they're pouring down her face. She doesn't make a sound—

no hiccupping, no sniffling, no howling—and when I hand her a tissue, she barely acknowledges me.

Jimmy returns with our main courses. He stops abruptly at the sight of Mim's tear-stained face and looks panicked. His instincts are telling him to turn around and run, but he knows he can't. Even though he's besieged by hysteria—weeping to the right of him, laughter to the left—he has to do his job. He's a professional.

I watch the emotions cross his face—terror, stoicism, resolution—and fight a smile. The last thing he needs now is levity. He puts the plates on the table with a minimum of talk, sees our empty glasses and suggests refills. This sounds like an excellent idea and I nod enthusiastically. Getting completely drunk is the only way to deal with any of this.

I pick at my crepes while Mim's steak gets cold and she struggles to regain control. Her efforts are valiant and brave but completely in vain. Something inside her has popped and emotion is pouring out of her like molten rock. Its progress is slow, steady and devastating.

It would be easier to watch Mim if she were wailing or moaning. Her silence, the way she's muffled her grief, is almost unbearable. Sadness is a tight knot that sits on your chest and you have to unravel the strands. Mim isn't doing that. She's holding both ends and pulling as hard as she can.

Feeling unsteady, I drink whiskey and wait. I've felt intense sadness before—when my mother died, of course—but it wasn't like lava traveling down the side of a volcano. My bursts of crying were severe, frequent, brief and loud, like summer thunderstorms or tornadoes.

By the time Mim stops crying, I'm out of tissues and napkins and have to fetch toilet paper from the bathroom. She mumbles thank you as she blows her nose. Then she takes several deep breaths to calm down. Her face is red and her eyes are puffy. Inside her rib cage, her heart is beating violently. I'm two feet away but I know this for sure. Sometimes you don't have to be closer than one table width to feel someone's heart pounding.

When Mim disappears into the bathroom to splash cool water on her face, I eat crepes and watch the patrons at the bar chat and drink. The restaurant is full now—every table is taken—but Mim's meltdown has attracted little attention. It was quieter than mine and more discreet.

She returns a few minutes later looking marginally better. The puffiness is still there as well as the redness and now her bangs are wet, but she seems calmer. There's an element of control that wasn't present when she left.

Her dinner is completely cold and I insist we send it back to the kitchen for reheating. She tries to resist but she's no match for my determination. I want to do something to alleviate her pain and this is all I can offer: a warmed steak.

Mim eats in silence, with none of the enthusiasm that accompanied the pumpkin soup. She takes small bites and chews everything thoroughly. There remains a vulnerable, schoolgirl quality about her—the booth is still large and imposing—but she looks older now and more worn.

She finishes her meal, the busboys clear the table, Jimmy gives us dessert menus and I begin to believe it's over. The heart-to-heart that I thought was coming next, the one that traditionally follows gut-wrenching crying jags, doesn't seem to be on the agenda. Mim, for all her tears, isn't prepared to open up to me. I don't know if I'm disappointed or relieved.

"The bathroom at Mount Rushmore," Mim says quietly and suddenly.

I'm about to wave for the check when she makes this

cryptic statement. I stop, put down my hand and look at her. For a moment I think she's carrying on a conversation that was interrupted earlier and open my mouth to correct her but then I realize what's happening and nod.

"The bathroom at Mount Rushmore, November 20, 9:28 a.m.," she says. "I spotted my first wrinkle. I'd gone in to wash my hands and while I was turning off the faucet I saw it, a crooked groove to the left of my mouth. It wasn't very long—only an inch in length—but it wouldn't go away, no matter how much I distorted my face."

Mim's head is tilted down. Her eyes are focused on her hands, and she seems determined not to look me in the eye. She doesn't want me peering ruthlessly at her face, trying to find the one-inch crooked groove to the left of her mouth. "It was a wrinkle, not a forehead crease or a laugh line. A wrinkle gouged into my skin and I couldn't stop staring at it. Peter was in the café ordering breakfast, but I couldn't leave the bathroom. I couldn't leave. And Peter had to come in there and get me. It was so humiliating. I ruined the whole trip. After the photo shoot for *Metropolis* we were supposed to have a rustic weekend in a friend's Black Hills cabin but Peter decided at the last minute that he needed to get back to his studio in New York." She laughs quietly and without humor. "Of course he did. Who'd want to spend a weekend trapped in a cabin with a wrinkled old hag?"

The mirror in the bathroom of the Mount Rushmore cafeteria wasn't enchanted. No wicked sorceress or evil fairy put a spell on it, but that doesn't matter. Mim looked into it and was instantly transformed into the witch from every Hans Christian Andersen story. Her sense of reality is off—faces don't crinkle in an instant like balled-up sheets of paper—but I won't try to convince her of that.

Mim's too smart. She knows the countdown has begun. This heart-stopping, breakfast-delaying, weekend-wrecking groove is only the first guest to the party. Soon there'll be dozens like it eating crudités and making small talk on her face.

Mim's terror is extreme and premature but I understand it. Coolhunters have a front-row seat to the incredible disappearing act of the old and older. Every day of our lives we watch sixteen-year-olds buy jeans and sneakers and sunglasses. Nobody stays young forever but somehow the kids in Williamsburg swing it. They never age. But Mim does. I do. We go from one target demo to another until we cease to exist. Once we turn thirty-five—that is, leave the coveted, hard-to-reach eighteen-to-thirty-four-year-old category—our value goes down. Advertisers who used to pay twenty-three dollars to reach one thousand viewers now pay nine dollars to reach us. It's a slow slide toward invisibility that doesn't stop until you're nothing but a ghost who haunts the grounds of the old family estate. Suddenly I get it. Snuff, accordion rock, capes—this is Mim rattling her chains.

There's a certain amount of freedom that comes with falling out of a target demo—people stop trying to manipulate your decisions—but Mim doesn't see it as liberation. She's tethered to unhealthy, materialistic ideals: The more they spend on you, the more valuable you are.

I consider explaining this to her but decide against it when I see tears forming again in her eyes. A Marxist interpretation of her grief isn't going to make it any less terrible. She needs reassurances that she's still vital and necessary. Despite appearances, her problem is not aesthetic. It's one of those things that cuts right to the bone.

Mim mistakes my silence for agreement and looks at me

with watery eyes. "It's true, isn't it? I'm a wrinkled old hag." She puts her head on her palm and sighs loudly. Her melodrama—so many times larger than the one-inch wrinkle in question—would be funny if her husband hadn't left her for a younger woman. You can't tell the deserted first wife that it's all in her head.

Seeing that she's on the verge of another meltdown, I sit on the cushion next to her and provide a shoulder to cry on. Mim doesn't take it.

"What happened with Peter?" I ask quietly, wanting to get out of the Mount Rushmore bathroom. The monument's faces promote an impossible ideal: weathered but smooth.

Mim shrugs. It's a familiar gesture—she's already done it several times this evening—but the information it conveys is brand-new. This isn't indifference. This is pain too deep for words.

While she pulls herself together, I read through the dessert menu. I'm still not hungry, but I don't want Mim to think that I'm waiting impatiently for her to continue. Jimmy doesn't recognize the ruse for what it is and drops by our table.

"Ready for dessert, then?" he asks, pen at attention.

I consider ordering coffee but decide I'm not quite ready to sober up yet. "Another whiskey," I say, handing him my empty glass. He glances quickly at Mim, sees she's in no shape to answer and leaves. He takes the dessert menus with him and drops them at a neighboring table.

When he's gone, Mim lifts her head. For the moment, at least, her eyes are dry. "December 12, 3:24 p.m. I came home early from work. Things had been really slow in the office so I decided to skip out and make a surprise dinner for him. Christmas was in two weeks and I thought it would be fun to try a new recipe, Pottage of Pompion. I'd cut it out from the *Times* the Sunday before. It called for pumpkin, cream, chicken stock and an assortment of herbs, which I picked up on my way home.

"Peter wasn't supposed to be there—he had an afternoon shoot in Brooklyn that was probably going to run late—but when I came up the stairs I saw his jacket hanging over the railing. This made me happy. I figured we could cook together like we used to and I started calling his name. He wasn't in the kitchen or the den or the darkroom. He was in the bedroom, of course." Her eyes are bright and watery but her tone is calm. I don't know how she's pulling it off—cool, indifferent, detached. "He was having sex. With one of the models from the Brooklyn shoot, it turns out. Everything had gone smoothly and they finished early, which was a relief to everyone."

There's no irony in her voice, no sarcasm or scorn or derision.

"With one of his models," she says without any heat. But her hands are shaking. They're tearing up one of the napkins she'd used to dry her eyes. "Can you believe it? With one of his goddamn models. I was so angry. I was so angry I can't even put it into words how I felt. If I had had a knife in my hand or a gun I don't know what I might have done to him and that slut." She inhales sharply, one long shuddering breath. "How dare he do this to me? Make me a part of that overdone, overworked scene. The unsuspecting wife in the doorway with the groceries—how dare he do that to me? I kicked him out. I threw his stuff out the window and told him to never come back."

Eyes shimmering with tears, nose red, face puffy—she seems defeated and overwhelmed. The drawbridge to the Mim stronghold is down. It's been lowered over the moat, and foot traffic—peasants, knights, merchants—are free to walk across. "Where's the anger now?" I ask, wondering if Helen has ever seen this Mim.

A quick, cynical smile darts across her face and disappears. Here's the irony and the self-deprecation and the contempt. "It's very easy when he's there in your bedroom with the model to feel anger. But when it's you alone in the bedroom with the memory of him with the model, it's harder. Because you feel so alone. And so old. And so unloved. And so ridiculously inadequate. I can't stand being there. Anywhere in the apartment. It's suffocating." She leans her head against the cushion. "It's big and empty and all of Peter's annoying little piles—his mail on the kitchen counter, his clothing on the bedroom chair, his photographs on the dining room table—are finally gone and I can't breathe."

"Sell it," I say.

It's obvious that this simple solution hadn't occurred to her and Mim looks at me with astonishment. I'm not surprised. She and Peter have been living there for ten years. It feels like home. Or at least it used to. "Sell it?"

"Sell it," I say emphatically, realizing this is what Mim needs: a to-do list. "Find a new place, put the condo on the market and take a vacation."

For a moment she brightens. The simple practicality of the list makes everything bearable. This is always the hardest part—figuring out what comes next. But Mim's not ready for level-headed action. She's still in the weepy stage of grief, and the thought of undertaking any large task— looking for a new apartment, finding a trustworthy broker, picking a secluded island—is overwhelming.

"I'm happy to help," I say quickly, when I see the defeated look creep into her eyes again. "A friend of mine just rented an apartment from a very nice broker. I could find out the name of the woman. I'm pretty sure she does sales as well. And I'd love to help you look for a new place. Looking at apartments is one of my favorite hobbies. Sometimes I go to the open houses on Fifth Avenue just to gawk."

Mim sighs deeply and stares at the clock on the far wall for a minute. Then she grips my hand tightly. Her fingers are hot and sweaty. "You're so kind, Meghan. You've always been very kind. But I don't think I'm ready to handle all that right now," she says quietly and slowly, as if articulating thoughts that have just occurred to her for the first time. "Living in the apartment and hating the apartment—it gives me something to focus on. Take it away and what happens? I start a new life? I start dating again?" she asks, in a horrified little voice as she lets me go.

I think of my father trying so hard not to run in place. That crushing excess of energy—I always thought it was a desperate fear of standing still. But maybe it's not. Maybe it's just him taking life in stride. "Yeah, you start dating again. Not right now, but eventually."

"I can't do that," she says. "I'm too old. I have wrinkles. Of course Peter left me."

"Mim, you're not—"

But she knows what I'm going to say and she doesn't want to hear it. "It's the truth and I might as well face it now rather than delude myself. I am old. I have wrinkles." She runs her hand under her chin. "My neck is starting to go all roostery. It's loose and sagging."

The skin around her neck is as firm as mine, and her desperate patting does nothing other than draw attention to that fact. Mim has ten years on me, but you can't tell by looking at us. The fact that she only just spotted her first wrinkle is testament to that. I saw my first one-inch line two years ago. Crooked and thin, it extended from my left eyebrow like a country road off a major interstate on a roadmap. The mark threw me for a loop—it was unexpected and ugly—but only for a moment. My mom was terrified of wrinkles. She had chemicals peels and eye jobs and face-lifts that left her so battered and bruised she wouldn't let us look at her for an entire week and died at forty-nine of some obscure lung cancer that only men who work with asbestos get. I understand Mim's fear— I've felt it myself—but I also know the truth: It's the lucky ones who age.

Mim closes her eyes and an errant tear runs down her cheek. Her halfhearted wrinkles are just a symptom, but she's got them pegged as the disease. Her formula is simple—no wrinkles, no desertion—but horribly flawed. Human relationships, her ten-year marriage, cannot be reduced to the lines on a person's face. And if they can—if the only thing Peter was checking out was ages on driver's licenses—then Mim had a bigger problem, one that couldn't be solved no matter how many enchanted mirrors she looked into.

"Are you talking to someone?" I ask.

"You. Now," she says, touching the skin under her neck again and then lowering her hand.

I shake my head. "An MSW or a psychologist, someone with a little professional experience to help you deal."

Mim's hand brushes against her neck for a third time. The movement is so quick and smooth she hardly seems aware she's doing it. "I *am* dealing," she says confidently and with a straight face.

I stare at her, fighting the urge to laugh dismissively. Mim is not dealing. In the course of this conversation she's developed a new fixation—floppy neck skin—and a lovely obsessive-compulsive habit to go along with it. "Are you sure?" I ask tentatively. I don't know what my friendship obligation is here—to nurture her confidence or to burst her denial bubble.

Mim sees my concern and brushes it aside. "I know I seem a little shaky right now, but I promise you I'm fine. I have my manic-depressive moments, like this evening, but most of the time I'm very even-keeled. I have my work, which is a lifesaver. The routine of Pravda keeps me sane. And I love my new office. It's a completely new space, with no bad associations. I can breathe there."

Her enthusiasm is real. She genuinely has no idea that she's been banished and isolated like a quarantine victim. "Work is going well?" My tone is neutral, almost indifferent, but I'm extremely interested in the answer.

"It's the only thing in my life that *is* going well at the moment," she says with an enthusiastic smile. Her eyes are still watery but they seem to be shimmering with excitement, not tears. "I feel so in control, it's wonderful."

For the past month, Mim has been treated like a rag doll. Helen has dressed her up, brushed her hair and stuck her in a closet, but despite all that I'm not surprised Mim feels in control. She has taken the basic tenets of trend-forecasting—the watching, the deciphering, the interpreting—and tossed them out the window. She's eliminated the X factors and the chaos and the uncertainty of the street by inventing the trends herself. It's not right. It's not how coolhunting is supposed to be done, but I understand the appeal. Being in control must feel good.

Mim has created this—a Shangri-la where mistakes like the Killington don't exist—because she's terrified Roger

Cooley is right. Her success depends a large part on her rapport with teenagers, and it would be devastating to her self-esteem if she lost it. I don't think she has. Mistakes are narrow cracks we all have to step over every day, but Mim has managed to turn one error into a yawning canyon. She's added the Killington to her wrinkles and Peter's infidelity and did what she always does: identified a trend—in this case, aging. Her reasoning is faulty—you don't see white sneakers, snowdrifts and a doctor in a pristine lab coat on his way to work and say white is on the upswing—but completely understandable. Anyone with a gift is afraid of losing it.

"Take the *Jawbones* project. It's very different from what I usually do and the most interesting thing I'm working on at the moment," she says, tantalizingly. I wait for her to elaborate—I'm extremely eager to hear about her other ventures—but she's too engrossed in *Jawbones* to digress. "I know you don't approve of how I've handled it, but I think I'm doing a good job. The Lonely Planet in Cambodia—it'll work, I just know it."

This is where I came in but I can't muster up the anger I felt before. I know now that Mim's head isn't in the game. She thinks it is, but it's not. Her capacity for clear thought has been undermined by grief and wrinkles. "But you're done now, right?"

"Hmm?" Mim asks absently. She's staring at her empty wineglass with confusion. I have more whiskey; why doesn't she have more chardonnay?

"The *Jawbones* project is completed, right?"

She waves her glass enthusiastically until she catches the eye of a waiter. Discreet, tactful gestures are in the past. "Most likely, yes."

"Most likely?" I repeat. This is not the answer I'm looking for.

"More than likely?" she offers, as if we're bargaining or bartering.

"Mim, this isn't a negotiation. We're not haggling over a vase in a flea market. When I say the *Jawbones* project is completed, you say right."

I'm trying to be stern and forbidding, but all the whiskey in my system makes that a challenge. The urge to laugh is perpetually present, and I have to squelch it in order to maintain a threatening persona.

Mim sullenly examines the stem of her wineglass for a moment. Then she says, "Right."

"I'll have to tell Ian, of course," I say. "As soon as we're done here, I'll go to his apartment and tell him what you've done. He's going to be very, very upset with you, Mim. You might want to have a statement ready."

"A statement?"

"A few prepared ideas. With Ian it's always better to have your thoughts worked out beforehand. He's a dirty fighter and if you don't say it all in one shot, you never get to say it at all."

"What's a dirty fighter?" she asks.

"One who walks away from you while you're still seething with anger," I explain. "One who doesn't let you make your point. One who doesn't try to make a point in return."

She tilts her head to the side. "Is that what he does?"

"It's what he excels in."

"Is that why you broke up?"

I shake my head no but don't say anything.

"Why'd you break up?" she asks, suddenly persistent. This isn't like Mim. The garden gate that keeps you out of her backyard keeps her out of yours.

I mumble an answer.

Mim leans in to hear me and knocks into my drinking arm. Whiskey drips down the side of my glass. "What?"

"Delilah Quick."

A devastated look comes over her face and she throws her arms around me. She's drunk and clumsy, and the force of her hug almost pushes me off the bench. I recover my balance while she pats my head comfortingly. "Oh, you poor, poor darling. You know exactly how it feels. I've been pouring out my heart like I'm the only woman who has ever been done wrong by her man and you just listened quietly. You poor, poor dear." She pulls away, but her bracelet is tangled in my hair so I go with her. Mim is momentarily disconcerted by this development, and she frees her arm with only a little bit of fuss and hair loss. "You must have wrinkles, too," she says, her eyes searching my face eagerly. The light in the restaurant is dim and my complexion appears perfect—so does hers—but Mim hides her disappointment beautifully.

Her relief at not being the only woman scorned at the table is so intense that I almost don't have the heart to tell her the truth. Part of me wants to leave it here, with Ian as the heartless villain in a love triangle, but I can't. Two hours ago his book was left in the coat of a murdered mechanic on Pearl Street. He's been ill treated enough for one night.

"No, no," I say. "Delilah Quick isn't a person. She's a character in *Jawbones.*"

Mim is thrown off by this. She looks at me blankly and repeats the sentence quietly under her breath. Then lightning strikes. "The emasculating bitch who betrays Rocco!"

"Yes, that's me."

"You know Rocco?"

Rocco is a secondary character whose life is loosely sketched. Nobody really knows him, not even Ian. But that isn't what Mim means. Fact and fiction—it's all a mess in her head. "He based Delilah Quick on me."

I'm prepared for her outrage and her sympathy and another punishing hug, but she just draws her eyebrows together. "That's why you broke up with him? You didn't like being a muse?"

The word *muse* gives the sordid affair an unacceptable patina of Greek culture. "I wasn't his muse."

Mim rolls her eyes. "You inspired him, no?"

This thinking is simplistic. "All inspiration isn't good," I say, trying to think of an example that supports my thesis but nothing comes to mind. It was that last drink. If I hadn't had it, I would be throwing out examples left and right.

"Come on. There has to be more." She laughs and leans in closely to hear the true story. "Why'd you *really* break up with him?"

Her lack of sympathy is unexpected and unfair. I listened patiently to her tale of woe. I patted her hand and said, "There, there."

"He fights dirty," I remind her peevishly.

"We've already covered this ground. Dirty fighting wasn't a deal breaker," she says sensibly. For a drunk woman who cannot distinguish fact from fiction, she has a remarkable hold on reality. "What's the real reason?" she asks, her expression resolute. Mim really wants to know. Maybe because she's genuinely curious. Maybe because my sob story will mitigate the pain of her own.

I don't feel comfortable telling my deepest, darkest secret to my boss but at the same time I'm not completely repelled by it either. The candlelit restaurant and Mim's honesty have fostered an atmosphere of intimacy. I'm not sure if the closeness is genuine or the product of too much liquor, but suddenly I feel the need to tell her everything. It almost seems like a betrayal not to.

I take a deep breath and say it. "He hates her."

This isn't the quite the revelation I think it is, and Mim looks at me, baffled. "Huh?"

Her inability to see the big picture in a blinding flash of understanding disconcerts me. I was prepared for sympathy, not confusion, and I bite back a growl of frustration. Mim's had a lot to drink. She's obviously not thinking very clearly. Otherwise she'd get it. What Ian's loathing of this inhuman thing he created really means—she'd get it in a heartbeat. "Think about it," I say. "The scathing way he writes about her, the derisive way he describes her—he really, really hates her."

Mim nods as though she gets it but she still doesn't have a clue. Although she's putting on a good show for my benefit, her eyes, puffy from tears and alcohol, are bereft of understanding.

"He hates her and he hates me, too. I am her," I explain quietly. This is the first time I've said the words aloud. They've been bubbling and boiling in my brain for eleven months but this is the first time they've passed my lips, and I'm unprepared for the way they make me feel—sad and a little bit hopeless.

It's funny. When Delilah Quick first appears in chapter two—when she steps off the elevator at Truth Inc. in her shiny black boots and her shoulder-length chestnut hair—I was flattered. She struts across the floor with attitude and verve and seems almost to have her own theme music. "Real Wild Child" plays in your head as you watch her. Here, I thought, is an idealized version of myself, and I liked the implication: that this is how Ian saw me.

But it cuts both ways. And when she turned out to be the Antichrist in Jimmy Choos, my mind jumped to the same place. The venom, the vitriol, the contempt—I'd never seen any of it before but somehow it was all very plausible. Delilah Quick made an after-the-fact kind of sense that embarrassed me. I should have seen her coming. I should have known she was there, lurking in the wings of Ian's subconscious.

Mim waves her hand in the air. It looks as though she's swatting a fly, but she's really tossing aside my concerns. I knew I'd get this response—from my father, from Bonnie, from Ian. On paper, my theory has the frayed dissociative edge of the fiercely paranoid. Delilah Quick as the embodiment of Ian's true feelings about Meghan Resnick—puh-lease. But I know it's not that simple. Delilah had to come from somewhere. Why not me?

While I'm debating what to do next—develop my argument, change the subject, sulk—Mim starts laughing. Her shoulders quiver and her voice trills and her eyes sparkle. Her amusement is less obtrusive than mine—no waiters are looking at her in fright—but it's just as keen.

After a few moments Mim notices that I'm not laughing, too. I am sitting next to her with a cross expression on my face glaring into my drink. I am serious. Too serious. Suddenly she stops and looks at me with drawn eyebrows.

"You're kidding, right?" she says, more confused than ever. "You're just making a joke."

I don't look at Mim. I avoid eye contact with her completely and continue to stare silently into my whiskey. Moments before, sulking hadn't been a genuine option—it was third on my list, a tossed-off alternative rather than a serious contender—but all of a sudden it seems like the only course of action. Even though I expected this reaction from Bonnie or my father, I am ill-equipped to deal with it. Nothing in my life prepared me for this—my worst fear being a very good punch line.

Mim watches me silently, her catlike blue eyes focused intently on my profile. She still doesn't quite understand what's going on—am I really not kidding?—but she's determined to make amends. This is how Mim was raised, with the beautiful, airtight manners of the Junior League. "Of course he doesn't hate you," she says now, laying a comforting hand on my shoulder. "Oh, honey, how can you even think such a thing?"

There are a million reasons for this extremely logical assumption, but I can't articulate a single one. In my head it all makes sense—obvious, embarrassed, wings, subconscious—but as soon as I try to express it, it becomes an ugly jumble of "you knows" and "likes." I stutter and ramble and fail to communicate anything other than my complete lack of coherence. At one point I get so frustrated I start to cry. The tears roll so softly down my cheek that I don't even know they're there until Mim wraps me in her arms and cradles my head against her shoulder. She runs her hand along my hair and assures me that everything is going to be all right. Her voice is gentle and soothing and full of conviction. I haven't been held like this in years—not since my mother died—and the sensation is almost too much to bear. It makes me cry harder. But Mim doesn't mind. She holds me and waits.

At some point the waiter swings by the table again, this time with our check. He leaves it hesitantly and without comment, but it's obvious from his look that he wants us to leave. It's a Thursday night, the restaurant is crowded, and we've monopolized a booth in his section long enough.

Mim insists on paying the bill despite my protests. It's her

fault we're here, but after a night of heart-to-hearts her trespasses no longer seem quite so egregious. The real offense
isn't tampered crime scenes; it's Peter's maltreatment of
her. Women aren't disposable. We aren't white cotton
T-shirts you toss out when the old one gets yellow sweat
stains under the armpits.

Before we leave, Mim excuses herself to use the bathroom. She stands quickly, with more speed than wisdom,
and teeters for a moment. Her balance is precarious and
she holds on to the table's edge until she feels steady. Across
the room, our waiter watches Mim's progress with a jaun-
diced eye. He smiles smugly as she regains her equilibrium;
then he leans across the bar and says something into the
bartender's ear. The two laugh. Although I am not close
enough to hear their conversation, I know they are talking about us. We haven't left the building yet but we're already a story: the overwrought ladies who can hold their
liquor but not their emotions.

Although I should be offended by such treatment, I am
not. My brain is tired—it's been doused with whiskey and
stretched out on the Mim rack—but I have enough sense
left to recognize the truth. This is exactly what we are: two
intoxicated women with awful wrinkles and terrible fears.

After I drop Mim off at her apartment—after I help her
to the door and leave her in the capable hands of John the
doorman, who is eager to supplement his income with large
tips—I go to Ian's apartment. His work schedule is a hodgepodge of weekdays in my mind, and even as I press the button I have little confidence that he'll be there. But he is,
and he buzzes me up after a short, confused conversation.
When I get to the third floor, the door is open and I let
myself in. Ian is sitting on the couch reading the newspa-

per and listening to the radio. The scene is so benign. It's so domestic and comfortable—the *New York Times,* the Foo Fighters—that something inside me tears. This could be mine. If he didn't hate me, I could do this, too. But he does and I can't and it's all his fault.

I take a steadying breath—I will *not* get upset again—and look him straight in the eye. "I know you hate me." My voice is calm. Unnaturally calm. This is me being Mim-like. "I know you hate me, and it's okay."

There's something else I'm supposed to tell him, but I can't remember what it is and turn to leave. I've said all there is to say and now it's time to go home and sleep off the whiskey. But Ian doesn't understand the plan. He thinks I'm here for a discussion, and he pulls me toward the couch just as I'm reaching for the door. He smells the liquor on my breath and asks where I've been.

He's trying to make small talk. Despite the fact that he hates me, he's trying to observe the social niceties. "Nowhere. It doesn't matter," I say, trying to stand up. Ian's grip is strong and tight and keeps me tethered to the couch.

I want to leave. There's nothing more to say—"you hate me, it's okay" is all I've got—and no reason for me to remain. Ian doesn't agree. He's trying to construct a conversation out of a few meager facts.

"I don't hate you," he says.

Ian is being kind. It's the first time he's ever lied to me but I accept it for what it is: a white lie steeped in kindness. "It's okay. I don't mind that you hate me." And there it is—my first lie to him.

"Stop saying that," he says angrily. "I don't hate you, Meg. I couldn't possibly hate you."

I abandon my freedom struggles, which aren't getting me

very far, and lean my head against the back of the couch. The cushions are soft and welcoming. "You hate Delilah Quick," I say, changing tactics. Let him deny that.

Ian laughs. "I love Delilah Quick."

I'm not amused by his cavalier treatment or the fact that he thinks I am so easily taken in. "No, you don't."

"But I do, really, Meg. Of all the characters I've ever written, she's my favorite," he says.

There's so much earnestness in his voice, so much sincerity, so much nothing-but-the-truth gravity, that I can only stare at him in wonder. I want to contradict him again but I'm incapable of speech.

"Her behavior is totally extreme—I love thinking up stuff like that. With each new outrageous thing I loved her more. She's not the most complex person in the book, which is a problem. I'm hoping in a couple of years I'll be more adept at writing over-the-top characters who aren't all one-sided. For the moment, though, I think her absurdity is wonderful. I'd write a whole book of Delilah Quicks but I know I couldn't get away with it." He sits down next to me and shakes his head. "I can't believe you thought I hated her. How," he adds quietly, pushing the bangs out of my eyes, "could I hate anything that reminds me of you?"

This turn of events—this harmless white lie morphing into the god's honest truth—is too much for my whiskey-soaked mind and I close my eyes. Ian has to hate Delilah Quick. She's evil incarnate, and except for a few über-villains and would-be superheroes who are seduced by the dark side, everyone hates evil incarnate.

But maybe not Ian.

With my eyes closed the room is peaceful and gentle. The song in the background is a soft ballad and it lulls me.

Ian runs a gentle hand through my hair and I find myself, without thought or volition, leaning against him. Then I'm sleeping with my head in his lap.

FIFTEEN

In the morning we're both awkward. I'm alone in Ian's loft bed when the wail of a fire truck finally wakes me up around nine o'clock. I'm disconcerted for a moment—it's the low ceiling that's only a foot from my nose that throws me off—but I quickly recall everything. Ian's on the couch. He has a cup of coffee in one hand and the newspaper in the other. The room is silent save for the fading siren and he hears me rustling the sheets.

"Hey," he says softly, lowering the paper a few inches but not all the way.

I respond in kind, but with a hoarse voice that's raspy. My head doesn't ache or pound but it will start doing both soon enough. Hangovers are pretty reliable things, and I have little reason to believe that a bender like this one will have no repercussions.

I stretch my muscles and climb down the ladder feeling very self-conscious. Last night's rant—and despite the calmness with which it was delivered, it was still a rant—is embarrassing under the cold light of sobriety. Ian's hating me is a bogeyman. It's a monster I invented to frighten me in the middle of the night and to make the fact that he didn't come after me bearable. The truth—indifference at twenty paces—is a little less intense, and a lot harder to accept.

No more eager than I for conversation, Ian hides his eyes in the newspaper. I brush past him on my way to the bathroom but he doesn't look up.

When I come out a few minutes later, he's refilling his coffee cup. He indicates with a gesture that there's enough left for two but I shake my head. This is the end—the real end, not the fake end I enact every time I stop by his bar—and I don't want to drag it out.

I put on my coat, pick up my bag and thank him. I don't say for what—I'm not sure exactly—but he doesn't notice. He tells me I'm welcome and stands with the French press in his hand, waiting for me to leave.

I'm turning the knob on the door when he speaks. "You broke up with me because of Delilah?" he asks out of nowhere.

I tighten my grip on the door. "What?"

"You broke up with me because of Delilah?"

He says it differently the second time. The first time it's a straight question. The second time it's coated with a thin layer of incredulity.

It's the disbelief that gets me. It's the intimation, however slight, that he had no idea. I drop my hand and look at him, angered by the implied lie. "Yes, why did you think?"

Ian shrugs. The coffee in his mug splashes over the side. "I didn't know."

"You didn't ask," I point out. This is why I don't believe him—because he never asked me why. I stood in the middle of his tiny kitchen and told him it was over and he said nothing. He *had* to have known. The only time you don't ask a question is when you already know the answer.

He accepts the truth of this with another shrug, but he turns away. He puts the half-filled coffee press into the sink and stares at his hand. "What good would that have done?"

"You would have known. I would have told you," I say.

"Yeah," he says, looking at me and smiling self-deprecatingly, "but I didn't want to hear it."

This avoidance, this not asking the question so you don't have to listen to the answer, is the old Ian. But the persistence, the not letting me leave—that's the new. "Hear what?" I ask, genuinely confused. The list of reasons why I'd break up with him is so short it only has one item.

"That you were bored with me. That you were tired of us."

The answer is so out of left field that it makes my knees weak. I grip the door handle. "What?"

"Change is the cornerstone of your existence," he says. His tone is quiet and matter-of-fact but there's an element of challenge in it, as if he's daring me to disagree. "It's what you do for a living."

"Oh, my God," I say, seeing it all in a flash, "I was right. You do hate me. That's why Del—"

He takes a step forward. He reaches for me but pulls back before contact. "Don't be ridiculous. That's not—"

"It is true. That's why Delilah Quick is evil. You look at me and see a person who isn't capable of any lasting affection. You think I change boyfriends as easily as I change clothes. God, I can't believe it." It was so simple and so ludicrous. After everything it came down to this—his lack of faith in me. And here, all along, I thought it was my lack of faith in him.

I take a few steps back and reach for the doorknob. Ian

is standing by the kitchen sink. He has one hand on the counter and the other around a coffee mug. His face is pale and his eyes are bright, but his mouth is shut. I wait for him to say something—to deny it, to admit it, to apologize, to ask me to stay—but he remains silent.

I shrug, turn the knob and accept the truth—you can pull a relationship behind you like a sack of grain for only so many miles.

"How insane. This whole thing is fucking insane," I say under my breath as I open the door. I want to leave on a cloud of dignified silence but I can't do it. I'm too pinned to the ground. I turn around and look him in the eye. "It's all just fashion. Every single thing in life—clothes, theories, thoughts—is just fashion. And all of it is subject to the mysterious erraticness of trends, philosophies as much as hemlines. But you don't get it. My life is not all about change. I don't hop onto every flatbed truck that passes my way." My hand on the door is trembling slightly. I can't remember the last time I was this angry. "A persistent belief in a fashion is a conviction. I have some of those, one was even that I loved you."

I close the door behind me and walk away. It's the second time I've done this, but I'm smarter now. I don't idle on the landing or take the stairs slowly. Ian isn't two steps behind me. He's not trying to catch up before I disappear from his life forever.

By the time I get to the office, it's eleven o'clock. A ten-minute drive-by stop at the apartment to change clothes quickly evolved into breakfast and a shower with a dash of poor-me time on the couch thrown in for good measure.

The two aspirins I took for my hangover finally kick in on the walk to work and I decide to drop in on Mim before heading straight to my desk. I'm embarrassed by last night's emotional orgy, but I want to make sure Mim is okay. Her outpouring was significantly more overwrought than mine and I'm only borderline fine.

When I reach her office, I stop in the doorway to take a discreet look inside. Mim is sitting at her desk, talking energetically on the phone and typing briskly at the same time. Inexplicably, she looks as fresh as a daisy. I'm relieved by this development—clearly she doesn't need me as a crutch—and try to get away without being seen. Mim might have recovered from last night with no ill effects but I haven't.

I'm halfway down the hall when Mim calls after me. I sigh and resign myself to yet another awkward conversation. Two before noon—this is not a good day.

"Hey," I say.

I'm standing in the doorway in an effort to put some literal distance between us, but Mim won't have it and insists that I sit on her couch.

"You got home safely?" she asks.

I hesitate for a moment before answering. To give her the long answer would be to just encourage more confessions, but I don't feel right lying to her. Mim has been told too many lies in the past couple of months. "Yes, I did. Thanks."

"Excellent," she says, with a relieved smile. "I was afraid you would go to Ian's to discuss things. You had said you were going right there. But I'm happy you didn't. I want to tell him myself."

At first I think she's talking about Delilah Quick and my total paranoid fantasy that turned out to be only part paranoia, but then I realize she means the *Jawbones* publicity scheme. I had forgotten about it entirely. "He's usually around in the mornings if you want to give him a call right now," I say, thankful that she's relieving me of the responsibility of telling him. I couldn't imagine the stilted awkwardness of *that* conversation.

Mim nods. "Yes, I'll definitely do it today. Not right now, of course, since I haven't prepared my statement yet. You did say that was the best way to communicate with him, didn't you?"

The reminder of last night's conversation—the intimacy and the naiveté—makes me blush. Mim sees the color wash over my face, sits down on the couch next to me and takes my hands. This only makes my embarrassment more acute but she doesn't notice. "I really think you kids can work this out," she says. Her tone is earnest and sincere. We're no longer in a crowded barroom drinking whiskey and chardonnay, but the drawbridge is still down. "This idea that Ian hates you is utterly unfounded. You mustn't let a silly misunderstanding get in the way."

Mim's insistence on the groundlessness of something that was discovered a few hours ago to be true is painful, and I mutter something about being late for work. Mim shoos me out of her office with an order to say hello to everyone for her. She doesn't notice anything is amiss.

Helen is rearranging the furniture in Mim's office when I arrive. Her new space is considerably smaller than her old one, and all week she's been leaving giveaways in the reception area. Today there are two vases and A and Z bookends from Pottery Barn.

Helen hears my voice and she sticks her head out of the office. "Ah, there you are, Meghan. Do you have a moment?"

I cringe at the upbeat familiarity of her tone. Helen thinks my helping her into a cab was a watershed event in our relationship. Yesterday she sought me out three times for friendly conversation. Once I was even asked to give my opinion on some questions on the teen consultant form—because I'm for progress.

I follow her into her office, closing the door behind me as I look for a place to sit in the crowded quarters. She's moved all her furniture into this confined space, even her oversize lacquered desk, and unless she starts leaving Marcel Breuer chairs in the reception area, there will never be room for visitors.

I stand awkwardly by the door and wait.

"I'm announcing MAD B 4.0 tonight at a press conference at the Waldorf–Astoria," she says, sitting down. Her large, leather executive chair is jammed between her desk and the wall, and she has to take a deep breath in order to squeeze in. "Tonight the National Society of Small Business Owners is having its annual awards banquet at the Waldorf, so this is an optimal time. The press corps will already be assembled."

"You're moving awfully fast," I say, trying to imagine what newspapers cover such a dry affair. Surely not the important ones. "Don't you want to look into it more? Isn't there some cost-benefit Excel spreadsheet program you should run first?"

Helen smiles. "You're cautious. I like that. But in this case I think it's better to move forward as quickly as possible. I don't want some other company beating me to the punch." She holds out a folder. "This is the most recent draft of my speech. Why don't you have a look? I value your opinion."

I take the folder. "Sure. And what about Mim?" My question isn't meant to be provoking, not entirely. I'm genuinely concerned about how she will react to this—the hijacking of her company. MAD B 4.0 might seem like progress to Helen and Josh, but to me it feels like obsolescence.

She wrinkles her forehead. "Mim?"

"Yes, what about Mim? Shouldn't you warn her about the new direction you're taking Pravda in? Or have you already?" I ask archly, knowing perfectly well she hasn't.

"You're very thoughtful, Meghan. I like that, too. But let me worry about her, all right?" she says, her smile falsely bright. Our new friendship extends to but does not cross the Mim line. "Now, if there's nothing else, I'd like to practice my diction."

The way she phrases it—like I'm imposing on her time—annoys me and I leave without saying goodbye. I return to my desk and switch on my computer, determined to get something useful done today despite the slow start and many distractions. But I don't get the chance. While I am waiting for my computer to boot, Mim comes striding into the Pravda office. She's making a beeline to my desk, and although she politely fields many cheery hellos from co-workers who are genuinely glad to see her, she stays true to her course.

"We have to go," she says quietly, standing in front of my desk with an eager expression on her face.

I don't understand. Did we make plans for lunch last night? "Go where?" I ask.

The entire room is straining to hear our conversation, but she smiles as if nothing is wrong. "Out," she answer breezily. "We have work to do."

I look at her confused for a long moment and then I notice it—the Burberry coat. Her attitude, eager and enthusiastic like Holmes telling Watson that the game is afoot, is another dead giveaway. "No," I say emphatically. "We're not doing this. This will not be done."

But Mim doesn't agree. She has her own take on the situation, and it's in direct opposition to mine. "Of course we are. Now come along, Meghan. We work excellently as a team." Then she walks to the elevator, where she presses the button and waits for me. She doesn't have to turn around to see if I'm coming. She just knows that I am.

I try to resist following. I sit at my desk telling myself that there's such a thing as free will but seconds later I'm running to catch the elevator. Mim is holding the doors for me. She's smiling.

I stand in the entranceway and keep the elevator from closing. "We're not doing this."

Mim pulls me into the car and the doors close quickly behind me. "The crime scene is only around the block. It won't take a minute," she says.

I look at her expression—the glowing features, the flash of anticipation in her eyes, the vibrant smile—and my stomach knots. Last night's confessions have done nothing to temper her recklessness. "You promised you wouldn't do this again," I say, my voice almost shrill. "Last night you swore that you'd never, ever do this again."

Mim has the grace to look ashamed. "I know I did. And that was rash of me."

"*That* was rash?" I repeat, just to make sure I heard her right.

She nods as her eyes watch the numbers on the display descend—four, three, two. "It was very rash."

"You're about to break into a crime scene and tamper with evidence in order to publicize a book, and you think promising never to do it again was *rash?*" I ask, appalled.

Mim blinks at me. She's surprised by the vehemence in my tone. "I should have promised to never do it again unless the murder happens right around the block from me. I left out a very important caveat, which was rash. I'm sorry."

Her apology is sincere but useless. "You can't do this," I say again.

The elevator doors open and she steps out onto the ground floor. "Of course we can. We've done it before, and very well at that." Her tone is still blithe. "You're an excellent cohort."

But I am not a cohort. Despite the way I trail after her, I'm not an ally or accomplice or a sidekick. Mim doesn't get this. The seriousness of the situation—its illegality, its immorality, its irrationality—has escaped her. She acts as if we're the invincible heroes of a beloved Saturday-morning cartoon. But this is not "The Extraordinary Adventures of Meghan and Mim," and we're not animated figures that can drop a hundred feet into a canyon and walk away unscathed.

I follow her to the door, wondering how I can put a stop to this. Reason, logic, simple facts laid out like evidence at a trial—these things don't work with Mim. She's too careless with the truth to be swayed by it. But I've never tried issuing threats. "I'll tell the police."

She halts dramatically with her palm against the glass and looks at me. "What?"

"I'll tell the police," I say, moving to one side to let other people into the building. "I'll go up to the first officer I see and tell him exactly what you're doing."

This gives Mim pause and she considers me silently for a few seconds. I can't tell what's going on in her head—her expression is suddenly blank—but her stare is disconcerting and I have to fight the urge to fidget. In the end, though, she doesn't capitulate. She doesn't admit to being outmaneuvered by her cohort. She just shrugs and pushes the door open.

"I mean it, Mim, I'll tell," I say again, wielding the only weapon I have even as I feel it slipping out of my grasp.

Mim waves her gloved hand. "Do what you have to. I understand."

Just as I'm about to assure her that I will indeed do what I have to—it's no empty threat this—someone taps me on the shoulder.

"Hey," a voice says, "can I talk to you?"

I spin around. It's Ian. He's standing with his hands in his pockets. His shoulders are hunched over and he looks nervous. The sight of him—anxious and here—is so unexpected and lovely that I can only stare at him. No, he might not have been two steps behind but he was back there giving chase nevertheless.

He takes a hand out of his pocket and waves it in front of me as if to break a trance. "Meg, can I talk to you for a minute?"

Of course I want to stay and listen to him say he's sorry for underestimating me so dreadfully, but I can't. Mim is getting away. "I can't do this right now b—"

"I have to talk to you," he says, not letting me get my excuse out, even though it's an unusually good one. "Something's going on, something really important, and you're the only one I can tell."

Mim's figure is growing smaller and smaller as she strides purposefully down Hudson.

Ian sees me turning away from him to look down the street and he mistakes it for avoidance. "This is important," he says. Everything about him is adamant—his stance, his tone, his expression.

Mim turns a corner and disappears. There isn't any time to lose. I grab Ian's hand. "Come with me," I say, starting to run. "I'll show you important."

Ian doesn't understand what's going on but he keeps pace and doesn't ask questions.

"Here's the deal," I say brutally, trying to fill him in on everything in the minute it takes to catch up with Mim. This isn't the way I planned to tell him. There's nothing gentle about the way I'm breaking it to him, but I have to work with what I've got. "Mim's been listening to a police scanner, she's been dropping by crime scenes and planting your book on murder victims."

Ian stops. His legs cease moving and he stands on a square of concrete looking white-faced and appalled. He doesn't give me any warning—he's like a car hitting a brick wall—and my arm is tugged painfully in its socket. I let go of his hand and rub my shoulder as he digests the information. We don't have any time to spare—even now Mim could be slipping by clueless police officers—but I give him a second to catch his breath.

"Oh, my God," he says, his voice hoarse. "Oh, my *fucking* God."

The look on Ian's face is terrible—ashen and distraught—and I reach out a hand to comfort him. But I don't say anything. I don't know what I could possibly say that would make this situation more bearable.

"Goddamn it, I spent the entire morning trying to convince Detective Williamson of the Sixth Precinct that I have no fucking idea why my book wound up at three murder sites," he says, looking down the street at Mim's retreating figure. There's a glint in his eye that I've never seen before—maybe it's murder. "I can't believe she fucking did this."

Then he breaks into a run. His legs are longer than mine and they're stronger, and within seconds he's turning the corner.

I follow as fast as I can. Mim isn't running—she's walking briskly without breaking a sweat—and Ian disappears into the building a few seconds after she does.

Breathing heavily, I check out the area, looking for a plainclothes detective or a uniformed officer or even a meter maid with ideas above her station. But I don't see one. The street is quiet. A super in the building next door is squinting in the bright sunlight and taking out the trash and muttering under his breath about residents who don't recycle. Everything about the scene is calm and peaceful and overwhelmingly normal. It's just another February day on Barrow Street.

I run to the building and quickly climb the steps, taking two at a time. The security door is busted—the knob is lying on the floor—and someone has propped it open with a Grand Union circular. The entrance is long and dark with weak fluorescent lights and dark gray walls. Above me I hear Mim and Ian. They're racing up the stairs and their footsteps—thump, scratch, thump—are echoing in the empty hallway.

Buffeted by the stillness—maybe Mim got the address wrong—I scramble up the stairs, my heart beating painfully in my chest. I'm not used to this kind of physical exertion. The equipment at the gym isn't like this. With all their technological innovations, the Stairmaster and the elliptical trainer can't reconstruct real life—the unplanned mad dashes after your unglued boss and your irate ex-boyfriend.

Above me the pounding stops, and my tired footsteps are the only thing disturbing the perfect silence of the building. I have no idea where Mim and Ian are, so I keep climbing. Second floor, third floor, fourth floor—each is a blur.

I reach the fifth floor and stop. The door to apartment number 23 is wide open and I look inside. Mim and Ian are here. They're at the end of a long hallway, standing on the threshold to another room with their backs toward me. They're stock-still. I come up behind them.

"Look, we can't be—"

Then I see it—*her*—lying on the bedroom floor. She's young, blond and motionless. Blood from her throat is still seeping into the carpet and the stain—already large, amorphous and deadly—continues to grow like a monster in a fifties horror movie. Her eyes, gray and blank, stare through me and the ceiling fan with complete indifference.

In *Jawbones* Ian describes corpses as if they're patchwork quilts—assortments of colors and textures—but that's not what they're like at all. Her cut throat isn't a pomegranate cleaved in two. Her bruised face isn't the Caspian Sea on a calm afternoon. Up close, death is more than a collection of similes. You only see a pattern when you're standing too far away.

Unable to bear the sight, I turn my head. I spin around and close my eyes and try to drown out the screaming in my head with simple practicality. Call ambulance. Check pulse. Stop bleeding.

Suddenly a door slams. It's terrifying and it's abrupt and it's followed by heavy footsteps walking slowly down a hallway—this hallway.

Ian reacts first. He grabs my arm in a painfully tight grip, pulls me toward the closet, pushes aside the curtain and throws me inside. It's a narrow space packed with silk dresses and plastic storage boxes and metal folding chairs. I have no room to move but I want none. I only want to stand here like a statue and stay alive.

He grabs Mim next. Mim—who I expected to disappear in a flash like the ray of light I always thought she was the second the door snapped. Ian pushes her behind the bedroom door for cover. It's an adolescent place to hide—where you go when you're playing hide-and-seek with your cousins—but it serves its purpose. She is sufficiently hidden.

Only Ian remains in plain sight, and he stands in the middle of the room as the heavy footsteps get closer and closer, not sure what to do. There are no more closets and no more doors, and just as the awful footsteps enter the bedroom, he dives for the bed. My heart stops beating in my chest as I watch. Not there! This is New York—everyone stores their cookbooks and air conditioners and luggage under the bed.

But Ian's gamble pays off. His body fits snugly beneath.

With my heart pounding I wait and watch. The gauzy red fabric is scant protection against a murderer but I tell myself not to assume the worst. We don't know what we're hiding from. Those heavy footsteps could belong to a cop or a kindly next-door neighbor.

But then I see the glint of steel. Afternoon sunshine is pouring in through the bedroom window. It's illuminating the room with a golden glow and shining off the blade of a sharp kitchen knife.

I can't see any of the details of the man holding the knife—hair length, eye color, shape of nose—but he's large and thick and totally at ease in the gruesome setting. With careful deliberation, he's erasing his presence—wiping off fingerprints, cleaning under nails, checking for stray hairs. His calm is so deep, so to the marrow of the bone, that the whole scene seems unreal. Any second now the director will yell cut from stage right and pull him aside. We'll step out of our hiding places—me from the closet, Mim from behind the door, Ian from under the bed—and go over to the craft services table for a bite to eat while the director tells Mr. Murderer-Actor that he's not really feeling the urgency.

Even the sound of approaching sirens doesn't disturb his preternatural composure. His hands remain steady as he picks up the phone—bloody and useless next to the body—and wipes it free of prints. My eyes are transfixed by his hands. I want to look away. I want to close out the whole terrible sight, but I can't stop staring at his latex-covered fingers.

The sirens grow louder and more piercing as he stands up. He sighs deeply and inspects his handiwork. His eyes travel fastidiously around the room, taking in everything: the bed, the door, the window, the closet. My breath catches agonizingly as his gaze meets mine through the red gauze. A loud rushing sound—like water falling or a train approaching—blasts through my ears and every muscle in my body stiffens. I don't know what this is for—this painful tensing, this shallow breathing. It's not fight or flight. It's just a lamb to the slaughter. But even as I'm making peace with this thing that has suddenly and inconceivably happened to me—death in the phone-booth-size closet of a woman I've never met—he's looking away. He's standing in the glaring, golden rays of the afternoon sun. I am not.

Slowly, my heart starts beating again.

The murderer turns his attention to the body. There is nothing rushed about his movements now either, and he gazes at the body with the careful scrutiny of a mother of the bride examining her daughter: Is the hair right? Veil straight? Eye shadow too subtle?

The scene meets with his approval—he doesn't change a thing—and the murderer leaves the room. I listen as his heavy work boots scrape the floor: clump, clump. I'm expecting to hear them stop and turn back but he heads straight for the door. Having arranged everything perfectly, he's not inclined to linger—the first indication that he knows he's done something wrong.

Even after the front door slams shut, I'm afraid to move.

Ian is the bravest of all of us, and after a moment of tense silence and blaring sirens, he shimmies out from under the bed, legs first. He indicates with a hand gesture that I should stay where I am, but I need no prompting. My closet is small, dark and safe.

Ian returns a moment later and tells Mim in a whisper— we're all afraid of making noise—that it's okay to come out now. Then he pulls me from the telephone-booth-size perch and wraps me in a hug. It's tight and bone-crushing and his arms are heavy on my shoulders.

"Damn it," he says softly in my ear.

While Ian is having a breakdown, Mim is recovering her composure. She's as freaked out as the rest of us—her face is pale and her hands are shaking—but she refuses to let that stand in her way. A little thing like almost getting killed will not deter her from her mission, and she removes *Jawbones* from her shoulder bag as she tries to decide where on the body to leave it.

I free myself from Ian's grasp, walk over to Mim and grab the book with a violent tug. "No," I say, my voice angry and harsh. I haven't forgotten why we're here. I will never forget why we are here.

Mim opens her mouth to argue.

"No," I say again, feeling as though I'm disciplining a dog or an unruly child. Mim looks me straight in the eye. She expects to cower me with her steady gaze and determination but I'm not that easy. I've stared down worse things today.

After a moment she shrugs—it's feigned indifference but I'll take it—and suggests that we get out of there. I'm relieved to hear that her publicity program doesn't include Ian getting arrested for murder, and I agree readily. Yes, let's get out of here.

While Ian and Mim discuss the relative merits of leaving through a window—Ian wants to know who's going to close it behind them; Mim wants to know why that matters—I stand in the hallway having aftermath. My legs are shaky and my head hurts and I can't think of anything but getting out of this death trap. Let's go now.

"It's one thing not to own up to your inadvertent material-witnessness," Ian is saying as he looks through the front door's peephole, "but it's another thing altogether to leave false clues."

I hear Ian's words but I don't understand them. The part of my brain that interprets things has been tackled and immobilized by the part of my brain that does things. Only my muscles are working.

Mim agrees with Ian's logic—her thinking mechanism is still humming—and she presses herself against him to get a peek at the hallway. There's nothing to see and Ian opens the door. Mim pokes her head out, looks both ways and tiptoes across the landing. Ian waits for me to follow suit—I do so quickly and eagerly—before silently closing the door with his sleeve covering his hand. Then we run down the stairs. We skip steps, taking two at a time, and jump to the landing when we're near the next floor. The stairwell is deserted. There's nobody here except the three of us—tripping and jumping—but I have the creepy feeling that someone is watching. We don't know where the murderer is now. He could be in the building with his own malicious eye pressed up against the peephole. He could be on the next landing with a knife raised in the air. He could be trailing behind us. He could be waiting outside. He could be anywhere. But that doesn't matter. The only important thing is getting out and getting away and getting home.

When we step outside, everything is the same as it was

before. The sun is still directly overhead. It's still bleeding into the eyes of the super and he's still taking out the trash. He's sorting aluminum cans from glass bottles as if nothing has happened. It's not right. My eyes have seen horrors. They have seen a slain woman and a murderer's meticulous satisfaction. Something should be different. The air should be heavier. The tint of the sky—as effortlessly blue as a child's drawing—should be darker. It should have a purplish cast, like the artificial sky in a cheap postcard from the Midwest.

Mim and Ian don't notice how wrong this is. That the world is askew by not being askew doesn't strike them, and they keep on going—past the super, past the neighboring apartments, past the police cars that are just pulling up.

Mim heads straight for the office. She turns the corner, walks up Hudson and pulls open the glass door without stopping. There's something automatic about her movements, an off-putting preprogrammed exactness as if she's a shuttle returning to the mother ship. But I can't go back there yet. My job—sitting at the computer, making telephone calls, agreeing with Helen—is inconceivable right now. My eyes have seen horrors (slain woman, meticulous satisfaction). They're not ready for spreadsheets and bell curves.

Ian follows me home. Although I tell him it's not necessary, he insists on seeing me safely to the door. But he doesn't say a word during the fifteen-minute walk. The unexpected events of this afternoon—the police interrogation, the warm corpse, the Mim treatment of his book—have left him in a shocked kind of silence. I want to give him upbeat platitudes or cheery reassurances or even heartfelt sympathy, but the everything's-going-to-be-all-right box inside of me is empty. Sometime in the past half hour, its worn cardboard bottom tore and all the little slips of paper fell out. Even the moral outrage of last night blew away.

When we reach my building, Ian says goodbye. "You'll call me if you want to talk?" he asks, his voice calm.

Ian seems almost composed—as if all he needs are fifteen minutes to pull himself together—but he's not. His hands are shaking violently and he doesn't seem to know what to do with them. One moment they're deep in his coat pockets, the next they're dangling at his side.

I nod slowly while he watches me. It's the same look as always—grass-green and steady—but there's nothing inscrutable about it. Fear, anxiety, a wrenching paralysis— they're all swirling around like colors in a kaleidoscope, and I marvel that I could have ever thought his gaze was hard to read. The way he deals with punches, taking them on the chin and moving on, is just a coping mechanism. It's a way of handling things. But I didn't get that. I thought it meant he didn't feel the blow.

"Yes," I say quietly.

Ian kisses me on the forehead, then walks away. He's leaving for the last time and I know it. The epiphanic moment I thought we were having this afternoon—the one in which he finally chases after me—was only more Mim fallout.

I stand on the stoop and watch until he disappears around the corner. I'm hollow inside and yet full of regret; things might have been different if I'd understood him sooner. But maybe that's the way it works—you get the flash of insight at the exact moment it ceases to matter.

When he's gone, I unlock the door, climb the stairs slowly and let myself into my apartment. It's the exact same place I left two hours before, but home—repository of dust bunnies, junk mail and soap scum—suddenly feels like the only safe place in the whole entire world.

Chilled despite the heat pouring out of two clanking radiators, I keep my coat on and sit down on the couch. I take off my shoes, put my arms around my knees and stare at the opposite wall. I'm looking directly at a Dufy painting of Nice—the Mediterranean, the promenade, the Negresco—but I'm not seeing it. I have other images in my head.

I stay like that for a long time. Hours pass as the sun moves across the room. First it's in the corner by the telephone stand, then it's in the middle of the floor, then it's on my face. The sun is hot and searing, but it doesn't matter. The cold I feel runs deeper than warmth on skin, and goose bumps develop along my arms. Around four o'clock the sun finally disappears behind the building across the street.

A few minutes later the silence is disturbed by a ringing telephone—my ringing telephone—and I stare at the device angrily for a second before getting up and turning the sound off. I do the same with the answering machine. Whoever it is, I don't want to talk to them and I certainly don't want them to talk to me. Standing is harder than I expected. My legs are stiff and achy from the day's abuses—running, stillness, terror—and I have to stretch several times to loosen the muscles.

Realizing my throat's quite dry—and has been for several hours now—I go to the kitchen. The bottled water in the fridge is too cold, so I fill up a glass from the tap and drink it quickly. Then I fill it up again and again and again. The sandpaper texture, the desert dryness—this thirst feels like acute dehydration but it's not. It's just more aftermath.

When my thirst is quenched at last, I rinse the glass and

put it in the drying rack. I'm not ordinarily so fastidious—using and cleaning rarely happen in the same afternoon, let alone the same five-minute period—but my options are limited. Either I wash dishes or sit on the couch. The latter is too difficult. I can't be there and not think. Thoughts, images—these flutter enticingly through my mind. One inevitably leads to another and before I know it I'm back—in the apartment, in the bedroom, in the closet.

Determined not to brood, I take a large glass bowl from the cabinet and put it down on the counter. I dig out the electric hand mixer—it's on the top shelf under the salad spinner—and an unopened bag of flour. I borrow Bonnie's red-and-white-checkered *Better Homes and Garden* cookbook from her room and flip through, looking for an easy cake recipe. I haven't done this in years—baking is something Mom and I did together on Sunday afternoons—but it's familiar and comfortable and engrossing. I am trying to whistle a happy tune.

But it doesn't work. You can't block thought with cups of flour and sticks of butter. You can't block it with anything at all. Stream of consciousness isn't a stream at all. It's a raging river and it will knock down every dam you build.

I look at the counter, which is now covered with ingredients. Eggs, butter, oil, vanilla, flour, sugar, salt, baking powder—they're all lined up neatly like schoolchildren on a field trip. But I can't do this. I can't stay at home and bake a cake. My eyes have seen horrors.

I lay down the wooden spoon, go into the living room and put on my shoes. I grab my wallet and a scarf.

With the sun gone, the air is even chillier, and I pull my jacket tightly around me as I walk to Barrow Street. I didn't realize this would happen. Sitting on my couch for all those hours this afternoon, I had no idea that something like this was in the offing. But I'm a shuttle, too. And this—this run-down apartment building, this dirty stretch of New York City road—is my mother ship.

There's a large crowd in front of the building when I re-turn. People are standing in the street and hanging out windows. They're blocking cars that mistakenly thought that Barrow would be an easy way to access Hudson.

This thick congregation of locals isn't what I expected. The murder happened four hours ago—it's practically old news—and the initial excitement of seeing speeding cop cars screech to a halt in front of your neighbor's apartment building has long since passed.

"They're about to bring out the body," a woman says as I walk by. She's a civilian, another street-hovering gawker in jeans, fleece and down.

Her friend has just returned from the supermarket. She's holding two large plastic bags with overflowing produce—stalks of celery, carrots and fennel. If it weren't for this mur-der, she'd already be inside making soup. "How do you know?"

The woman leans in for the answer and I slow down to hear it. "The M.E. went in about forty minutes ago. It has to be any minute now. How long can it take to declare a person dead?"

Seconds—it took only seconds.

I push my way through the crowd, annoyed with myself and with them. I hate being here. The circumstance, the reason, the collective morbid need to see the corpse of a dead neighbor—everything about the scene is appalling. Death is something you hide your eyes from. You don't seek it out. You don't stand for hours on a curb in thirty-degree weather just to get a glimpse of a black body bag.

The police officer who was charged with keeping rubberneckers away from the building is enjoying his job. He's standing in front of the blue police barricades answering questions with a sort of good-humored patience that you rarely get from New York's Finest. He isn't letting anyone without a badge by—not even a gray-haired gentleman whose driver's license proves he lives in the building—but the crowd is respectful and patient.

I stand a few feet away and watch. I tell myself that I'm still scoping out the scene, but the truth is I'm terrified. Now that the moment is here—now that there's nothing left for me to do but go up to a man in uniform and declare my material witnessness—I'm paralyzed with fear.

I close my eyes and take a deep breath. I have to do this. I can go home now and pretend that I don't, but I'll just be back in a half hour.

The gray-haired man goes to get coffee, leaving uninterrupted space between me and the officer. I accept the inevitable, with all its unfortunate physical side effects—the painfully beating heart, the uncomfortable chills, the sudden nausea—and approach the barrier. I lean against it, gesture for the police officer's attention and open my mouth to say it: I was here. I saw him. I'm a witness. Take me away.

But then I see the most astonishing, inconceivable sight. I gasp and hold on to the barrier for support and ask the police officer for confirmation.

"That's the murderer," I say, watching the plainclothes detectives lead a man in handcuffs from the building. "That's the murderer."

The police officer turns to me. He takes in my pale face and shaking hands and breathless voice and jumps to the wrong conclusion. "Been watching your crime shows, have you? Yes, that's the murderer, all right. But don't worry, miss, we've got him dead to rights," he says comfortingly. Others around us gasp as they hear this information. "He won't be back on the street anytime soon to terrorize other young ladies."

"Dead to rights?" I say, unable to take my eyes off the man. He has his head down and is avoiding eye contact, but still I feel like he's staring at me, just as he did in the bedroom.

"Confession and everything," he says with satisfaction. "He's not going anywhere for thirty years to life."

I think of the knife, the fingernails, the careful perusal of the entire room. "He confessed?" There's patent disbelief in my voice but he doesn't pick up on it. All he sees is a freaked-out young woman who's terrified of being raped and murdered in her own bed.

"Yeah, we got a confession. We knew going in it was the boyfriend," he explains. "Got that from her call to nine-one-one."

The bloody telephone—not so useless after all. But still not useful enough.

"We only had a first name but it was clearly a dispute of a domestic nature," he continues. "We talked to the neighbors and found out that she was seeing a guy on the floor above her, so we knocked on his door."

"And he confessed?" Despite this logical-sounding sequence of events, it's still an impossible thing for me to believe. You don't clean under the fingernails and then confess.

The police officer smiles. "Not right away, of course. He tried to deny it, even went so far as to say that he'd never met the victim. But we caught him in that lie easily enough. She had a picture of the two of them on her nightstand. We applied some pressure, made a few threats and he crum-

bled like a baby. Most of these murderers do," he intones
wisely to the fascinated crowd. I'm the only one asking
questions but every bystander within fifteen feet is listening attentively to the story. "You see, it's true what they
say—most criminals really want to get caught. Take the
knife he used. It was from his own kitchen. We found five
others in his drawer. Not the smartest way to hide your
guilt."

"You think he'll be convicted?" I ask. Before I go home,
I want to be sure. Before I put all this behind me—as if
that's as easy as it sounds!—I want to be absolutely posi-
tively sure.

He nods enthusiastically. "Like I said, we've got him dead
to rights. Even have the statement of her sister, who says
she heard him threaten to kill her last week at the movie
theater. The man has a temper. Lucky for us, men with tem-
pers never make good killers."

The relief I feel is almost overwhelming. It's sharp and
prickly and it makes my knees weak. But I don't fall. I lean
against the barrier and take steadying breaths and watch the
murderer disappear into the police car. That there are these
small doses of justice in the world doesn't make everything
better—I still don't think I can go home and bake a cake—
but it makes today bearable.

The gray-haired man returns with two coffees, and he
shoulders his way to the front. He squeezes in next to me
as he hands one cup to the obliging officer. I step back to
give him space. I don't need to be in the front row anymore. After my conversation, I don't need to be here at all,
and I walk away just as the crowd starts to twitter excitedly.
I don't have to look to know they're bringing out the body.
I've already seen enough today.

SIXTEEN

I stop by Shanghai Tang on the way home and pick up a quart of beef with broccoli. My appetite hasn't returned yet, but a hunger strike—without political objectives or moral intentions—isn't going to help anyone.

On my way to the stairs, I pick up the mail. There are only a few pieces, mostly advertisements and solicitations, and I toss all but my credit card bill into the trash. I put the Chinese food on the counter, take off my coat and turn on the television. I'm doing everything from habit—watching, eating—but it feels okay. It's progress. It's not sitting on the couch like a comatose patient and staring blindly at the wall.

I kick off my shoes and leave them in the middle of the living room floor. The TV is tuned to the local news channel—weather, traffic and more weather—and I pick up the remote control to find something less dull. My goal is simple—mindless and fun—but I never get there. A news report on channel two stops me dead in my tracks. I stare at the television, heart pounding, hands shaking, and slowly sink to the rug. Here, in a day full of horrors, is the thing that finally brings me to my knees.

On the screen is the police commissioner. He's standing at a podium with a book in his hand and discussing their efforts to catch the Jawbones Killer—that's what they're calling him: the Jawbones Killer. My brain struggles to understand what's happening. What I'm thinking—it can't be right. I have to be missing something.

But I'm not missing anything. My assessment of the situation is accurate—the New York Police Department truly believes there's a serial killer on the loose. Thanks to Mim, they think a crazed killer is leaving Ian's book on all his victims.

Oh, God, *Ian.* I reach for the phone and call him. His line is busy but I press flash and instantly dial again. While I do this—get busy signal, press flash, dial over and over and *over*—I sit on the floor and flip through the channels. Everywhere I turn there it is: the cover of *Jawbones.* It's on every channel, local and national. NY1 is covering the serial-murder story full-time, except for weather breaks every ten minutes. It even makes CNN's Headline News.

I try to settle on one channel to get the full scoop, but I can't. The need to flip is compulsive and uncontrollable and I can't stop no matter how hard I try. It's only after all the local six o'clock news programs have moved on to other stories—subway fair hikes, Bronx Zoo spending cuts, school board upheaval—that I'm able to keep the television on one station.

The story—gruesome, terrifying, sexy—is a no-brainer for news directors.

"The most disturbing thing about this case," the NY1 newscaster is saying after footage from the police commissioner's press conference earlier is run for the fourth time, "is how disparate each of the murders is."

One of the men at the roundtable—because this is what they've done already: established roundtables and called in experts—steps in to address this issue. He's a former FBI special agent and the author of the book *Tracking Justice.* "Yes, exactly. Ordinarily a perpetrator has a preferred way of committing a crime—we call this his modus operandi—and he tends to repeat himself. We in the FBI would look for similarities amongst the cases and create an overview of the perpetrator, which we call a profile."

The newscaster nods. "But in this case that will be difficult."

"I'd say next to impossible. Nothing is similar here, not the victims or the murder weapons or the method." He sighs wearily and looks the camera straight in the eye. "I'm afraid we're dealing with a genius here."

The other men at the roundtable concur with equal gravity. Oh, my God.

After fifteen minutes of watching *Jawbones* coverage and trying to get through to Ian, I give up. I throw down the phone with a frustrated shriek, put on my coat and slam the door behind me.

His apartment is only ten minutes from mine, but I run most of the way and get there in five. When I arrive, I'm completely out of breath and it takes several tries before I can form a coherent sentence into the intercom. Ian is restrained and suspicious and won't buzz me in until I answer a series of questions that only I'd know.

I enter his apartment just as the national news programs are starting. He's on the phone with his older sister, listening with a patient and weary expression. When he sees me, he waves hello, locks the door behind me and tells Susan that there's no reason for him to enter the Witness Protection Program.

I look at him sharply, but he just halfheartedly rolls his eyes. Ian is tired. He's pale and drawn and seems on the verge of collapsing.

"Sorry about the third degree," he says softly, covering the mouthpiece with a finger so his sister won't hear. "I'm terrified reporters are going to show up. My editor checked in to the Soho Grand under my name. It was an obvious ploy but so far it's worked. Apparently there's a crowd of paparazzi out front. The hotel is loving the exposure."

His sister calls his name repeatedly and he listens patiently for a few seconds. "The thing is, Susan— Yes, I know. I've got to—" Ian breaks off as she interrupts him again. He pulls the phone away from his ear and closes his eyes for a moment. From five feet away, I can hear Susan Cumberland chattering on as if her brother were hanging on her every word. "Yes, I know that as well. And I love you, too," he says, when he has enough fortitude to listen again. Ian usually doesn't treat his sister like this. On days when his book isn't the only clue in a serial killer investigation, he has long, thoughtful conversations with her. "Same to Joe and the boys. Yeah, bye." He hangs up the phone, cutting Susan off in midsentence, and turns it off before she can ring back.

"She thinks I'm the next victim," he explains with a sigh as he sinks into the couch and covers his face with his hands. "She's panicked and terrified, convinced these murders are a sick, twisted love letter to me and the killer is just biding his time before coming after me. Of course Uncle Barney agrees." Ian laughs but the sound is harsh and without humor. "I tried explaining that things aren't what they seem but she wouldn't listen to me. And I'm too tired to make her."

I've never seen Ian looking like this—defeated and helpless and exhausted—and it makes me feel useless. I want to *do* something. Raise a magic wand, twirl it in the air and go poof: no Jawbones Killer, no Mim publicity scheme, no dead woman in the apartment.

But making a quarter disappear if my palms aren't sweaty is all the magic I'm capable of, so I ask who Uncle Barney is in an attempt to distract him. During the year we dated, I met only one Cumberland, his sister, and it's weird to hear him mention another.

"An insurance investigator in Providence," he says with disgust. "He's another outcast who didn't toe the family line."

I want to smile at the contempt in his voice, but it's too sharp for levity. It must be difficult to do this—pretend that you don't care about your parents' indifference.

Ian leans his head against the couch and stares at the ceiling. "God, Meghan, can you even believe this is happening? I can't. I would swear on my life that this is just a bad dream and that I'm going to wake up any second. But it's not happening. This dream persists in seeming real. It's got the DNA sequencing of reality so down pat that it might as well be reality. The entire fucking day has been unbelievable and I just can't deal anymore. I know I should have called Detective Williamson an hour ago but I just can't bring myself to pick up the phone."

Before I can respond, the image of *Jawbones* flashes again on the screen and we stare transfixed as Peter Jennings sets up the story. Peter Jennings!

I take the seat next to him and curl my legs underneath me. "This is insane," I say, but Ian's not listening. He's too busy watching the taped news conference. There he is at the podium yet again—the police commissioner in his navy blue suit and tasseled Gucci loafers.

ABC cuts to an expert who says pretty much the same thing as the other experts—missing modus operandi, puzzling profile, diabolical genius. My fingers are itching to change the channel—how are the other national news programs handling it?—but I don't. Ian is too enthralled for channel surfing.

After the expert gets his fifteen seconds, they cut to the reporter, who sends us back to the studio.

"Thank you, John, for that insightful report," Peter says. "Let me ask you this… Have you read *Jawbones?*"

The reporter nods enthusiastically and holds up a copy he has in his hand. "Yes, I have, Peter."

"What can you tell us about it?"

"It's a very dark book but well-written and engrossing."

"Can you see anything about it that would drive a person to murder?"

"Well, Peter, that's the question law-enforcement officials in New York are asking themselves tonight. I myself have located several passages that I think would resonate in the mind of a maniac but I can't say for sure. But I'd like to leave you with this," he says. Then he opens *Jawbones* and reads the last paragraph. "This is how it was. This is how it would be. You think you're at the edge of a cliff—dangling, darting, dodging—but you're really in a dark room. Alone. Eviscerated. With the shades drawn. With the doors locked. But that's how it was. That's how it would be.'"

"Who knows, Peter," he says finally, with a sad shake of his head, "what darkness lies in the hearts of men."

Peter Jennings gives an equally baffled shake—who indeed does?—and thanks him again before jumping to the next story. While he's talking about social unrest in the Middle East, I flip to NBC and catch the tail end of its coverage. A woman is at the scene of yesterday's murder. She's standing in front of yellow police tape that's blowing erratically in the early-evening wind.

"No clues tonight," she is saying as the camera pulls back from her face to take in the garage, "only fear and hope that this murder spree—one of the bizarrest in this city's history—will end soon. I'm Tricia McDonald in New York City. Back to you in the studio."

We don't see the story on CBS. Either it was on earlier in the broadcast or they didn't cover it. The latter is highly unlikely, but we cling to the possibility that not everyone thinks the Jawbones Killer is major national news. It's not a wide swath of silver but it's the best lining we can come up with.

At seven o'clock, I turn back to NY1, whose roundtable discussion has widened to include an NYU professor who has written a best-seller called *Modern Analytic Interpretation for Dimwits.* He's reading passages of *Jawbones* aloud and deciphering hidden messages in the text. Next to me, Ian whimpers. This isn't what Ian wanted for his book—for it to be treated like the Beatles' "Helter Skelter." Any second now Professor Marcus Turnbull is going to start reading *Jawbones* backward.

"What is it," the moderator asks, "that the killer is trying to tell us by leaving this book behind? What does he want us to know about him?"

The professor furrows his brow in an endearingly academic fashion—he has had excellent media trainers—and considers the question carefully. "That he's alone in the world, that the sense of alienation he feels, the alienation that modern society has unthinkingly thrust upon him, has turned him into a killer. He identifies with Bones McGraw.

He sees Bones's struggle as his own and where Bones has failed, he has failed."

Ian jumps up from the couch and starts sputtering. His face is red and angry and his hands are clenched in fists at his side. "Bones doesn't fail. He makes a connection with the waitress. *Analytic Interpretation for Dimwits,* my ass," Ian says disparagingly. "Look in the mirror, man, and see who the real dimwit is."

The relationship between Bones and the waitress is understated and formed mostly through half-finished sentences. The novel doesn't end with wedding bells or even the chirp of morning-after alarm clocks, but there's a sweet note of optimism in the way Bones decides to walk by her apartment when he knows she isn't there. Some people might not think the romance is developed enough or they might need more details for a happy ending, but a professor who prides himself on interpreting works analytically should be hip to subtlety.

"And so *what* if he wants to be alone," Ian asks rhetorically, well into his outrage now. "People are allowed to be alone. Not everyone wants to be surrounded all the time by screeching suburbanites and drunken spring breakers. For God's sake, isn't that what this country was built on? The right to be alone? And being a loner doesn't ipso facto make you a serial killer. There are other factors at work. I mean, this guy probably—" He breaks off with a tortured expression, buries his face in his hands and drops back onto the couch. "Oh, God, what am I saying? There isn't a serial killer."

I know obsessively watching the Jawbones Killer coverage isn't healthy—Professor Turnbull and his clucking ilk are making matters worse—but I can't turn it off. It's like a train wreck, only we're on board.

My cell phone rings and I go into the bathroom to answer it, leaving Ian alone to rail at the television or nurse his grief.

It's my father, calling to warn me about some disturbing news. I tell him I'm already aware that a serial killer is leaving Ian's book as a souvenir and get chastised for my levity.

"This isn't a laughing matter," he says, disappointed that I've chosen this moment to find my sense of humor. "Have you spoken to Ian?"

I assure him with proper sobriety that I have.

"How's he doing?"

I peek into the living room. Ian is lying on the couch. He's turned his face into the cushion and piled a stack of pillows on top of his head. He can't turn off the television either. "He's dealing."

Dad isn't convinced. "You should go over there and make sure he's all right. He might say he's okay but he probably isn't. Think about it: This must be devastating. He has to be wondering if it's his fault that three people are dead."

In the other room, Ian groans loudly. Even through the pillows I can hear him. "I'll go to him right now," I say.

"Good," he says. "And tell him that I'm worried about him and to call me if he needs anything."

"Will do."

"And, Meghan, be careful. We don't know what kind of sicko we're dealing with."

I promise not to take any reckless chances with my person and hang up. The phone immediately rings again. This time it's Clarissa, also asking if I'd heard the news about Ian. I try to keep the conversation brief, but Clarissa has a copy of the book—she bought the very last one over the objections of an elderly gentleman with a wooden cane less

than a half hour ago at the Astor Place Barnes & Noble—
and wants to run through it chapter by chapter looking for
clues.

"This Delilah Quick," she says, despite my insistence that
this really isn't the best time for a *Jawbones* exegesis, "she
seems awfully familiar. Could I have met her at the bar? I
remember meeting one of Ian's ex-girlfriends. She was tall
and curvaceous with deep gold hair. She was really gorgeous. There was something not quite right about her,
even menacing. At the time I thought it was because she
was so obnoxiously beautiful. You know how some people can be beautiful and discreet and others are up in your
face with it? But now I'm thinking maybe it's because I
sensed that she was evil. What do you think? Isn't it possible that she read about herself in Ian's book and decided
to exact revenge? She might even be trying to frame him.
When you speak to Ian find out where he was at the time
of each killing. And make sure he has airtight alibis. That's
where they always get you, with the weak—"

"Listen, Clarissa, my other line just beeped in. Thanks
for the call. Talk to you soon. Bye," I say, hanging up before she can get another word in. Delilah Quick—tall, curvaceous, gorgeous ex-girlfriend. Yeah, right.

As soon as I press End Call, the phone rings yet again. I
sigh and check the caller. It's Bonnie.

"What is happening?" she asks, her tone sharp with
anger. "*How* is it happening?"

"Mim," I say, feeling capable of only monosyllabic conversation.

Bonnie digests this silently. Then, with unusual calm:
"What did she do?"

For a moment I consider giving her the whole rundown.
She already knows the crime-scene, yellow-tape half, and

64 *Lynn Messina*

it would only require a few sentences to fill in the rest. But I can't muster up the energy. "It's just too big…. Don't worry. I'm handling it."

"Yeah?" she says, not at all convinced. She hears the hesitation in my voice and the fatigue. "How's Ian doing? Have you spoken to him? Did they bring him down for questioning? Oh, God, they don't think he did it, do they?"

"No, they don't seem to. He talked with them this morning. He needs to…" But I don't know what he needs to do, and I trail off. "He's fine. I'm with him now and he's fine."

"I'm glad you're there," she says. "Stick close."

There's something about her earnest approval that makes me realize she hasn't given up on me and Ian, the couple. She still thinks we have a future. I would clarify the situation—with details this time—but it's another thing I don't have the energy for.

I promise to call her later, turn off my phone and go into the living room. I look at Ian in his sad, if-I-can't-see-it-it-can't-see-me position and sigh. This solution—hiding under pillows on the couch—doesn't have long-term viability. Despite his Soho Grand dodge, the world will find him here eventually.

I lift his legs and sit down. When he doesn't shift or protest, I realize he's asleep and mute the television. No, I can't turn it off, but there's no reason why it should offend all the senses. Even with the sound off, the images still tell a narrative and I follow it easily. Press conference, book jacket, roundtable—the endless cycle is interrupted only by weather reports.

Ian mutters and flips over, tumbling the pillows onto the floor and driving his knee painfully into my thigh, but he doesn't wake up. His sleep is deep and persistent, which is not surprising. He started his day with a visit to the police station, spent lunch hiding from a murderer and now contended with this—twenty-four coverage of the Jawbones Killer.

And it's not over yet. We still have to go to the police. I look at Ian's peaceful, sleeping form—mussed hair, unfurrowed brow—and realize that we don't have to go. I can do it myself. My telling the police everything is not fairy dust or enchanted beans, but it's a start. It won't solve every problem—Detective Williamson will still want to talk to him, the TV pundits will still bandy about his name—but everyone will stop treating *Jawbones* as a spur that incited a man to murder. They'll stop examining every paragraph, sentence and word for evidence.

It's only right that I go to the police. This mess, this disaster, this fictionalized serial killer who's terrorizing New York, is my fault. I should have helped Ian when he asked. I should have understood how important *Jawbones* was. I should have stopped Mim.

My stomach grumbles—the first hunger pang of the day—but I ignore it as I turn off the television. I can't watch anymore. I have to *do* something.

I find a sheet of scrap paper to write a quick note but I don't know what to say. Nothing I come up with—the truth, a lie—seems appropriate, so I crinkle the paper into a ball and throw it into the trash. I put on my coat and let myself out quietly. The door locks behind me.

I run down the stairs, impatient and anxious. Doing this—going to the police, confessing all, being a fine, upstanding citizen of the city of New York—feels good. I came close earlier today. When I finally dragged myself off the couch and returned to Barrow this afternoon, I almost earned a gold star. But almost doesn't count. Climbing a sixteen-foot ladder and standing on the diving board doesn't get you wet. Only jumping does. And I didn't. I walked to the edge and looked down and felt dizzy from the height and went home. I thought the murderer's arrest cleared my conscience. I thought it wiped the slate clean and gave me permission to walk away from the Mim ugliness, but the Mim ugliness followed me home.

I leave Ian's apartment intending to go straight to Detective Williamson in the Sixth Precinct station house, but I find myself standing instead in front of Mim's building. I'm not really sure why I'm here. The hole that we're in now— this deep, wide, awful sinkhole—is of her making. But things are different now. A serial killer is on the loose, and her plan, although never exactly harmless, is suddenly detrimental. Mim—crazy, stubborn, irrational Mim—will want to undo the damage, too.

She isn't at home when the doorman rings. He holds out the phone and asks if I want to leave a message but I'm already walking away. If she's not here, then she's at Pravda. There's nowhere else Mim can be.

At the office building, I impatiently press the elevator button several times. I tell myself that I'm only being fair— Mim deserves the opportunity to turn herself in voluntarily—but a part of me is afraid that I'm just trying to put off the inevitable for as long as possible. Despite my high-minded determination, I'm terrified of what happens next. It seems entirely likely that I'll have to serve some jail time. Overnight in a New York City holding cell—that alone will give me nightmares for the rest of my life.

It's a little after eight on a Friday evening, but Mim is still at her desk. She's eating a focaccia sandwich and flipping through a glossy magazine. Her office, quiet and still, is lit by a single gooseneck lamp on her desk.

Here in her office, Mim seems completely removed from the rest of the world—hibernating is the new cocooning—and I'm reluctant to intrude. It's obvious from her relaxed posture that Mim doesn't know yet what has happened. The Jawbones Killer and all of its insanity doesn't exist for her. But that's about to change. Her obliviousness is a clear sylvan lake and I'm here to throw in a rock.

"Hey," she says when she sees me at the door. "Come in. Sit down. Tell me how you are doing."

I'm disconcerted by the warmth of her smile. So much has happened today that I've forgotten about this—the lowered drawbridge.

"I'm all right, thanks," I say, wishing she didn't look quite so eager to have a pleasant chat with me.

"Good. That's good. I was afraid you might be still be upset about…well," she pauses awkwardly, "you know, before."

"I am still upset," I say sharply, annoyed that she thinks that any part of "well, you know, before" could be gotten over so quickly. Hours ago, when I watched the murderer being led away, I'd believed I could leave this terrible experience behind me. But I was wrong. The horror of this afternoon isn't an exit sign you drive past on the highway. It's a passenger in the car with you.

She nods. "Yes, I can see that."

Mim and I aren't following the beat of the same drum, but her concern is sincere. Her afternoon was just as horrific as mine, and it's not her fault that she's affected differently. "They arrested the guy," I say, leading with the good news. It's always best to start on a high note. "He confessed and everything."

"Yes, I know."

This calm agreement is the last thing I expect, and I stare at her in surprise. It doesn't seem possible that she did what

I did—return to the crime scene, watch the murderer being led away in chains—but it's the only explanation. "You know?"

"I heard it on the radio."

"Oh," I say, looking around her office. I'm not sure if she means police scanner radio or radio radio but I see no incriminating evidence of the former. There's a little Sony cube sitting on her desktop to the right of her computer. I stare at it, watching the time change from 8:07 to 8:08 while a niggling doubt begins to gnaw at me.

I stand up, walk across the room to her window and look out. A line of cars is stopped at a traffic signal. A taxi's off-duty light switches on just as a businessman in a gray overcoat reaches for the door. "You were listening to the radio?" I ask, my back toward her. I'm feeling jumpy and nervous—this is the niggling doubt gnawing.

"Yes, before," she says, unconcerned. My agitation hasn't communicated itself to her. "I was listening to the classical music station. They break in every half hour with news updates."

"So you know?" I ask, turning around and leaning against the windowsill. The niggling doubt is growing. It's becoming a serious qualm in record time.

She tilts her head. "Know?"

"What's happened."

"Yes, I know what's happened."

Mim's composure is so entrenched and nonchalant that it makes the conversation seem farcical, as if we're talking at cross-purposes for the amusement of an audience. I'm discussing the serial killer she unwittingly created and she's discussing the butler who's hiding in the maid's parlor with a twenty-one-year-old heiress. "You know about the Jawbones Killer."

My statement changes nothing—not her stance, not her understanding, not her coolness. She smiles slightly. "Yes."

"You know," I say flatly.

"Of course I know. They've been talking about it on the radio for hours."

"But you haven't mentioned it," I say, my alarm growing. Her behavior—peculiar and unpredictable—makes me uneasy and I grip the window ledge with my fingers. Perhaps I'm overreacting. Mim could be embarrassed by the havoc she's wrought or horrified or unsure what to do next. Or her placidity could be a defense mechanism. Maybe there's more bubbling lava underneath the surface crust.

"Really, Meghan," she says chastisingly, "I'm not the sort to crow over my successes."

"What?"

"I'm not the sort to crow over my successes," she says again. "I thought you knew that about me."

I lean my head against the windowpane and look at her. She's the same old Mim but something is different. It's the smugness. Despite her claim, she is crowing. "Successes?"

"Yes, of course." She examines me curiously. "You knew the plan. Why are you reacting so oddly?"

I take a deep breath and fight this. She will not make me complicit in her successes. "The Lonely Planet in Cambodia, Mim."

"Yes."

"That's what you said, the Lonely Planet in Cambodia."

"And that's what it is."

"No, Mim," I say dampeningly, "the police think there's a serial killer on the loose. They're looking for a murderer who doesn't exist and overlooking real ones in the pursuit. That's *not* the Lonely Planet in Cambodia."

Mim shrugs. The action is appalling and my jaw drops. "There's no Khmer Rouge in Manhattan, Meghan. Someone had to start coming up with an explanation sooner or later."

"*That* was the plan?"

"You know this. We talked about it last night. I can't understand your surprise now," she says, in the tone of injured innocence.

But Mim is being disingenuous. We never talked about this. Last night we only skimmed the surface of the plan. If I hadn't had so much to drink, I would've noticed there were details missing. Planting the book on dead bodies—it sounds like half a plan now.

Just thinking about it brings back the horror of this afternoon and I shudder. "God, Mim."

"You must have realized that leaving the book on murder victims failed to serve a purpose if nobody talked about it. Trust me, Meghan, this is what we wanted to happen. All publicity is good publicity."

There she goes again, making me a part of this. "No, Mim, I didn't want this to happen. I didn't want any of this to happen." I look at her in the center of her art-installation office—pristine, sleek, indifferent—and try to find a crack in her armor. But she's chain mail from head to toe. "I have to put a stop to it," I say decisively, standing up straight.

In her seat, Mim jumps. She turns to me sharply and stares at me with wide alarmed eyes. "What?"

Mim's reaction—reasonable and natural—gives me hope and adds credibility to the elaborate-defense-mechanism theory. Maybe her response is just plain old fear wrapped up in the shiny cellophane of apathy. "I'm going to the police," I say gently. "We have to tell them everything, Mim."

She stands up, reaches out and grabs my hands. Her grip is tight and sweaty. "You can't."

Mim's mouth is drawn and her skin is pale and her eyes are watering. Suddenly she's Mim from last night—vulnerable, frail, wrinkled, distressed—and I feel horrible for doing this. Peter and Helen, even Roger Cooley, have already put her through enough. "This has to end, Mim. Trust me, it's for the best," I say comfortingly.

She nods enthusiastically, her head bobbing up and down as if on a spring. "Yes, yes, of course. I'll never do it again. I'll toss out my police scanner," she says. Mim is eager and hopeful, like a thirteen-year-old promising never to throw water balloons off the roof again.

But her offenses are more serious than a harmless teenage prank. "We have to go to the police. We have to tell them everything."

"We can't," she says, her hands tightening painfully on mine.

"We have to, Mim. Think about it. Leaving *Jawbones* on those dead bodies—it's obstruction of justice, planting false evidence, interfering with an investigation." My heart beats faster with each new charge and I take several deep breaths in an attempt to steady myself. But it doesn't work. "God, it might even be accessory after the fact. I don't know."

Mim pales as I run through the list. "They'll put me in jail. They'll put me in jail." Terrified, she starts crying. "Please don't do that to me. Don't let them put me in jail. I can't survive jail. How would someone like me survive it?"

I know how she feels—of course I do. I'm consumed by the exact same fear. But this isn't about us. "We shouldn't assume the worst. We have no idea what's going to happen. First, we'll call your lawyer," I say, remembering how a to-do list calmed her down last night. "You have a lawyer, don't you? That guy who draws up your contracts for Pravda. We'll call him and have him meet us at the station. You won't go to jail, Mim."

My voice lacks real conviction, and she starts to shake. "Oh, God, Meghan. I've done awful things. I've planted false evidence and obstructed justice. Accessory after the fact—they could put me away for the rest of my life for that, couldn't they?" More tears fall. "And I was only trying to help Ian. You know that, don't you? I was only trying to give your boyfriend the help you refused him."

"Yes, I know," I say softly, feeling swamped by the old, familiar guilt. "I know you were only trying to help Ian. But the way you helped was wrong and there are consequences. Let's go down to the police station and face them together. I'll be there with you the entire time. I promise."

My tone is soothing but everything I say only agitates her more. "What about Peter?" she spits out. "What he did was wrong. Worse, really, because he made promises that he broke and he told lies. But he gets to go to glittering galas with that slut on his arm. What kind of facing the consequences is that?"

She's confusing the issue, mixing apples and oranges, but her heartrending plea for justice gives me pause. I don't know what to say. That life isn't fair is a lesson you're supposed to learn as a preschooler, not as a thirty-nine-year-old businesswoman.

As Mim watches me with tears streaming down her cheeks, I'm overcome with a crushing sense of uselessness. Mim's problems are enormous. Her terror of aging, her fear of being out of step with coolhunting, her heartbreak over being discarded by Peter—it has all coalesced into a perfect storm of devastating inadequacy and there's nothing I can do to make it better. Mim needs more than hastily thought-up to-do lists.

"Please," she says quietly, pleadingly.

Perhaps if I hadn't seen that woman in a pool of her own blood only hours before I'd be moved by pity, but the image is too clear. Murder—the thing that strangles you in the night, not the abstraction one talks about over the newspaper—is too fresh in my mind. "No," I say with resolution. Although it requires some effort, I'm determined to be strong. There's no point in both of us falling apart. "We have to go to the police."

"But it's not—"

"No, we have to do this," I say firmly.

For a moment I think my implacability has worked. Mim immediately lets go of my hand and stops crying. She straightens her shoulders, smoothes her hair and stiffens her upper lip. She has the calm, resolute air of a soldier about to face a firing squad, but she doesn't put on her coat or turn off the gooseneck lamp. She sits down at her desk and studies me carefully for a long while. The expression on her face—calculating, cunning—chills me to the bone and for a second I see myself dead at her feet with a copy of *Jawbones* tucked discreetly in my coat pocket. The image is only a flash, a split-second flight of fancy that flickers and dies, but it picks me up, twirls me around and drops me in a different place altogether.

My hands are shaking. They're trembling fiercely and I put them in my pockets so she won't see. I'm not really afraid of Mim—even in her chain mail armor she embodies total Mimness—but her aloofness unnerves me. I take a deep breath and try to calm down. Mim's not planning my demise—it's a long shuddering jump from finding corpses to making corpses—but I can't help thinking that the woman we found today must have believed the exact same thing. We fear strangers, not familiars.

As she watches me, Mim's expression softens. It loses the bone-chilling look of cunning and calculation and seems almost friendly. But my hands don't stop shaking.

"All right," she says, warmly and with a sad sort of resignation in her voice. "Do what you have to do. I understand completely, Meghan."

It's the same speech as earlier and the exact same I-don't-believe-you'll-really-do-it expression, but neither one affects me this time. The cold look of calculation, the swift transition from hysterical to calm—both have raised red flags. I've always thought I had Mim sussed out. If she kept part of herself separate, it was the insignificant part that baked banana bread and shopped for lingerie. But now I'm not so sure. It's possible the change is the result of panicked scrambling, a desperate eleventh-hour attempt to extricate herself from an ugly situation. But something about it feels more like cool-headed manipulation. Her back straightened too quickly. Her tears dried up too fast. Suddenly Mim seems like a collection of unknowns, like a crossword puzzle with only a few boxes filled in. Her erratic behavior could be the final stage of a protracted breakdown—maybe this is her succumbing fully to the pressure of the past few weeks. Or maybe this is just her. That's the thing: I don't know.

I take a deep breath and look away. None of this matters anymore. It's inevitable that the police will find out what's going on. If she doesn't tell them or if I don't, then Ian will the second he wakes up or his editor will as soon as he checks out of the Soho Grand. Mim's world isn't a climate-controlled playhouse. We're not actors following her script.

"Well then, I've got to go," I say matter-of-factly, impatient to leave. The moral clarity of confessing all to the police seems refreshing compared with Mim's opaqueness. "You should come with me. It will go easier for you if you come forward yourself."

It's a reasonable argument, but Mim shakes her head. She's sitting calmly at her desk, staring at me from across the room with cool detachment—the same cool detachment that Helen has been driving a battering ram against for thirty years—and nonchalance. Maybe this is why she's always been so much better at spotting trends than the rest of us: because all she does is watch from ten feet away.

"It's all right. I know you have to do what you have to do. And I forgive you," she says, playing the guilt card with all the sympathetic understanding she has in her—a considerable amount.

But it doesn't work. Even though I don't know which door the real Mim is behind, I recognize this for what it is: fey manipulation. "Yeah," I say, nothing but tired now, "I forgive you, too."

Mim doesn't respond. She watches me with acceptance and kindness and waits patiently for me to give in. She doesn't realize what's happening. In her head, the play isn't over—we're still somewhere in the middle of act three.

There's no reason to stay, and I turn sharply on my heels to leave. In the hallway I literally bump into Helen. I apologize absently for the unintentional collision, but I don't linger. Even though I came sauntering in at eleven-thirty today and ducked out of work at noon, I don't stop to explain. I can't waste the energy or the momentum or the righteous anger that's swirling inside me like a tornado.

But Helen stays frozen where she is. She remains glued to the spot, and when I step into the elevator a half a minute later, she's still standing there in the hallway with a thoughtful look on her face.

Helen holds her press conference at 10:00 p.m. and announces a major break in the Jawbones Killer case.

"My fellow New Yorkers, there is no cause for alarm. The Jawbones Killer is a fiction," she says from a wooden podium in the Waldorf-Astoria ballroom. "He is, in fact, an illusion created by my colleague Mim Warner in a misguided attempt to create interest in a book she's representing."

A shocked buzz travels through the room and is picked up by NBC's microphones. I'm in the bustling bull pen of the Sixth Precinct, but I can hear it clearly. On-screen, Helen fights a smile and waits for the noise to die down.

"In a moment I will go into details," she says, looking up from her prepared statement to make eye contact with the ladies and gentlemen of the press. "I will tell you exactly what Mim Warner did and exactly what she hoped to achieve, but first let me assure you, my fellow New Yorkers, that this information is new to me. I only just learned of it an hour ago. When I did, I rushed to make it available to you."

Helen's speech makes this news conference seem like civic duty and public responsibility, but it's not. It's the final nail in a thirty-year-old coffin.

The detective who's taking my deposition gestures to the television with his chin as he jots down notes. "What's her deal?" he asks, but he really wants to know why she's not here with me, why she's giving the Mim exclusive to the entire tri-state area rather than the authorities.

"They're rivals," I say, watching Helen's performance with increasing disgust. For the first time I see it—how she and Mim are two sides of the same coin. "They've always been rivals."

Detective Williamson nods. He gets it. In his job he sees the worst of human nature all the time. But I do not, and the encompassing horror I feel chokes me. Pravda on Monday morning at 10:00 a.m.—I can't do it.

Helen runs through Mim's publicity scheme. Her grasp on the details is weak—she keeps repeating the phrase "Lonely Planet in Cambodia"—and I realize suddenly that she overheard my conversation with Mim. She only knows what we talked about, and although she filled in several of the finer points herself, a fair amount is missing. Journalists notice this during the Q&A, but Helen retains her cool and sticks with the facts as she knows them.

The press conference is short—only fifteen minutes long—but Mim catches every second of it. Before she can formulate a response, before she can pull together a thought, before she can even see past the angry red tide that overtakes her, the police are at her door asking questions. She stutters and stammers as they take her down to the station house and press charges. Her fury with Helen is thick and heavy and ferocious. It takes up residency in her bloodstream and swirls around in heady circles, but it's quickly supplanted by gratitude the second the early editions of the *Post* and *Daily News* hit the street with her face on the front page.

For the first time since she entered the bathroom at Mount Rushmore, Mim feels one hundred percent visible. She's no longer disappearing, and she clings to her fifteen minutes with clenched fists. Pleading not guilty, fainting at the bail hearing, stretching her day in court to a three-week circus—each event is a column's worth of material. Her defense against four counts of obstruction of justice is temporary insanity and by the time her high-profile lawyer is done painting her famed photographer husband as a heartless, egotistical, philandering cheat, the jury buys it—as does Hollywood. Mim sells her story for 1.8 million dollars and moves to L.A. to become a producer at a well-known studio that admired her chutzpah. Helen goes, too, leaving Pravda in the capable hands of Josh, who is more than happy to rename the company after himself and pay Hildy Young Younger an exorbitant salary to fetch his coffee.

Mim is frequently pictured now in the tabloids, her few insurgent wrinkles semipermanently quelled by Botox and chemical peels. In every photo, Helen is there. She's in the background. Her face is out of focus and her left arm is cut out of the frame, but she's there and she's smiling. This is what she always wanted—Mim in her debt, Mim in her custody, Mim in her pocket.

But I don't know any of that yet—Mim's staggering media success as the *Jawbones* mastermind is barely a glimmer in the *Post*'s editor's eye—and when the police finally let me go at one in the morning, I trudge home exhausted and hungry.

The bars on the Bowery are full, and the streets are crowded with well-dressed hipsters smoking on the sidewalk. A couple is waving erratically for a cab on the corner of Bleecker as I walk by. The light changes, the traffic stops and I cross the street quickly. On the other side of Bowery is Mott Street and I have to force myself to pass it without stopping. I could make up a reason to see Ian. Even though I called him from the police station three hours ago and gave him a full report, I could easily invent a plausible pretext for buzzing. But I don't. Manufacturing excuses, dropping by at one in the morning—I won't do that anymore. It's over. I get that.

The apartment is dark and silent when I let myself in. I slide my coat off my shoulders and leave it where it falls on the floor. I don't have the energy to hang it up. I can't remember the last time I felt this exhausted. And the thought of the future—that gaping hole yawning widely before me—wipes me out completely. I close my mind to it. I'm tired of thinking. I'm tired of being awake.

I take the Chinese food out of the fridge and stick it in the microwave for three minutes. Except for a stale dough-nut at the station, I still haven't eaten at all today. While the beef with broccoli is heating, I go into the living room and pick up the remote. NY1 is still covering the Jawbones Killer, only now it's the Jawbones Swindle. On-screen is an-other roundtable. The topic: How easily the police were fooled.

I flip through the stations while standing a few feet from the television and settle on FX, which is showing another *M★A★S★H* repeat. The program cuts to a commercial just as the microwave beeps. I sigh, put the remote on the Par-sons table and turn around. Then I see it. The only light in the room is the flickering glare of the television screen, but I can see it clearly—Ian on the couch sleeping.

It's startling and stunning and it takes my breath away.

But sometimes that's the way it happens—you walk into a room and there's Roy Rogers and Trigger and a table full of free hot dogs.

Also available from Lynn Messina

Tallulahland

Tallulah West thought she had life figured out. That was until her world was turned upside down (again). Now she is doing everything she can not to follow in her dad's footsteps careerwise, and is considering abandoning the big city for a plot of undeveloped land, to follow her mom's dreams. But what's best for Tallulah?

Praise for Lynn Messina's *Fashionistas*

"Fashionistas **has genuine style, plus wit and wisdom."**
—*Time Out New York*

RED DRESS INK
™